'Til It
HAPPENS
To You

'TIL IT

HAPPENS

To You

A NOVEL

To: Khara
Thank you for
supporting my novel.
Such a pleasure meeting
you. Peace + Blessings—
Kristofer

Kristofer Clarke

Second Twin Publishing
Landover, MD

9-29-12

ALSO BY KRISTOFER CLARKE

Less Than Perfect Circumstance

Published by **Second** Twin **Publishing**

Cover and Author Photography by Emmanuel Fisher
for Photography by Emmanuel
photographybyemmanuel.com

Cover design by James Jefferson for
PlatinumPixels, LLC

Typesetting: Heir to the Throne Publications

ISBN 978-1-4507-4937-4

[May 2011]

First Edition

ACKNOWLEDGMENTS

God is good. I truly understand and believe that, without him, nothing is possible. I give thanks to God because HE is above all others. Thank you for blessing me with the gift of creativity, and allowing me to entertain through words.

I have been blessed with the greatest family on earth. The best love any one person can ask for is unconditional love. It is everlasting and limitless. You mean more than the world to me, and I'm always proud to call you my family.

Thank you to my mother, Paulette Clarke-Ranglin, for being my rock, the epitome of perseverance, and for always being in my corner.

To my sisters and their families: Maxine and Ian Weakly, Xenia Weakly, Shanya and Khentrell Graham, Senae Graham, Khentrell Graham, Jr., and Kason Graham for always filling our conversations with laughter. Thank you all for your unwavering love and support.

Thank you to relatives, old and new, who have supported, encouraged, guided, and loved me in your own way. It's good to know I can always count on your love.

To my Great-grandmother, Edna May Brown (Mama), and my Great-grandfather, Wilfred Brown (Papa), we all miss you and love you very much. Your beautiful spirits live in us all, and I love seeing you in my dreams. Heaven became even brighter when we lost you, but now we have our personal angels.

Thank you to friends who always have my best interest at heart. You are like family, and I am grateful to have surrounded myself with such great beings. Thank you all for your support, for understanding my focus, and for helping me lose focus when I needed to.

Thanks to Troy for always listening to my ideas, giving me feedback, and telling me when something just won't work. I appreciate you, your friendship, and your honesty.

Thanks to Janice. You have some of the craziest stories, and you definitely know what to say to make me laugh. Thank you for always praying for my success. Bingo!!!!

To the greatest group of friends in the world: Maurice, Dr. Regina, Dr. James, Wyman, Auden, Marcus, Tanisha, Marimba, Elliot, Reggie, Syreetta (unofficial official personal assistance...Go Duke!!!!), Lorraine, Jonathan, Darwin, Shannon, Selena, Dwayne, Jean and James Howard, David, Jabari, Thomas "Smitty" (mentor), Ty, Matthew, Jacques, Cardell, Isaac, Kuji, Kendrick, Brian, D'Antoine, and Joseph (I know your play will be a great success. I can't wait until the world knows who you are).

Thank you to Emmanuel Fisher, my friend and photographer, for taking great pictures and for bringing the concept for the cover to reality. Thank you for always giving me your best shot. Lookout!!! Emmanuel is making his mark one model at a time. I wish you much success.

To the models, Dominique Reece, Donlee "DonDevon" Sessoms, and Walter Redd for making the cover look so good. It was fun, wasn't it? Don't forget these names or the faces. They are up and definitely coming.

Thank you to a great team of professionals: Clarence Haynes, editor; Jenetha McCutchen for Quill Editorial Services, proofreader; James Jefferson for Platinum Pixels, graphic designer; and Traci Lewis, first reader/editor.

Since the release of my first novel, I have been privileged to meet some good people in the literary world. Thank you to authors

Trice Hickman, Karla Brady, Clarence Nero, and Rahiem Brooks for welcoming me, and for willingly sharing your knowledge and resources. Your guidance has been greatly appreciated. You are talented writers, with kind/humble spirits.

To Sharon Lucas and the ladies of The Reading Divas Book Club, thank you for the exposure. I am looking forward to your Annual Literary Brunch in October.

Thank you to Tanya and the ladies of Sistahs' Literary Book Club in New Jersey for selecting my novel and supporting me.

To Susan Parsons-Ritter, Meg Storey Groves, Georgia Best, Middlebury College and fellow alums for supporting my endeavors and me.

Thank you to Thomas, Walter and the members of the DMV. Continue to help each other achieve more.

This past year has been filled with meeting new and interesting people. To everyone who purchased a copy my debut novel, I want to say thank you for trusting the artistic creativity of an unknown. I hope you will continue to support me and enjoy these characters and the journey through their fictional life. Thank you for allowing me to take you on yet another literary ride.

Love, Peace, Happiness

"My heart could not think of anything better to do than love you."

Anonymous

'TIL IT

HAPPENS

TO YOU

PROLOGUE

I've heard people say if the lines in the palm of your hands connect to form the letter "M" you're going to be rich. I'm not sure if I believed that. I did find myself sometimes wondering what the palms of Donald Trump, Bill Gates, and Will Smith's hands looked like.

I never lived my life by words written in red on the tiny strip of white paper found inside the fortune cookie at my favorite Chinese restaurant. I didn't worry about analyzing dreams that woke me in the middle of the night or sometimes left me disturbed when I woke the next morning. And I was just as skeptical about palm readers who swore they could tell me about aspects of my life that were unclear to me; predicting my tomorrow when I was still trying to wrap my head around my yesterday.

"Why would I even want to know?" That was the question I asked myself as I stood at the front door of Forecast, a palm reading service in Manhattan, New York. I wasn't sure if I just didn't want to know, or if I was afraid she was going to confirm something I had already known. Until then, I had always frowned upon the idea of having my palms read. I've always thought palm-reading was a craft; I just hadn't yet convinced myself it was a craft I believed in. What exactly could she tell me by carefully observing the three or four unconnected lines in the palm of my hand? I had been looking at my hands all of my life and they hadn't told me anything.

So I was supposed to walk through these doors, up these steps that looked like they were borrowed from a scene in *The Exorcist,* hand this woman my fifty dollars, and she would be able to read me? I was supposed to extend her my left hand so she could tell me about my past, or my right so she could tell me my future? Or was I supposed to give her my left hand so she could tell me about relationships that never worked, aren't working, or aren't going to work out, or my right hand so I could be told about my education or experience? Exactly! Confusing!

I sat down in the chair across from her and I was almost certain I wore skepticism like a new facemask. But there I was sitting in front of this woman, with my right hand stretched out before me, listening to her telling me the year was going to be rocky for us, but next year our love would prevail, and that there are some forces working against my relationship. How was I supposed to process this information I had received? Her revelations built a web of confusion. I wasn't sure if the "us" she was referring to was the "us" that never really was; the situation I was walking away from. Or if she was predicting turbulence ahead in the relationship I was leaving to pursue. Either way, she gave me plenty to think about. Love is such a crazy thing - that was the one true conclusion I had as I walked back down the dimly lit stairs.

1

Goodbye's the Saddest Word

Jackson ...

"Maybe you should take him to talk to somebody." That was my stepfather's suggestion, and I listened, waiting for my mother to come to my defense.

"Then I would be admitting there's something wrong with him."

"Is that what you think?"

I stood at the window in a corner of my room listening to my mother and her husband discussing me like I was some case study. My stepfather stood holding the rake in both hands, the handle resting under his chin. My mother busied herself raking over the same spot on the lawn, stopping only to make her next statement.

"I don't know what I think."

I was only twelve years old, but old enough to remember if I'd told either my mother or my stepfather I needed to talk to anyone. I wasn't confused, and I had nothing I needed to figure out, if that was what they were implying. I knew who I was. I didn't need to engage in an hour-long conversation, sitting in a faux leather chair telling my personals to a stranger who thought he knew me from the few stolen words and one-liners he had written on a notepad, looking at me over his granny glasses saying, "hmm, hmm," and nodding his head as if he understood me. What was he going to do, fix me like he did my mother and my father's marriage? And where was my father now? Maybe it was my mother who needed someone to talk to, and rather than talking to my stepfather, she should have been talking to me.

I knew what spawned their discussion.

For the last three days, my mother and I had been walking around the house as if nothing happened. But something had happened. She'd walked into the house and saw what I wasn't ready to reveal to anyone, at least, not yet.

"What in the world?" Mother said, screaming at the top of her lungs. She paused. "What's going on in my house?"

Her abrupt presence startled me.

I was a young boy who saw nothing wrong with what I'd just done. Still, I stood there, frozen, with my adolescent hands covering my private part. Although there were more parts of me uncovered, like shame and guilt, there was nothing I could do to conceal what was just revealed, and to my mother of all people.

Words had never been more difficult for me than in that moment. I stared at her, wishing I could disappear. I stood looking at my reflection in the hallway mirror, then back at my mother, then the hallway mirror again. I wasn't sure what I was looking for.

"I have to run back out," she said. I was still frozen. "I forgot to…" she paused. She doesn't forget easily. "I'll be back," she said. She turned around, quickly walked back down the hall, and almost ran back down the stairs.

I knew my voice wasn't the only voice Mother heard as she walked up the steps and down the hall. I had just come out of the bathroom across from my bedroom wearing nothing but the smooth skin I was born with, leaving my best friend Bradshaw Ashan Donaldson in the shower. I never told her there was an early dismissal from school that day. That was a part of the plan. I wanted to satisfy Bradshaw's curiosity, and my own cravings. Oh, I was curious, too. I didn't know what was going to happen next, but my mother foiled my afternoon by keeping her own half-day work schedule to herself.

Later that evening, when she came home from her great escape, 'cause that's exactly what it was, I was sitting in the living room where I knew she couldn't avoid speaking. Well, she did. She looked at me, shook her head, and walked into the kitchen. In that moment, the idea that I was my mother's perfect son vanished from my mind. I followed behind her and stood, my body framed by the kitchen doorway, watching her put away the few things she did pick up from wherever she'd gone, her place of refuge. I stood there and accepted her silent treatment for as long as I could, and then made myself disappear into my own sanctuary, my bedroom.

I stood listening to the rest of my mother's conversation with her husband. When I couldn't take any more of what I was hearing, I lay across my bed, staring out the window into the darkening night, their conversation becoming a faint whisper. When she came inside, Whitney Houston's "I Will Always Love You" belted from the speakers of a small stereo that sat on my dresser. I've always loved that song, and I thought, *Hmm, how appropriate.*

"Can I talk to you?" my mother asked after lightly tapping on my door.

I didn't respond. I sat up in my bed, staring at my hands in my lap.

"I hope you know you can tell me anything." She stood at the door as if she were waiting for an invitation to enter.

"Maybe I should go talk to Mr. Kirkwood," I said, still not looking in her direction. "Since you think he has the answers for everything. Next time you plan on having some discussion on how you want to cure me, let me in on your plans, or at least make sure I'm some place I can't hear you."

"Watch your mouth, young man. What are you talking about curing you?" She walked over and sat on the edge of the bed. "Do you believe I think something is wrong with you?"

"If you didn't, why are you suggesting that I talk to someone?"

"I'm your mother, and as much as we hate to admit it, mothers always know. Sure sometimes we pray we're wrong, and sometimes we are, but for the most part when you think we don't already know, we're just waiting for confirmation."

I raised my head and caught her silken eyes. I dropped my head feeling that somehow, I had disappointed her.

"I've watched you grow into the little man you are now, so nothing you do surprises me...well, except for the other day. You know, that's not the way I expected to find out."

"That's not the way I planned on telling you." I looked up, again, and into my mother's eyes. "And why would you pray to be wrong?"

"Come here," she said, tapping her hand on a spot on the bed next to her. I eased my body down the length of the queen size bed and sat beside her. She gently cradled my head against her shoulder. "You're my son, and I brought you on this earth because I loved you from the moment you were conceived. And no matter what you are, or whom you decide to love, I'm never going to love you any less than I love you right now. And that's a promise."

"I love you, too."

"I love you more, Junior. And don't you ever forget that. You hear me? But you have to know not everyone is going to be as accepting. There are people in this world that can be unforgiving sometimes. They can be cruel and abrasive, and I prayed because I don't want you becoming a victim to that. Not everyone is going to understand."

"I'm not worried about what the world thinks."

"Maybe not right now. But sooner or later you're going to find yourself explaining to people who shouldn't matter, or defending your lifestyle because people think it's just not right. You're going to find yourself surrounded by those who say it isn't what God intended, as if they had sat down and had their little talk with Jesus and knew His intentions personally. I just want you to be prepared."

That was the night I stopped keeping hardly anything from my mother. That was also the first time my mother and I had tea, with lime and honey, on the back patio, the night my mother really started listening to me. I've always thought she heard me, but I never thought she really listened.

Now sixteen years later and I felt like I was about to have a repeat conversation with her. I made sure my decision was final. I was no longer wavering, ultimately convincing myself this was what I needed to do, what I had to do. I now had to let her in on the change I was about to make in my life.

It was an early Sunday morning in May. Mother sat in her patio chair, her white robe tied loosely around her waist and her right leg crossed over her left with her pink house slipper dangling from her foot. Her hair was combed back into a ponytail, revealing features that didn't stop at her high cheekbones and full lips. I always thought my mother was beautiful. She held her teacup between her palms, as if to keep her cold hands warm. She sipped her tea. She looked up. She looked back at me and smiled. I loved her smile. I smiled back at her, and I tried to hide the edgy feeling I was drowning in.

"Just in time to catch the sunrise with your mother," she said, looking past the rooftop of our neighbor's house to the cluster of evergreens nearby.

My relationship with my mother was built on sunrises and sunsets, early morning tea and conversations, laughs and smiles.

"I thought I'd missed it," I responded, closing the patio door behind me.

The morning had a cool, fresh breeze, the kind early morning runners enjoyed. They said it was good for the lungs. I sat down next to her. I was not as relaxed as she was, but tensed and erect, which was an unusual posture to assume in her company.

"It's only 6:30," she said, looking at her wristwatch. She always wore her watch. I once asked her why, and she told me it was her way of making sure time was on her side. I left it alone, never contending her explanation.

My cup of hot tea sat on the table in front of me as I watched the steam rise up and then vanish into the cool morning air.

"I have to tell you something," I said. I'm not sure what she was expecting to hear. Either way, I wasn't going to torture her with the awkward silence. "I'm moving in a couple months," I said, letting it out like I had just swallowed my stomach.

"You're moving?" she repeated. "Why? Where?"

"D.C.," I said, taking a sip of tea. I gave her the most information I could without telling her everything that was going on in my mind. I watched the smile from her face disappear. My mother and I sat in silence, gazing into the sky, and I tried not to let my news ruin the moment.

"What's wrong with Connecticut?" she finally asked, looking at me from the corners of her eyes.

"Nothing," I said insistently. There was nothing wrong with Connecticut except that the people who had mistreated my love had made living here less than ideal for me.

My mother wasn't pleased with my decision and my explanation didn't win any applause from her, either. Over the next several months it became obvious she didn't want me to go, but she hadn't figured out exactly how she was going to convince me to stay. She never understood from whom I was fleeing, and she certainly didn't know towards whom I was anxiously running. Truth is, the person I was leaving behind no longer belonged to me.

Her house was becoming empty one child at a time. Devaan, my older sister, had graduated from Yale University with a doctor's degree in investigative medicine. A clinical research manager at Delta Pharmaceutical, she saved most of the money she needed, and with help from my mother and Mr. Kirkwood, had put a sizable down payment on her own house. She moved from her room in my mother's house and into a three-bedroom, two-and-a-half bathroom stone-front colonial on Cypress Creek Court in a gated community in Wallingford. She did exactly what she had planned, and what my mother had wanted her to do, and that was the same plan my mother had for me. Now she was watching those plans evaporate.

2

Wish You Were Here

Trevor....

My mother was a strong black woman from Savannah, Georgia. Her grandmother called her Clara because it "rolled off the tongue like honey pouring from a beehive." That was her grandmother's explanation. My mother hated that name, but she never told her grandmother because she didn't want to offend her.

I loved talking to my great-grandmother about my mother. My grandmother knew a lot, but it seemed my great-grandmother remembered everything. All it took was a picture and the stories came flowing from her mouth like water through a sluice. After my great-grandmother passed, I held on to the stories. Often I would close my eyes just to hear my Mama Markie's voice in my head. Sometimes she was there even when I didn't expect her to be.

"Pass me my good church hair." That was usually the last request Mama Markie made of Clara just before heading out the door and on their way to The Great Ebenezer Worship Hall. Clara would stand tiptoe, reaching for the curly black wig that her grandmother hung from the closet door after roller-setting the curls. She hated the way the Georgia sun frizzed her long, natural black hair, not that it had any mercy on the curls in her wig. Mama Markie would lean over, looking in the dresser mirror, tucking her hair under wig, pulling and tugging until it was just right.

As a child, my mother played church girl on Sundays, flanked between her mother, Cynthia-May, and her aunt Daphne. Clara went to church because she had no choice. Daphne only made it to church when she felt she had a sin that needed forgiving. She could have just repented in prayer and save herself a trip since she didn't pay attention to anything said in church anyway.

Of course, she wasn't the only one whose focus was somewhere else. While everyone else belted out the second verse to *"Glorify Thy Name"*, young Clara sat with her eyes titled towards the ceiling, comforted by the thumb that never left her mouth, thinking more about the words to Minnie Riperton's *"Inside My Love"* than to the Lord she had come to praise. My mother nursed a huge crush on young Robert Seymour Harrison, an army brat from Texas who had moved just around the corner on East Perry Lane. She was probably preoccupied with thoughts of him, too.

Church was always too long for Daphne, and wordlessly, Clara agreed. Clara didn't mind going to church; it's what would happen every Sunday following the service that she hated most. Rather than rushing home, both her mother and grandmother would stand outside talking considerably about the service, as if those they engaged in conversation hadn't just sat through the same sermon. Or they talked about some shindig at Sister Eden Dwyer's place, another opportunity to flaunt her money.

Clara usually sat on the last step of the stair, just outside the church, with her legs crossed at the ankles, praying they would hurry. She hated sitting in the hot Georgia sun, in the middle of August, when she could have been sitting on her own steps waiting for Robert to ride pass on his bicycle. He would wave to Ms. D, who was usually sitting in the corner of the veranda in my grandfather's chair with her favorite man, Jack Daniel's, her Sunday evening teaser.

I loved looking at old pictures of my mother. I was sitting at the small dinette table under an open window. My father was standing in the kitchen, pouring another glass of wine. He always drank wine after breakfast. This morning he prepared homemade waffles, poached eggs and hollandaise sauce, and sliced strawberries. A widow for so long, he'd always cooked for himself. Practice had made him chef-perfect. It was only fitting he knew his way around the kitchen, since he liked to carry his belly with him wherever he went. That's what my grandfather always told him.

I stayed the night at my father's house after having one of our Saturday night hangouts at our favorite spot, Ace of Spades, an upscale bar and eatery on the corner of Salisbury and 7th Streets. We went there whenever we needed to catch up, for the two-for-one drink specials, three-dollar Red Stripes, and four-dollar cosmos. Our last visits had been different. We no longer expected to see my friend Sidney rounding the corner, balancing a service tray of bottled drinks and liquor glasses, wearing a friendly smile that never disappeared. Collin, our usual mixer of potency, was now the owner of Club District, his own upscale bar near Wyoming Ave in southwest D.C., catering to a list of clientele from the nearby embassies and their congressional cronies. But his replacement Tress Symonds did not disappoint.

"This one is my favorite," I said, holding a small picture of my mother. I stared at the picture before holding it up to show my father exactly which one I was talking about. My mother's dress was a bright bride white. She had a single flower in one hand and her arm around a small dog.

"That's Hocus," Robert explained. Hocus was an English beagle given to my mother one Halloween, so I guess the name was appropriate. "That was the first time I really paid attention to your mother," he continued, laughing.

"What do you mean? Didn't you say you knew she had a crush on you?" I asked, turning around.

"Yes. But I was waiting my turn. See, your mother had a crush on me, but all the neighborhood boys had a crush on her," he said, handing me one of the two champagne glasses he had in his hands. He took the picture from me and looked at it as if he were seeing it for the very first time. "She had curves like the petals of red roses. One afternoon she went yelling down the street shouting for Hocus. We spent hours looking for him. After circling several blocks, we came back to your mom's house to find Hocus sitting on the veranda, lying with his head between his front paws, staring at the front gate. You should have seen the joy in her face when she saw him."

"Mom was beautiful." I have to admit these same pictures that often brought a smile to my face sometimes saddened my heart. It was always like seeing them for the first time.

"So, did you and mom talk about having more kids?"

"I wanted a basketball team, my own starting five." My father handed the picture back to me and sat.

"And mom?" I asked.

"When we heard of the complications she was about to face with you, she just prayed you were all right." He smiled. "You would think she wanted only you from the very beginning."

"I wish she were still here."

"I wish she were here, too," Robert said, brandishing a smile.

"You do? What about Natalie?"

"What about her? I never stopped loving your mother. And I don't have to stop loving her to make Natalie my…"

"Your wife?" I interrupted.

"One step at a time." Robert paused and took a sip from his wine glass. "I was going to say fiancée, but I'm not ruling that out, either."

"My old man's taking a dive into the old marriage pool again," I said in a giggle, shoving him playfully with my elbow. "It's about time. Set a date, already," I added, muffling my words as I spoke into my wine glass.

"I heard that, and your man's not that old."

"Speaking of Natalie, where is she anyway?"

"Adrian is home for a quick weekend break from school, so she's spending the day with him." Robert looked at his watch as if he had been anticipating her return. I loved that he had found someone to share his life with, but I loved having these moments with him more than anything else.

I looked at my watch and realized time had been slipping away. I still had a busy Sunday evening ahead. My father was one man I cherished having in my life. He had been in my life since birth. With some men walking around dropping babies left, right and center, and then walking away from their responsibilities, leaving these women to play daddies to little girls and teach boys to be men, I was proud my father didn't fit into the deadbeat-dad category. Besides God, my father was the only other person on whom I could bet my life was never going anywhere. I began placing the pictures back in the lockbox.

"What's the rush?" he asked.

"Did you forget?"

"It all depends. What was I supposed to remember?" I could see him hiding his smile.

Yes. My father had forgotten. "Today is the day," I said, hoping that alone would remind him.

"Today is what day?"

"Pop, I told you Jackson was moving here today." We'd had several discussions about this. I guess with everything going on with him and Natalie, he had pushed this day behind everything else. But it wasn't his excitement to remember, so I wasn't going to hold it against him.

"Are you ready?"

"We've spent the better part of two years getting ready," I said with a wide smile.

"And what about Kelvin?"

"You know, that's the same question Denise asked me, as if something about him is supposed to concern me. He hasn't concerned me in a long time, and that's exactly how I intend on keeping things. Sure, every now and then I may wonder how he's doing, but I'm human, not evil, and those are natural thoughts. I hadn't done the ashes to ashes, dust to dust thing on memories of him, like I had our relationship, but I haven't thought about Kelvin in the context of him and me. Hell, I don't even think about him in the context of him and Lawrence."

"Just making sure. If I remember correctly, that was Jackson's concern earlier," Robert said. He picked up the two empty wine glasses and began walking back towards the kitchen.

Jackson's concerns were legitimate. Had I been on the outside looking in, as Jackson had been, I would've had those same concerns. But the last thing Jackson has to worry about is a Kelvin and Trevor sequel. I had moved on, and Kelvin doesn't get a do-over. Sure there were feelings I thought weren't going anywhere, but it's good to know I was wrong. I saw Jackson struggling to understand them. It made no sense to him, especially since Kelvin was miles away with his new love. So, If I hadn't put things into perspective, I would have lost Jackson. I would have lost myself. But distance and time was all I needed, just like my father had told me. There's no better feeling than completely flushing someone out of your system.

I thought about the last real conversation my father and I had that actually involved Kelvin. That night another phone exchange with Kelvin reminded me I had cared so much about him that I had forgotten how to care about myself. I had allowed Kelvin to rain on my parade, something he had done so many times before because I let him. I told my father about Lawrence's letter to Kelvin I had found while boxing up Kelvin's belongings a few days before he moved. I didn't know it at the time but I was packing Kelvin off to be with Lawrence, my replacement. For whatever reasons, some beyond my control, at least that's how I felt, I struggled to disconnect myself from Kelvin. But my father was right when he told me I was a lot stronger than I thought. I can't tell you how much I needed to hear those words. Isn't it funny how some love just makes you weak sometimes?

I placed the pictures back into the lockbox where they would be preserved for years to come, carried them back upstairs to my father's room, and placed them in the back of the closet where he always kept them. I stopped in front of the dresser and stared at the picture of my mother and me. She was still lying on the hospital bed, with my tightly wrapped body close to hers. I could tell in the picture my mother loved me the moment she laid eyes on me. I looked at my watch again and smiled as I thought about Jackson's arrival.

3

By the Time I Get to...

Jackson....

I hated the feeling I got whenever I came home, like I had opened the door to lonely. It bothered me that I wasn't able to be with the new object of my affection the very moment my body yearned for his touch. I never thought I would do this for anyone, but from what I knew, Trevor was worth it. Trevor and I, so far, had all the makings of a good thing. I'm not sure if that says a lot since this was the same sentiment I had at the beginning of past relationships. However, it said enough to help me make the decision about Trevor.

For a long time I thought if I hung on and showed interest in one man, he would eventually come around. When that didn't happen, I spent the rest of my time trying to get over the idea, the hope, and the fact that the "we" I wanted so badly would never be. I often wondered *"if broken hearts ever mend?"* or *"where do broken hearts go?"* I finally figured it out. You spend time thinking about the memories you created. You convince yourself you would never find another like them, because they had been the one you prayed for all your life. A few tears make their way to the curve of your chin, but then eventually, that zigzag line that dissects the familiar symbol of a broken heart begins to straighten, disappear, and the heart is whole again.

I had a lot I still needed to tell Trevor. He knew something about the hurt I experienced, but by whom and how badly never made its way into many of our conversations. If I were going to leave what was never mine in the first place, I needed to keep whom I was leaving behind to myself; for now, that was the plan.

It was hard for me to leave. I felt no one else would understand what was happening to me, and so, I kept my pain silent and suffered inside. The one person I thought would have understood, the one who told me he would always be there, was always too busy to hear my cries that usually came at night when I found myself alone wondering where he was. I was young and in love—he was only interested in himself. Through all the hurt, the frustration, and the disappointments, I had proven to this one man I wasn't going anywhere. As I stayed in that place, his eyes wandered, his mind followed, and eventually, so did his heart.

I was a ball of emotions, but still I embraced the excitement I felt about the changes that were happening in my life. I had postponed this day several times over, and it had finally arrived. This was the day for which I had impatiently waited, and it was met with a level of eagerness I hadn't experienced in a long time.

The night air still lingered as the sun started to show the same ugly head that brought the sweltering heat as the month of July ended and August began. I walked from the house to the car with my possessions in both hands. I was on my way to starting anew with Trevor, and that was exactly how I packed. I loaded only the essentials: clothes, shoes, a container of the dinner my mother prepared, and bottled water. A family portrait of my mother, my sister, and me lay perfectly on the passenger seat. A picture of my father, the man everyone said couldn't deny me at birth even if he tried, was lying under that.

While I prepared for my departure, I tried not to look in my mother's direction. I knew it was hurting her to see me leave. It was hurting my heart as well. But what I think hurt her more was not being able to figure out what she was losing me to, and any explanation now would be obscured by the ache we were both feeling. So much for never keeping secrets. She wouldn't have understood had I told her she was losing me to needed sanity, a mended heart, and tearless nights. Well, maybe she would have understood, but still I offered her no explanation. I just knew I had to go, and that was good enough for me.

Saying goodbye to my mother was hard, too. Our embrace was long, and when I was ready to let go, I felt her resistance as she tightened her hands around me. She didn't need words.

"You can let go now. I'm going to be okay," I said, but she never responded. If she did, I didn't hear her. I was too busy holding back my own tears. She slowly loosened her grasp. I bolted to the car, closed the door, and never looked at her. I adjusted the rearview mirror and backed out of the driveway.

When I started down Elmore Street, I talked myself out of looking back. I drove with my eyes staring at the open road that stretched out before me, looking, at times, in the rearview mirror as my mother and all I was leaving behind became miniatures, and finally disappeared out of sight as I turned left on Dulcaster Drive, and then right onto Ponder Terrace. I could have turned right on Camden Court and headed back home, which would have delighted my mother, but instead I turned left and headed toward happiness and my own love. When I realized the decision I made, the tears came. The more the tears flowed, the faster I drove.

I drove in silence until thoughts flooded my mind. I tried unsuccessfully to drown them in music, but everything on the radio reminded me of the very thing I was trying to get away from. There was one other person I needed to talk to about my decision.

My sister Devaan and I had been close growing up. She was always protective (not that I thought I needed her protection), and believed her purpose on earth was to save me from everything (not that I thought I needed to be saved). One day she did. I was sitting on the floor in front of my bed, weakly calling my sister's name. I knew if anyone would hear me, she would, especially since her bedroom was right next door to mine, and she always slept with her door open, unlike my mother. I had slid the knife smoothly across one wrist, but pain and fear had stopped me from doing the same to the other.

I sat there watching blood discharge from my arm, coloring the carpet around me. When I felt myself slipping away, I yelled louder. Devaan walked in, saw me and dialed 911, summoning the paramedics to the house before waking my mother. When I woke, my sister stood holding my hand, while my mother was asleep in a visitor's chair in the corner of the room with a bleach-white hospital sheet thrown over her. That night wasn't something my sister or mother ever talked about. I still have the marking from that desperate attempt to keep my father in our lives, and even then, he never returned.

Devaan was five years older, and had she been at the house as I was leaving, she wouldn't have allowed my planned departure to occur—at least, she would have tried her hardest to persuade me to stay.

"Hello," I answered, adjusting the Bluetooth to my ear.

"What is this I'm hearing? You've left home?" Devaan began in a soft, comforting tone.

"Is that all she told you?" I asked.

"Yes. And that you would tell me the rest. What's going on?" she asked, her voice becoming overwhelmed with emotions. "You could have at least called to say goodbye."

I apologized to her for leaving without her knowing, not that I needed to consult with her first. I had a plan, and I was going to be okay. But I decided to make one last promise to her.

"If this doesn't work, I promise I will come back home," I said.

● ● ● ● ●

If I drove the posted speed limit, I calculated the drive from home to D.C. to be about six hours without traffic. *There shouldn't be much traffic on this Sunday afternoon.* That was the thought I had as I drove down I-91 and onto I-95, heading towards New York. An hour later, I was driving into a sea of brake lights as I approached the George Washington Bridge. Until then, I was making good on time. *Great*, I thought. I hadn't planned on making any stops, other than filling up on gas at one of the gas stations on the Jersey Turnpike. I had enough gas to take me that far, and it was always so much cheaper. I rarely allowed the gas needle to go below half a tank—that was part of my emergency plan, along with bottle water, Tylenol, and a flashlight I kept in the trunk of my car. Still in traffic, my car hadn't moved more than ten feet in the last twenty minutes, and I wondered what was causing this jam. As I approached, it became clear. I guess deciding whether to take the upper or lower level of the bridge was a bigger decision than I thought.

I needed something to take my mind from the snails-pace traffic. I fondled with the radio dial before settling on "It Don't Hurt Now", my mother's favorite Teddy Pendergrass song I'd adopted. I found myself singing out loud and tapping my feet as he sung, "Well there's no more sleepless nights, no more heartaches, and no more fights… I found someone to ease my pain." Before I would sing those words hoping I would find someone to ease pain that came so easily. Now I was singing in truth because I had found that someone in Trevor.

I met Trevor Rene Harrison when his head and heart belonged to someone else. He was standing with a wall built around him, looking like he was trying to hide his own pain. The dancing lights took turns brightening his light brown sugar complexion. I took my time getting close enough to stare into his dark brown eyes. He looked like love was missing. Once I made it past his pretend rough exterior, he made something inside me come alive again. We danced to music that made us both feel good. We disconnected ourselves from the outside world, and for a moment, shut out the hurt. Damn, the DJ had us falling in love, though we weren't sure that was a place we were ready to be, or needed to be. The first month was a rocky start, but the past year-and-a-half had been filled with amazing love. Here I was allowing love that, against my will, was taking me to Washington, D.C.

4

Happy Days, Lonely Nights

Jackson...

Before Trevor, I thought I was happy. At least, I had spent time convincing myself I had found the happiness I'd been looking for. As I loved, I concentrated only on those behaviors that supported that thought, and avoided, even dismissed, the ones that proved otherwise. Needless to say, I fell in love with blind eyes and deaf ears. My UCONN education had prepared me for many things, but dealing with bullshit came with experience—three bad ones, but it's time to stop counting.

Loving Trevor was easy, even from a distant. Everything was perfect, which was good, since perfect hadn't existed for me in a long time. I waited for Trevor's heart to open up to me, and now that it had, I was going to love him right. I was entering a new situation with this new man, and I was entering with optimism. How else was I supposed to think about the new life I was getting ready to start?

A neo-eclectic colonial on a cul-de-sac was where Trevor called home. This composition of brick, floor-to-ceiling windows, and red French doors stood erect with money-green grass, winter shrubs, and strategically placed Eastern redbuds at the end of the driveway on either side. When I pulled my car into the driveway of 1084 Willow Crest Court, I pulled up the parking bake and headed to the door. Before I could extend my finger to ring the doorbell, the door swung open. Trevor's smile extended from one side of his face to the next. He stood in the doorway wearing only FAMU basketball shorts, which hung below his behind, exposing blue beagle print boxers.

"What took you so long?" Trevor asked. I didn't respond. I pulled him close to me and smiled. Trevor had made himself a prisoner in his own home for as long as it took me to get there.

"I didn't have the road to myself. And I drove as fast as I..." Before I could complete my thought, Trevor's lips were already on mine. I became overwhelmed with passion. He placed one hand at the back of my head and another under my chin. His kiss was breathtaking, just as it was when we first met. "And it's nice to see you, too," I said, after I had a moment to finally catch my breath. I began walking back to the car to grab a small carry-on bag since we had agreed I would stay my first night with him.

"Jackson," he called out as if he wasn't going to see me again.

"I'm coming right back. I'm just going to grab some things from the car."

"Look, you've had a long drive, and I'm sure you want to get out of those clothes. I'll get that stuff for you." Trevor kissed me again as he grabbed the keys from my hand and headed towards the car.

I was standing under the shower with my arms folded across my chest. I hung my head with my chin resting between my collarbones, allowing the water to massage my head and the back of my neck, wondering if I had made the right decision.

"Hey, do you need anything?" Trevor asked

"A towel and washcloth would be nice, unless you expect me to use my hands," I said, jokingly. The shower muffled his response.

I heard the bathroom door open and then close. I wasn't sure if Trevor was in the bathroom or not, but I didn't think I was alone.

"The towel is on the towel rack when you get out," he said, confirming my curiosity.

"Thank you. Where's my washcloth?" The shower door opened, and Trevor was standing in front of me with the washcloth clenched between his teeth. I smiled. He was staring up into my eyes, and then at my 6'9" muscular frame.

"You don't mind, do you?" Trevor asked. My eyes became immediately filled with lust.

Of course I didn't mind. If I did, watching the water flow over every manly curve of Trevor's body had taken my voice away for the moment. His eyes went from my eyes and then to my now hardened penis.

"I'll take that as a no," he said, smiling.

I reached around Trevor for the shower gel that had sat in the soap holder. I began to lather my hands, and before too long, I was massaging parts of his body he probably didn't know hurt.

He felt tense.

"Ooh, yes. Right there, baby," Trevor directed as my thumb dug into the muscles in his shoulders.

"Right here?" I asked, making sure I was following his commands as I aimed to please him. Trevor didn't repeat. He closed his eyes, inhaled, held his breath momentarily, and then allowed it to escape his body once again. Before long, I allowed my hands to slide down his body and rested them at his waist. He opened his eyes and stared up at me. If he hoped his expression had given me the permission I needed to invade his body, it had. When I obliged, he closed his eyes, again, and enjoyed it all.

When I stepped into the dining room finally fully dressed, I was met with quite a surprise. Trevor was a man of perfection, and that's exactly how dinner went. The rack of lamb with caramelized shallots, the lemon-butter green beans with pine nuts, the perfectly sliced hasselback potatoes, seasoned with paprika and thyme leaves, all tasted as if they came from the kitchen of some five-star restaurant. The candles stayed lit throughout, and their constant glow brightened the face of my new love. It pleased me to see him smile like he had been since I arrived. A bottle of Cabernet Sauvignon chilled on ice in a corner on the table, and it wasn't long before that bottle was sitting empty on the table. So while I drove, Mr. I-can't-boil-hot-water transformed himself into America's top chef. To simply say I was impressed would be an understatement.

After dinner, Trevor and I settled in the chaise lounge. His head rested comfortably in my lap. I leaned over and smiled, kissing him from time to time. I loved kissing his lips. His face was in close proximity to my manhood, but his eyes remained fixed on mine.

"So the house is ready for you to move in?" he asked.

"Everything should be delivered tomorrow. But if moving in means I won't have this, then I'd rather just stay here." I smiled.

I was ready to make 2634 Lansing Crossing home. A rebuilt section in SE DC, near to the Barracks and M Street, the community was close-knit. I had met a few neighbors on several early morning stakeouts of the neighborhood when I visited Trevor. There was the young couple that waived politely as they jogged past. I met Jaris and Celeste Woolford, an elderly couple from across the street that held a long political conversation as my agent, Trevor, and I removed the "SOLD" sign posted in the front of the yard. They were cordial too, and I thought they must be the eyes of the neighborhood, the ones who see and hear everything.

"You might get tired of seeing me and need your space other than a room on the other side of this house."

"Oh, you're right. I might need to get away from you at times." I stroked Trevor's head and stared at him. When he raised his head and kissed me, I tasted love on his lips. When I thought he might stop, I held on to the back of his neck and kept his lips pressed against mine.

5

You Know How to Love Me

Trevor...

I smiled whenever I say Jackson's name. After Kelvin, I felt my heart was irreparable, but in time it had been mended by my own self-love, and the love Jackson was giving to me. I knew Jackson loved me, but I didn't know he was going to fall as deep as he did. With his love, I knew I had avoided the pain of falling out of love when love didn't work.

It's already been a long week. I spent Monday with Jackson. The trucks came one after the other, and I watched him as he directed deliveries into one room and then another. On some days, nights seem to come sooner than on others. Jackson didn't seem like he was missing home yet, but there were times he was reminded he had no one close by to call family. I had introduced him to my father and his fiancée Natalie, and her son Adrian. Being around them made his first week of settling in easier than he thought it would have been. Jackson knew my father and I were close, but now he was able to see just how close we were, even alike in many ways. Sometimes I'll catch him staring at my interactions with my father, looking as if he were wishing he and his own father were as close. Jackson rarely talked about him.

I loved my nights with Jackson. They were usually quiet, which I didn't mind. I loved listening to him breathe. Some nights I pretended I could read his thoughts when we lay there in the hush of the night. Jackson always had a story to tell. I loved listening to the stories he told about crazy coworkers trying to figure him out, or equally crazy friends, the few he'd kept close to him. Sometimes those stories kept us awake longer than we intended.

Dinner, as usual, was delicious. The half bottle of Ramandolo left over from Sunday's dinner now sat empty in the kitchen sink. That wine did something to Jackson. He admitted he always liked the way a few glasses of wine made him feel. It gave him a sexual feeling, which he didn't mind since I was right there next to him and didn't object to giving him that sexual healing. Drinking wine did something to me, too. Jackson was lying down in bed, naked, like he always was whenever I was with him, if he wasn't in boxers that usually hung just below his waist, revealing that v-shape that seemed to go on forever. I rested my head in the center of his chest, my right hand gently massaging where his heart was beating rapidly.

"I love being here with you," Jackson said, his hand moving across my back.

"Are you sure this is where you want to be?" I had no reason for asking that question, but I was curious how he would respond.

"Hmm... let me see." Jackson paused. "I can't think of anywhere else I want to be other than here with you." He sounded genuine.

"Are you trying to make me blush? 'Cause if you are, it's working."

"Not trying to make you blush at all. I'm trying to make you happy. I wouldn't be here if you, if this, weren't what I wanted. Just promise me this?" Jackson paused.

"Anything." I didn't usually make promises, but I didn't intend on breaking anything with Jackson.

"If you wake one morning feeling that right here, with me, isn't where you want to be, promise you'll tell me," Jackson said, and I could sense a change in him, as if a moment of sadness had set in.

"You don't have to worry about that. I don't intend on not being here with you. I love you, Jackson-Chase Demetrius Bradley." I smiled and kissed him. "If this is where you want me, then this is where I will be."

"I love you, too, Trevor, Trevor Harrison," Jackson said, and kissed the top of my head as he chuckled, remembering my introduction the first time we met. As he laughed, something else about that night made me beam. I thought about how we danced, and how we moved about the crowded dance floor as if we were attached, like a couple of teenagers or early twenty-somethings. I thought about how in meeting Jackson, I had met the chance to love again. Just when I thought I would never be happy again, I had met Jackson.

As I looked into his eyes, I began searching for any hint of a man who might hurt me. We were lying in the dark, in silence. I was breathing hard, deep. Jackson's heartbeat had slowed, and as he drifted off to sleep, he held me tight. I took a deep breath and exhaled, allowing my body to soften into his. He hugged me tighter whenever my body shifted, as if he thought I was moving away from him. I smiled.

"Goodnight, Trevor," he spoke, sounding heavy-eyed.

6

This Love Is So

Jackson ...

I was more tired than I thought. I was tired from the drive on Sunday, from unpacking all week, and spending time with Trevor's immediate family until late last night took its toll on me. But I wasn't too tired to dream.

Dreams of my father came too frequent, and I had all but convinced myself that was the only way I was ever going to see him again. The dreams always started and ended the same way, and in the middle there was nothing but confusion.

I was a young boy walking through the woods beside my father. It was dark, wet, and I had nothing shielding me from the elements. I had no idea how we got there. He was trying to explain something to me, but while his mouth moved, sound did not exit. "Talk louder," I said, but he just disappeared. There I was standing in the dark, damp woods by myself, turning around and screaming, "Dad, where are you? I'm scared, dad." He never answered, and he never returned.

That's what happened in the last dream, and the dream before that. And although in the beginning of my dreams I am always fully clothed, in the end I was naked as the day I was born.

I woke feeling cold from sweat that came even though the night had cooled. I lay in bed staring through the darkness, trying to untangle the mysteries embedded in these dreams until sleep returned.

I slept through Trevor getting ready for work. I was dead to the world for a good eight hours, and enjoyed every minute of it. My mother always told me I could sleep through an earthquake. Apparently, she was right.

I sat up in my bed and stretched my arms above my head. "Thank you heavenly father for waking me up this morning, and allowing me to see this day you created just for me," I prayed out loud. I didn't actually think God created the day just for me, but I was claiming it anyway. That's how I felt.

I took all week to work on my bedroom, putting each peace of furniture in its perfect place. I still had a few bits and pieces to add here and there before I could say I was done. A trip to T.J.Maxx had made it to the top of a to-do list I had created only in my mind. There was still so much to do, starting with figuring out the quickest route to my new job at the hospital. I'd heard about the traffic in this area, and sitting idle in morning congestion wasn't my idea of an early morning commute to work. I needed to shop for groceries, get a new work wardrobe, and spend some time downtown scoping out restaurants. Trevor had already warned there were plenty from which to choose.

I was about to roll out of bed and pull myself together when my cell phone rang. I was a bit startled. I started searching for the phone, which I thought I had thrown into the chair in the corner of the room, only to find it under my pillow, where I would usually put it after talking to Trevor late into the night. Then I was just too lazy to get up. Now it was just habit.

"Hello," I answered after looking at a number I didn't recognize.

"What happened to my phone call?" Devaan began as soon as she heard my voice. In my last conversation with my sister, I promised her I had a plan. What I didn't share with her were the details behind the airtight master plan Trevor and I had devised.

"Good morning to you, too, beautiful," I said with a smile on my face.

"Oh, don't even give me that. I waited a whole week to hear from you, and I had to call. What's that about? Why haven't I heard from you?"

"I planned on calling you today, but now I don't have to," I began, walking downstairs to the kitchen with my phone pressed against my ear. I opened the refrigerator and removed a bottle of spring water. I twisted the cap on the bottle, walked over to the breakfast island, pulled out a chair, and sat.

I loved talking to my sister. After my father left, it was always just the three of us—me, Devaan, and my mother—until Mr. Kirkwood made the trio a quartet. I didn't think we needed a fourth person. My sister and I had a special bond. We had been to hell and back, hell being our parents' divorce.

"So, tell me about this new man in your life?" Devaan suggested. "How have you been? Are you all right?"

"Hold up, big sis. Which question do you want me to answer first?"

"I don't care. Just start talking."

"Trevor isn't that new. He's been around for two years."

"So why am I just hearing about him? And I'm going to assume Mother doesn't know too much about him, either."

"I haven't told her much of anything. It took us, Trevor and me, two years to get to this point. We had some kinks to work out."

"So is that where you went when I couldn't find you on some weekends? You could have let us in on your plan. We wouldn't have judged."

"This is Devaan I'm talking to, right? When have you not judged?"

I told Devaan about the house, about my relationship with Trevor, and that I had already begun to feel like part of the family around Trevor's father and his father's fiancée. I told her the story about Gavin and that I needed to get away in order to maintain my sanity. I told her about the lies Gavin told, and how I believed everything—all the bullshit he dished out. It took me a long ass time, but I finally got tired. I got tired of spending Saturday nights alone wondering if the man I wanted to be with wanted just as much to be with me. I got tired of waking up Sunday mornings wondering why he didn't love me the way I thought I needed to be loved. And I got tired of having all these damn feelings and never doing anything to stop myself from feeling that way.

With my revelation, Devaan had only one other question for me.

"How's Trevor treating you? He's not hurting you, is he?" she asked with an I'll-kick-his-ass tone in her voice.

"No such a thing," I responded in my best Harpo imitation, the voice I used when trying to make her laugh. A better question would have been how was I treating myself.

"Listen, Jackson. I'm sorry you had to deal with the heartache Gavin caused all by yourself," she said, sounding more sincere.

"I appreciate that. I also appreciate the lessons I learned. I know what not to accept the next time. Most importantly, he led me to Trevor, who has shown me every chance he gets what love feels like. Sorry for keeping such distance between us. I just needed to figure some things out."

I knew my sister was there to listen to me. Sometimes though, you have to accept that people have things in their lives they have to figure out. You have to force yourself to work through the many things that causes you pain, even if it causes you more pain. Sometimes that is part of the process.

"And it sounds like you have. Your happiness and sanity is all that matters to me, and if it means moving as far as you can away from pain, that's what you have to do."

I had told Devaan about the new important person in my life, and now I had my own question for her too.

"So, who's the new guy adding to your happiness?"

"Well, there is this person…"

"You're calling the new man in your life 'this person'?" I asked, taking another sip of water. She chuckled. "Tell me about him. And I assume Mother doesn't know about him yet, or else she would have said something to me. Who is he?"

"Oh, Jackson, you're going to love him!"

Hmmm. I'll make that decision for myself. You're not going to build me up to let me down, I thought. "Is that all I get? Does this love interest have a name? You know I have to give him the once-over to make sure he's right for my big sis," I said jokingly, but I was serious.

"His name is Telly."

"I can't wait to meet this Telly person." I removed the phone from my ear and looked at the screen. A call from Trevor's office had chimed in. I ignored it and continued my conversation with Devaan.

"I can't wait for you to meet him, either. And when will I meet Mr. Trevor?"

"Soon, I promise."

"All right, baby brother."

"You're going to have to stop calling me that real soon. I love you."

She laughed. "I love you, too."

7

When You Really Love Someone

Trevor...

I was adding a few items to the bottom of an already long to-do list when his picture appeared on my cell phone screen. I had received a text message from him earlier, but between talking to Wesley on my way in, sending Jackson a quick text, and then talking with Caela about lunch reservations, it had slipped my mind to respond to him.

"Hello," I answered, placing the cap on my Waterman élégance black and silver pen. The pen was a gift from my father. "Every serious designer needs a good pen," my father had said as I anxiously tore through the wrapping like a kid expecting a gift from his wish list in a letter to Santa. *Don't you mean every good writer deserves a good pen?* I thought, but I wasn't going to correct him. I had just finished signing my first contract after cutting the ribbons from the doors of my vision, officially opening the glass doors to The Harrison Agency.

Double R Architectural and Interior Design had exclusively become The Harrison Agency, and had a name that was now synonymous with success. Ventures with mogul Curtis Millington that culminated in two lucrative projects had brought notoriety.

Notoriety came with a price and a clientele that now included developer Lew Wolff and Investor Jeffrey Picower. We were just waiting for Donald Trump to come knocking on our doors or ringing our phones. I sat back in my chair and attempted to give the caller my undivided attention.

"Too busy to even return a text?" Dexter asked, but I knew he was joking.

"Not true at all, man. I planned on responding, but I got sidetracked," I said. I hated that I had just described my conversation with Jackson as a sidetrack, even if it were just a text message. "What's going on in your world, my friend?"

"I can't call it," Dexter said, his usual response when he had something on his mind but isn't exactly sure if he wanted to talk about it.

"Everything okay with you and Giovanni?"

"Gio and I are fine, for the most part." Dexter paused. *For the most part,* I thought. *Wasn't that codeword for shit isn't going the way it's supposed to be?* I wasn't sure if he was waiting for a response, or if he was collecting his words to continue. Regardless, I remained silent. "I got another phone call from him yesterday," Dexter continued.

"From Patrick? Did you…"

"Of course I didn't accept it," Dexter interrupted, "But something inside me wanted to. I just don't want to step back into the past. I've finally gotten to the point where I can think about what happened and not get upset or angry at him. I'm where I have forgiven him, although he doesn't know it. Can I ask you something, Trevor?"

"Sure."

"Is it possible for love to stay the same, even though people change?"

"It's quite possible."

"Then that's my fear. I don't know that not talking to him, if not seeing him means I've stopped loving him. And I'm afraid him knowing I've already forgiven him will put some crazy idea in his head that there's some possibility of reconciliation."

"After two years, do you think he still thinks like that?" I asked.

"You don't know Patrick, and if his messages are any indication, yes," Dexter confirmed, and with that, he was silent again. This wasn't the conversation I was expecting to have with Dexter this morning. He didn't talk about Patrick often, but when he did, I didn't have a problem listening. It was because of what Patrick had done to Dexter that had led to our chance meeting.

There was one question I needed to ask Dexter. "Do you love Giovanni?" I could almost see Dexter's face deep in thought, playing the question in his mind. I don't think he had even asked himself that same question, and if he had, he'd never answered.

"I want to be...."

"It's a yes or no question, Dexter."

"I want to be in love with him."

"If you want to be in love with him, leave Patrick in the past where he is. Leave him wondering about what he did to you. Leave him feeling how he feels now that he has lost you. Don't make the same mistake I almost made. Don't hold on to someone who's already had his chance. Love does a lot of things, but what it doesn't do is wait."

The conversation had reached another level. I was asking someone to live by words I heard from so many. Damn, they were right. Hindsight is 20/20.

"Okay," Dexter said. That was all he said.

"Listen, I have a staff meeting in thirty minutes that I need to finish preparing for. Why don't we have dinner this weekend?"

"We?" Dexter questioned

"Yes, as in you, Giovanni, me, and Jackson. You can check with Giovanni, and I'll check with Jackson, but we'll talk. And listen…" I demanded.

"I'm listening."

"Leave Patrick in yesterday. Even if you still love him, he doesn't need to hear that in your voice, or see it in your face. Got it? He's had his chance."

"I got it. Have a productive meeting."

"And you have a great day, my friend."

8

Press Pause on Life

Jackson ...

I was sitting in my newly furnished office space, surrounded by walls painted in Wasabi, and trim the color of Vintage Wine, my new favorite colors. I still felt exhausted from moving furniture and hanging artwork. I was eager to occupy my new place. I didn't want to make the same mistake I'd heard so many others make, friends included: meeting some guy they barely knew, and after a few months of telephone conversations, even nights where phone calls went unanswered and whereabouts went unexplained, moving with no job or home on an empty promise of love and relationship. I just wasn't ready to spend most of my nights sleeping in this house by myself, especially since Trevor and I were closer now.

Trevor had spent the first few nights with me in my new house, a luxury we didn't have with miles of Eastern real estate separating us. He didn't mind waking extra early on workdays to make the forty-five minute drive to The Harrison Agency. Even with the unemployment rate slowly creeping upwards, the stagnant climb of the stock market, The Harrison Agency was still thriving, which allowed him to keep his staff employed. The projects he completed for Curtis Millington was done under budget and about two months ahead of schedule, and he had agreed to head another project for Charney Copeland Enterprises, Curtis's cousin whom he was introduced to when the Millingtons invited him to a celebratory dinner.

Trevor now owned his architectural and interior design company outright after buying Kelvin out of the partnership. He was no longer doing business as Double R Architectural and Interior Design, a name he and Kelvin created by combining the first letters of their middle names, Rene and Rasaun, which Kelvin rarely used.

The excitement in his voice was intoxicating when Trevor called me with the good news. That was the last thing keeping him connected to Kelvin. Fortunately for Trevor, buying Kelvin out of his share came easier than falling out of love with him.

I still had some large and small pieces of furniture that sat untouched in one room or the other. Those were the ones I kept hiding from Mr. Robert since he insisted on assembling anything that came with screws and directions. I don't know if he thought I had left my tool belt or ability at my mother's house. He also insisted I stopped calling him Mr. Robert. I thought it would be disrespectful, but Mr. Robert thought we were all adults. I didn't argue with him.

I still had one more day before I started my new job as a Clinical Pharmacist at the University Hospital. Although I had many other things I should be doing, I poured a glass of Joseph Phelps Insignia and retired to what I had decided was one of my favorite places in the house.

I was sitting on the natural Tigerwood hardwood floor with my legs stretched out in front of me. I don't know why I found sitting in this position so comfortable. I picked up my Moto Q and dialed in to Trevor's office.

"Don't tell me you miss me already," Trevor answered, laughing, his voice sounding more awake now. By now he already had a fresh cup of caffeinated Columbia flowing freely though his veins.

"Aren't you full of yourself? But to answer your question, of course I miss you." With Trevor, I had no shame in telling him exactly how I felt.

"Oh, before I forget, my dad and Natalie have invited us to dinner on Thursday. Are you free?"

"Sure. I'm looking forward to it already."

"Good. I'm sure one of them will call you, but I promised I would mention it to you."

"Listen, do you have time to grab lunch today?" Trevor asked. It wasn't 10:00 am yet. He'd barely finished breakfast and he was already thinking about lunch.

"But of course I do. Do you have a place in mind?"

"I didn't think beyond you saying yes. I'll ask Caela to make reservations and have her call you with the details."

"Cool. I will see you then. Enjoy your morning."

"Enjoy your last day of freedom. I love ya."

"I love ya too, Trevor."

A few moments after ending my conversation with Trevor, my cell phone rang. Since I didn't recognize the number displayed on the screen, I allowed the call to go to voicemail.

"Junior," the familiar voice called out as I listened. "If you're there, please answer," she demanded. Click. Click. The caller hung up.

I hadn't spoken to my mother in a little more than three days. I hadn't heard from her since leaving my new phone number on her voicemail at work. Calling her back was on my to-do list, right after calling Devaan and my friend Colton.

When I returned the call to the unfamiliar number, I was greeted by a generic voicemail. *Now we're playing phone tag,* I thought, and attempted to call the only other number I had for my mother. The number had been changed to a non-published number, and I was instructed to check the number I had and dial again. I wasn't going to do that. I was certain I had dialed the right number.

There was a sense of urgency in her voice, and being the concerned son I was, I needed to make sure my mother was okay. I walked from my office to the kitchen, poured a glass of freshly squeezed orange juice and removed my planner from the briefcase. I dialed my mother's office number, and after several rings, a male voice unlike any I've heard before answered.

"Hello. Mrs. Bradley, please." After a few seconds of silence, my mother spoke.

"Mother!" I said in a cheerful but equally concerned tone. I had been calling Mrs. Bradley "Mother" since I was a little boy. Some people thought it was some wealthy, uppity thing I had picked up. I was already too damn old to be calling some woman "mommy." Anyway, my way of addressing my mother didn't bother her.

"Yes dear," she replied with equal pleasantry. "Junior, is everything all right?"

For as far back as I could remember, I couldn't recall Mother calling me by any other name. I was born Jackson-Chase Demetrius Bradley. Jackson was my maternal grandfather's first name. Chase was my daddy's father's middle name. Demetrius Bradley belonged to my father. I could never explain why she called me junior except that she saw me as a small piece of the men who came before me. Or maybe she was trying to appease my father, as if he was ever worth appeasing. She did call me Jackson when I got into some trouble I had no business getting into, which rarely happened.

"You're going to thank me one day," Mother had said one evening while we sat across from each other at the dining room table. As she spoke, she waved the fork for emphasis, as if she couldn't have gotten her point across without such a threatening gesture. Devaan sat looking at her, and then at me, waiting to see our next reaction. I wasn't intimidated. I just sat like a stubborn mule impervious to the whipping I had received. I can't exactly remember what I had done. Though I was saddened by the consequences that usually followed, I was comforted by the thought that soon, my father would walk through the door, and before long, would convince my mother to "let the boy alone." A few days later, the same father who had often rescued me, had ran out on my mother, my sister, and me, leaving her a heartbroken, single mother, adjectives she never thought she would use to describe herself after she and my father were married.

"Junior, are you there? I asked how you were doing," Mother interrupted.

"I'm here. I'm fine."

"Your sister is worried about you. Have you heard from her?" she asked.

"I spoke with her earlier."

"Well, needless to say, she doesn't call or visit as often since you left. I heard from her two days ago. She called to sing about some gentleman friend she had been seeing for a couple months now and that she couldn't wait for us to meet him," she said with a bit of uncertainty. "If she was so excited, why are we just hearing about this man?"

"I have no idea, Mother. She just wasn't ready, I guess."

"Anyway, I have a new cell phone number."

I reached for a pen and jotted her number in my planner next to today's date.

"Aren't you a bit curious who this guy is?" she asked.

"Curious? Yes. But it sounds like you want me to be worried, and I'm not."

"Well, why aren't you?"

"Because I trust her judgment."

Devaan was no fool. She sounded happy. She didn't date a lot. The men she had met, the ones who hadn't worked, were just men who simply weren't compatible. She was smart enough to leave them before she invested too much, if she invested anything at all.

This was my opportunity to give my mother some insight on the decision I had made. She was at work, and any desire to question my reason would have to be put off until later. At least I would've had some hours to prepare my response. I finally told her about the heartache I endured and how badly I needed to get away. She was disappointed I didn't trust our relationship or her love enough to tell her what happened. It was hard for me to explain everything since I hadn't quite figured out certain things in my own head. Then I told her about Trevor, about the new job at the University Hospital, and the new house.

"You know no matter what, I will always love you," she said.

"Yes Mother, I know. It was never your love I was questioning. I just..." Before I could finish my response, another call beeped in. I asked my mother to hold and swapped calls.

"Hello," I answered.

"What's going on, baby brother?" Devaan greeted.

"Hello, lovely. I have your mother on the other line. Hold on a sec." I clicked back over and wrapped up my conversation with my mother. She promised to call me later. I promised to be here when she called.

I clicked back to Devaan and engaged in our usual question and answer conversation.

"Work is going ok?" I asked.

"There's talk about a promotion, but I keep reminding myself they had that same talk last year."

"Maybe this time it's real talk."

"Maybe." She paused. "Hey, did your mother tell you Aunt Whitney has been asking about you?"

"You mean she's fishing for new information to gossip about? I hope Mother hasn't told her anything."

"She knows better than to go to her with questions about you."

My Aunt Whitney and I haven't had the best relationship in years, and she used to be my favorite aunt, that is until she decided to make me her hot topic.

Their whispers usually didn't bother me. I paid as much attention to them as I did the other things I cared nothing about. They didn't make or break me, and if I were broken, I wasn't giving them the satisfaction of seeing me in pieces.

It was always my aunt Whitney. She was more like a nosey neighbor than a family member, always in somebody's business and never paying attention to her own disheveled life. She had nothing else to do but sit around and thrash out what is and what isn't in the lives of people who barely knew she existed. But I had some pity for her. The one man who had stayed around long enough to muster an ounce of care left seemingly without a trace.

And her own son pulled the same disappearing act about five years after, calling her only on birthdays, Mother's Day, and Christmases because, after all, she was still his mother. Her one true friend, her abettor, Janae DuBose, and her daughter Mackayla Conner were the only two women willing to lend an ear to her misguided conjecture.

"That man did something to that boy. I swear he hasn't been right since," Whitney said, talking out the side of her mouth.

"And I hear he's into them men."

"And where did you hear that?" Janae asked, crossing her legs and soaking up the scandal.

"Contrary to what people believe, we aren't the only ones talking," Whitney responded, taking a sip from a tall glass of apple martini. "And I don't think he knows what he's looking for in them."

"What makes you think he's looking for something?" Mackayla pitched in. I hadn't decided if she was on my side.

"Oh, now you want to play dumb with me."

As always, they were sitting in a corner during another family gathering, separating themselves from everyone, making them the outcasts they've become known for. And they wondered why they rarely got invited. Their conversation would continue. Only a look from my mother in their direction could bring pause to their banter.

But my Aunt Whitney was right. They weren't the only ones engaged in careless whispers.

"Blame his father for the way that boy turned out," my grandmother said three weeks earlier.

I'm not sure what had preceded my grandmother's statement. I walked into the kitchen unabashed by the overheard. My grandmother was sitting in the kitchen drinking her usual cup of green tea. My mother stood with her back against the kitchen sink. I walked over to the refrigerator, grabbed an orange, and walked out as if I had heard nothing. I felt their eyes following my quick departure. I stood outside briefly waiting for either to speak but I heard nothing. Regardless of what she said, I was still grandma's boy. I knew what she said was said out of love. This much I could say about my grandmother. I couldn't say the same about Aunt Whitney.

After talking with Devaan, I listened to the voicemail I had received. It was from Caela.

Mr. Bradley. I have made reservations for you and Mr. Harrison at Smith and Wollensky at 12:30.

I returned to the kitchen, grabbed the glass of orange juice, which was now room temperature warm from sitting on the counter top, and poured it in the sink. I poured another glass to half-full and made my way back to my office. I turned on the flat screen LCD television that hung on the wall between two five-shelf bookcases. I sat back on the floor with my legs stretched out before me and watched as they dissected Presidential candidate Barack Obama's readiness for the oval office. From what I gathered, pundits had already assumed he would not be prepared to tackle problems created by his soon-to-be predecessor. He hadn't even won and he was already being written off left and right. When I had had enough, I muted the television and directed my attention back to reviewing my agenda for the first days at work. I had two hours to kill before my lunch date with Trevor.

9

Brand New

Trevor...

When I wanted a quiet lunch and good food, Smith and Wollensky always stood on the top of my list of favorite downtown steakhouses. It was located on 19th Street in northwest, DC. Without a reservation, you needed luck on your side, or some connection to Jada Pinkett-Smith to get a seat by just walking in.

I was waiting for Jackson in an area outside the restaurant only used during the summer months that extended into late October, or the occasional unseasonably warm January days that, every now and then, visited the area. The lunch menu featured anything from classic steaks to catches from the sea, and after having eaten here so often, I had sampled everything. The marinated Cajun rib-eye was my favorite. Jackson had only been here on one other occasion.

"You didn't have to dress to impress me, sir," I said in greeting as he walked up to me.

"I hardly call this dressing to impress. I haven't unpacked everything just yet," Jackson replied. I got up and gave him the hug I'd been waiting to give him all morning. "And who said dressing had anything to do with you?"

He wore a white striped fitted shirt, with sleeves folded neatly up to his elbows. His caravan-colored stretch cotton dress pants covered legs that went on forever, and his burgundy belt secured his pants to a waist any woman would be glad to wrap their arms around. He still had that confidence, that focused and calculating walk I can now admit I loved the most about him.

As we walked into the busy restaurant, I could feel piercing stares, mostly from the ladies with the usual questions in their heads. *Damn! Any chance those two are available?* Or, *they must swing that way. Where are their lady companions?* Some of the men had their questionable expressions, too, as if homosexuality had made it unconstitutional for two fine-looking men like us to dine together.

"Reservation for Mr. Trevor Harrison," I said as I approached the maître d'.

"Here it is. Reservation for two," he said, looking up at me, and then at Jackson.

"Yes, sir," Jackson confirmed. He looked at me and smiled.

"Follow me, gentlemen," he directed.

As we were seated, the maître d' carefully placed our menus to our right on the table and mentioned the name of our waiter. "You gentlemen enjoy your lunch," he said with a warm smile, and then excused himself.

London, our waiter, stood 6'2". His skin was fair. His perfect teeth were hidden behind sexy pink lips. Without even trying, he looked as if he were posing for a face shot. His deep, dark brown eyes sat deep in his face, shadowed by far-reaching eyebrows.

"Can I get you gentlemen something to drink?" he asked under a soft tone that forced you to listen.

I requested a bottle of Brunello di Montalcino, and since we had been perusing our menus, we placed our orders at the same time.

"I'll be back shortly with your wine," London said, and walked away as if he were practicing his runway debut.

"Model?" I asked Jackson.

"If he isn't, he should definitely consider it." Jackson turned his head, looking over his shoulder at London. When he turned back around, I could read what I'm sure was supposed to have been an inward smile all over his face.

"What is it?"

"Did I tell you about this one time I was approached about modeling?"

"No."

"This guy told me I had 'the look' and I waited for him to tell me what exactly was this look. I was quite sure the look varied from one person to the next, or else everyone in the latest issue of *Vogue*, *Elle*, or *GQ* would look exactly the same."

"You didn't believe him?"

"I did. He said his name was Travis Price. Called himself a model agent, but I'm sure it was his mastered pick-up line and he thought I looked gullible enough for it to work."

"You must have thought about it for a minute?"

"Of course, but I knew at my height, I would have been a hard fit. Plus, I was with Sarina Crafton, and if you knew Sarina Crafton, you would have thought about it for only a minute too."

"Sarina Crafton," I repeated. "I think the name says enough."

"Pretty much. She had her own bent ideas about male models. If they weren't on one of the pages of *VIBE* magazine representing Enyce, or holding one of the sexy Apple Bottom models, they didn't qualify. She thought being a personal shopper for a still unnamed star had made her the juggernaut in the industry. I hated Sarina's sometimes self-centered, hypocritical thoughts. Her younger brother was a model, and as much as I liked him, he was nothing like those models his sister's mouth watered for. But his ads were plastered on billboard under the bright lights of Times Square because he had the smile and the body that made you buy shit you didn't need. And I think I'm sexy as hell in underwear."

"Sounds like jealousy was her middle name."

"I have a middle name for her but trust me, jealousy isn't what I'm thinking." Jackson laughed.

Jackson was smart and athletic. He was the super athlete in high school, once dominating the quarterback and wide receiver positions for his Stonewall Hardy Senior High School Panthers varsity football team beginning in his freshman year. That wasn't the school he was supposed to attend, but after his father left, Jackson's desire to please his father and graduate from his alma mater Plymouth High went also.

Jackson was as sexy as anyone in his practice gear, which included a panther t-shirt cut short enough to expose abs he had obviously worked hard for all summer. (I'd seen pictures.) Swimming was his passion, but he concentrated on football, the sport most adored by his father. Jackson was 6'9", a solid two-hundred-and-five pound, with skinny yet very firm legs, sporting a curve that began just where his knees ended. He had a great personality and a very attractive demeanor, which helped him survive when it seemed his world crumbled after his father left. He had a nose that complimented lips that, when he smiled, showed a gap that probably would have been unattractive on anyone else. He had eyes that always seemed distant, yet they had the power to pull you in, enthralling you unintentionally. And if the picture of his father was any indication, he had a lot more good-looking years ahead of him.

"Well, I think you would have had the modeling world ablaze, just like Tyson Beckford and Bobby Roache."

"I know," Jackson agreed, rubbing his chin and smiling. I needed to say something to wipe that smile from his face.

"So your last day of freedom," I began. "You ready to go back to work?"

"Not going to say I'm ready, but the bills have to get paid. And honestly, I'm running out of things to do around the house."

"What are you talking about?" I asked. "You still have boxes to unpack and furniture to assemble."

"Blah, blah, blah," Jackson said, and laughed.

London returned with the bottle of wine in one hand and two wine glasses in the other. He poured a glass full. Its color was a rich ruby. Its natural aroma tickled my nose. A quick taste left a lasting impression in my mouth. I nodded in approval.

London continued to fill our glasses, placed the bottle in an ice bucket on the table, then left to get our meals.

"So, listen. You've heard me talk about Dexter, right?

"Yeah. Your friend from the accident," Jackson said. "Yeah, I remember you talking to him."

"Well, if you're not busy this weekend, we're trying to make dinner plans with him and Giovanni."

"Giovanni?" Jackson asked.

"The man he's talking to. I told him I needed to check your schedule first before I could commit." I felt my personal cell phone vibrate in its case. I always leave my phone on vibrate or silent mode on workdays. Usually on lunch breaks I would turn down the volume, but since I was having lunch with Jackson, I left it on the setting it has been on since I arrived at the office at

8:45 a.m. I ignored the vibration and continued to focus on Jackson.

"So, we're already having dinner with your dad and Natalie on Thursday, and dinner with Dexter and his beau on Saturday. So where in between that do we try and find time for us?" Jackson asked with a smile, but I could tell he was serious.

"All you have to say is no and we can do something else. Dinner was my idea. I wanted him to meet you, the person in my life."

"Boy, stop getting so serious. I'll check my schedule tomorrow and let you know. Deal?" Jackson asked, winking his left eye. I smiled and took my wine glass to the head.

The marinated Cajun rib-eye was finger licking good, though I dared not lick my fingers in the presence of these fine diners. Jackson's Miso glazed Chilean sea bass smelled as good as it tasted. He didn't have to ask once before I was reaching across the table with my fork, boldly stealing one piece of the succulent cut sitting to the side of the plate.

If I didn't have work to finish, or if I didn't have another afternoon meeting with my partner Wesley and a potential new client, I would have definitely spent the rest of the day with Jackson. And I'm certain he wouldn't have minded.

10

What's My Name?

Trevor ...

I walked through the doors to my office at exactly 2:30. One of the best two-hour lunches I have had in a long time. Okay, the best two hours, since getting there took some time. As quickly as I was seated, Caela appeared at my door.

"Quick message, Mr. Harrison," she said. "Mr. Monahan wanted you stop in his office once you returned."

"Did he say what for?"

"He didn't say. But he did have a huge smile on his face," Caela said, turning and heading back to her desk. After a few steps, she turned back around, walked closer to the office, and leaned on the side of the door. She lightly tapped her pen in the palm of her right hand. Caela was left-handed.

"Yes, Caela," I said. I was standing behind my desk running lines through the items on my to-do list. With two meetings, a phone call, and lunch with Jackson, I hadn't made much of a dent in my errands and the day was almost over.

"How was lunch with Jackson?" she asked, smiling.

"It's not everything I'm going to tell you, Caela."

"Yes. But..." she said, and flashed her girlish smile. She paused, waiting for me to disclose.

"It was lunch, Caela," I said, walking past her, heading towards Wesley's office. She followed. "We ate, we talked, and we made plans."

"Plans?"

"Yes, Caela, and you're passing your desk," I said, turning around briefly to face her.

When I reached Wesley's office, I knocked to announce my presence, even though his door was open. I figured he was busy on the phone describing his morning to Erin. You know how people are when they get into a new relationship. You spent morning, afternoon, and evening on the telephone wanting to learn everything about them, as if you were racing against time. That's how it was for Jackson and me. I figured straight men did the same thing. Before Erin, the ladies who came into Wesley's life stayed on the bottom of his list of priorities, but this was never something he kept hidden from them. His business came before girlfriends, but Erin was so much more.

Once he acknowledged me, I walked into his office and sat in one of the dark leather chairs in front of his desk. He had a childish grin on his face.

"Guess what?" he said.

"What's that?"

"Mr. Copeland finally agreed to the design changes we proposed."

"How did you get him to do that?"

"He called this morning asking me to give my honest opinion. I told him none of my opinions had been dishonest," Wesley said. "I showed him how he could make the same statement and save a few bucks at the same time."

"And he went for it?"

"Like he should have in the first place," Wesley added.

Wesley Monahan stood 6'3", a little on the thick side, but could probably find a bulging muscle or two if he searched hard for them. But Wesley loved his size, and so did the ladies. He spent days at the gym, but just long enough to get his heart pumping. He wore suits Monday through Friday, and his idea of dressing down meant wearing his suit sans tie. The faith Wesley had lost in love, relationships, and marriage was restored when Erin Lanning came into his life. He allowed himself to do with Erin what he hadn't allowed himself to do with any other women he had met: he allowed himself to fall in love. Though he was working on his relationship with his father, a process he started a year ago, their interaction still had a few rocks, if not boulders, in the way. One in particular was his father's wife.

Wesley had already admitted he didn't see mending fences with his stepmother in his near future. The man who two years ago thought marriage was for the birds was getting ready to build a nest with Erin.

"How do you like working with him?" I asked.

Wesley convinced me to contract the Copeland project. I agreed, on one condition: He had to head the project from start to finish—designs, negotiations, and presentations were all on him. With Kelvin and Jackson already occupying my emotional space, I definitely didn't want to add the conundrum that was Charney Copeland, not as a client or otherwise. Wesley agreed.

"Working with him isn't that bad. He brought Thorpe Flynn to our last meeting, a guy he introduced as his partner. He didn't specify if Mr. Flynn was his business partner or his partner in the bedroom. I don't care either way, but if you ask me, I would have to say, both." Wesley paused. "Whatever makes the brotha happy, you know."

I looked at Wesley and smiled. I did know.

"Are you ready for your 3:15?"

"Nothing to really get ready for. We're just going to meet these guys, see what it is they are looking for or expecting, and I guess we can go from there."

We were meeting with the Milner Group, a nonprofit organization interested in expanding the recreation center just outside of Marcel's hometown. They didn't have a lot of money and needed some companies to donate their services. Marcel was Dexter's nephew and had spent most of his evenings after school and Saturday mornings perfecting his basketball skills. I was doing this as a favor to Dexter, my way of giving back.

"You are still coming in with me, aren't you?"

"I got you, partna," Wesley said, and winked.

11

Distance and Time

Jackson ...

Some people just don't get it. Even though it came sooner that expected, I expected this phone call from him. I hadn't completely cut myself off from him, at least not yet. I had purposely placed distance between us and I hoped time wasn't too far behind. Unlike many, I knew the truth. I had fallen plenty of times with him and because of him. I had fallen in love, fallen in hurt, and finally, I had fallen out of love. That last fall was the best fall I had ever experienced with him.

"So when were you going to tell me you were leaving, or that you had left?" The word hello hadn't even fallen from my lips.

"What difference would it have made if I had stayed?"

"Now we'll never know."

"That doesn't sound like something I need to worry about," I said matter-of-factly.

"Did you leave because of me?"

I wasn't going to give Gavin that much power or any credit for the choices I made. "I left because of me. I needed to start over and starting over has been going well so far. You know I almost forgot what it felt like to be loved, and because of the bad taste your love left in my mouth, I almost ran from it."

"It wasn't always bad," Gavin said.

"Well, I remember most of the bad because the good was few and far between, and towards the end, the good never existed."

"You know something, Jackson…" And he was silent, as if he were sitting on the phone contemplating if he should say exactly what was on his mind. I wasn't going to do anything to encourage him.

"Are you there?" he asked.

"I'm here. You asked me if I knew something. I didn't think you needed a response to continue."

"I miss you," he admitted, and I could tell he regretted those words the moment they were spoken. I was surprised he would say something like that.

Who he missed was the person I became during the five years I was with him; the guy who knew truth but accepted lies. He missed the man who held on hoping both him and his love would come around soon, and the person who went to bed asking why he couldn't be the one. If Gavin missed anything, it's that I was no longer there to play his fool.

"That's nice," I said. I think he expected more than that.

"That's it?"

What did he mean if that was it? What else did he want or expect me to say? I knew how Gavin's mind worked. I would be saying I missed him, and he would be hearing something completely different. He was notorious for hearing whatever he wanted to hear. That had been the cause of many of our disagreements because nothing I said was ever heard exactly how I wanted him to hear it. So many times I had stopped myself from telling him how I felt when most of what I felt was pure hurt.

"What else is there for me to say, Gavin?" I had gotten to where I just didn't care anymore, and it pleased me that Gavin was feeling what it felt like when your feelings just don't matter.

"You just don't say 'that's nice' after someone says they miss you."

"But it's always a nice feeling to be missed. Don't think I was going to lie and say I miss you, too, because I don't. You just don't get it, do you?"

"What are you talking about?" he asked, and for a moment he had convinced me he hadn't a clue what I was talking about.

"Gavin, ten years ago I came into your life to love you. There was nothing ordinary about the love I had for you, or the love I gave to you. I never thought I needed to take caution when it came to love, not with you. But leave it up to you to prove me wrong."

"Why do you keep talking about us in the past?" he asked. If I knew him as well as I thought I did, he had been thinking about this conversation, rehearsing it over in his mind.

"First of all, there is no 'us'. All thanks to you, of course. And I keep talking about you in the past because that's where I left you. Isn't that where you wanted to be? 'Cause you damn sure didn't act like you wanted to be a part of my future. I spent five years loving you, two years wanting you back, not realizing I never actually had you. I spent another two years trying like hell, and not without failure either, to get over you, and then one year finding the self I lost from loving you, and finally loving me again. And as hard as I've worked to get here, with everything else going on in my life, repeating you isn't something I want to do again."

"I'm sorry," Gavin said.

"It's too late for I'm sorry, Gavin. Maybe your apology would have meant something to me, you know, back when I needed to hear it, even if you didn't mean it. Right now, it really doesn't matter."

"But I am sorry," he repeated.

"You don't have to be sorry. I'm not." He was silent, like he always was when he knew I was speaking nothing but the truth.

I had been sitting in the car pulled over to the side on P Street NW, in the popular Georgetown section of D.C., getting ready to hit the shops. Students from the nearby Georgetown University were getting settled into the routine of classes. Freshmen who'd left home for the first time were taking advantage of their newly found independence.

"Will I see you again?" Gavin asked.

"I'm not sure that's a good idea. Maybe not this soon, but we'll see."

"Take care of you, JC."

I smiled and shook my head. "Who's going to take care of me if I don't?" I asked, not expecting him to respond. "Take care, Gavin."

12

Wish He Never Met You

Trevor...

What I thought was a heavy breeze was actually a hard rain. I sat up on the couch, my head resting in the fold of my arm, my eyes piercing through the vertical blinds, staring at a tree that swayed easily by a late September breeze.

I had just gotten off the phone with Jackson before the rain began. He had spent the rest of his day shopping for a new work wardrobe. He had prepared dinner when he got home and spent some time unpacking boxes. I wanted Jackson to be well rested his first day on the job, so I decided I would sleep in my own bed tonight, between my pillows. I heard the disappointment in his voice, but he knew it was best. It wasn't always possible to lie beside him and keep my hands to myself, which meant we would both be awake later than we needed to be.

The raindrops glistened as they freefell past a bright light in the front yard. A television movie I had planned on watching failed to keep my attention since all I could think about was Dexter and the conversation we had this morning. Across the street a couple ran from their car trying to escape the elements. When my cell phone buzzed, I had no intention of entertaining the caller. Although my mind was busy in thought, I was still enjoying my peaceful night until the vibrating phone interrupted my tranquility.

"So, you're the man who supposedly loves him? Don't think he's there for you to hurt him. If that's what you have in mind, do yourself a huge favor and leave him alone," a stranger began. "He's dealt with enough of your type in his life, and as much as he tries to avoid your type, you always seem to find yourselves in his radar. If you're looking for someone to hurt because you're still figuring out how to love, he's not the man for you."

"I don't know who this is, but don't you think it's time you stop hiding behind messages and ill-gotten phone numbers?"

"Oh, baby. I'm not hiding."

"I'm not your damn baby," I corrected. "And if this isn't hiding, then what do you call it?" I got up from the couch and walked to the refrigerator, searching for anything that would settle the nerves I had allowed this interloper to fluster. I had ignored his messages and phone calls, even the one that came today while I was having lunch with Jackson.

"For your own good," he warned, "loosen him from your pretentious grasp before…" the caller paused.

"Before what?" My interest had peaked. I stood in front of the refrigerator, the light revealing the tightness in my face.

"You'll be hearing from me again," the stranger promised.

"Hello? Hello?" I called out, but the phone was silent. I removed the phone from my ear and stared at the screen. Still disturbed by his audacity, I tossed the phone on the ceramic countertop. I removed an opened bottle of Pinot Gris I had gotten from The Wine List, poured a glass full, and then began making my way back to the couch. Before my nose could be tickled by the fruity fragrance, and my tongue completely wrapped in the sweet taste of vanilla, my phone vibrated again.

I rushed over to the counter. "Look, damn it!" I answered in fury. "I don't have time for you or your simple ass games. Get some balls and tell me why the hell you keep calling me."

"That definitely isn't the way I would greet my best friend."

"Definitely not," I said, smiling when I heard Denise's friendly, tranquil voice on the other end.

The familiarity in her voice brought a pleasurable smirk to my face. Some time had passed since our last conversation and we had some catching-up to do. Work, Caela, and my relationship with Jackson had kept me busy. I couldn't think of an excuse for Denise, although I was sure if I asked she probably had a good one.

I knew Denise would overreact to these menacing phone calls I had been receiving, so I kept that piece of information to myself. The phone calls, although I hadn't admitted it, were raising some questions about Jackson. Before he moved here, I wasn't receiving calls like that.

"So what's new with you?" Denise asked.

"I was going to ask you the same question," I said, deflecting her inquisition.

"I'm doing all right, and I'm definitely enjoying the people out here."

Moving to Houston was never in Denise's plans, but when opportunity came knocking, she opened the door and let him in. I hadn't had a chance to focus on missing her. But every time I spoke to her, that was the feeling I got in my heart.

"What about your love life?"

"Nonexistent. Next question," Denise responded hastily.

"Wait a minute, speedy Sally. You're not going to walk out of this one so easily. You were supposed to be working things out with Toni. Denise, what happened? What are you not telling me?"

"Like I told you," Denise replied. "DeRon Winters happened."

I did remember the last conversation I had with Denise. DeRon Winters had entered Toni's life and had thrown a monkey wrench into the happiness she enjoyed with Denise.

Toni Dale Hadley's hire at Texas Children's Hospital came with a salary increase, a seat on the hospital board, and eventually, DeRon Shane Winters. While Denise was busy negotiating contract deals for basketball center Shane Wheatley and guard Delroy Wallace with Los Angeles, Toni was busy becoming DeRon's bedfellow, cementing her place as the first Mrs. DeRon Shane Winters. Late evenings spent romping in DeRon's bed were covered up with lies about life-saving emergency surgery or board meetings that ran extremely late. Her involvement with DeRon stirred something in some of the jealous hens and cocks around the hospital. They were careful what they said about her and who were around when they said it. Those who thought she was a sleep-your-way-to-top kind of girl smiled in her presence and offered pleasantries like free government cheese, but smeared her name the moment she turned her back, or when the only thing lurking was the scent of her Angel perfume. The low jabs and insults came back to Toni as fast as they were breathed from the mouths of her haters. They, too, had their eyes on becoming Mrs. DeRon Shane Winters.

Toni's name was chewed up and spat out like last night's broccoli, at least that's what her inside-man, Kendal Bellfield, told her with eagerness, and then wondered what she did to make the women so bitter towards her—as if he didn't know. For whatever reason, Kendal paraded himself like a gossiping lady on a corner stoop just to get the latest scoop. He delivered rumors faster than an anchorwoman on the five-o'clock evening news, as if he had something to gain from Toni's rise or her impending nuptials to DeRon. DeRon was an eligible bachelor until Toni slithered her way in Texas Children's, and into his arms and heart.

I walked into the living room and settled in the chair facing my television. My right elbow rested on the arm of the chair, the wine glass held loosely between my fingers. I took a sip of the wine and waited for Denise to divulge.

"Maybe moving here was a mistake."

"Denise, what happened?" I asked again. She was never the type of person to second-guess herself. Any decisions she made were thoroughly thought out. She weighed the pros and cons, the ifs and buts, all to avoid making mistakes.

"I thought it was something she needed to go through since she'd never explored this idea of being with a man. It was a fling I thought, or hoped, would die out sooner rather than later."

"So you were okay knowing your girl had swung from dildo to dick?" I asked. I didn't mean to make a joke of it, but at some point, Denise expected me to do just that.

"None at all."

I sat on the phone and listened to Denise tell me about the end of a relationship I envied, between two women I admired.

Denise told me about the evening Toni never made it home for dinner as she said she would. She had called Toni several times, but each call went straight to voicemail. Knowing Toni's schedule, Denise didn't think anything was unusual. But when her calls weren't returned, usually within the hour, she knew something was wrong. She sat around the dinner table watching the candles burn to a ball of wax. She had emptied wine glasses of red wine to chase glasses of red wine, trying to stop her mind from wondering why one was enjoying dinner meant for two. Then, just before midnight, Toni came walking through the door as if she owed no one an explanation.

"What exactly did you say to her?"

"Are you going to let me tell this like it happened or what?" Denise snapped.

"Sorry. I shouldn't have interrupted," I said. I stayed quiet for the moment and allowed her to continue.

"Honey, you should have seen me. I wore a one-shoulder pink cocktail dress I had bought especially for this dinner she and I had been planning for weeks. I was sexy as hell."

"As you always are."

"Thanks sweetie, but I don't need your help." She laughed. "When I tell you it hugged my body and revealed curves you know I rarely show. I was standing in front of the large floor-to-ceiling window staring into the courtyard, feeling taller than tall in my backless silver shoes. I had an almost empty bottle of cabernet sauvignon in one hand, and held a wine glass close to my lips with the other when she opened my door and walked in. I turned my head slightly, looking over my left shoulder. Trevor, what she said next took my feet from under me."

"I'm not sure I want to hear this," I said, but I had my ears glued to the phone.

"Well, neither did I. But right now, you have no choice."

"Continue." I held my breath and prepared for the worse.

"Toni simply held up her left hand exposing her vintage diamond engagement ring and told me he asked her to marry him…and she had said yes."

Hearing what happened to Denise and Toni had left me without words.

"I don't understand why you're just telling me this," I finally said. Denise's angel had broken her heart. "I thought you guys were back on cloud nine by now. Why didn't you tell me?"

"I needed to work this out on my own. I thought she'd realized what we had and come back, but apparently life with the good doctor was sweet enough for her." There was a sadness I had never heard before in Denise's voice that was becoming familiar.

"No regrets, right?"

"None whatsoever," Denise said, pausing for a moment.

"So you have a wedding to prepare for?"

"Trust me. I'm not checking my mail for an invitation."

"Don't you want to be the one in the front to waive her hand after the pastor ask the congregation to speak now or forever hold their peace?"

"I don't need to be the one telling Toni she's making a mistake, even if that's what I truly believed. It'll come across as selfish. Whatever will be, will be."

"Spoken like a trooper."

Whenever I spoke to Denise I'm reminded why she had become the friend I would always want in my corner.

"Listen," she spoke softly. "When you answered the phone, you sounded like you were expecting someone who had already gotten on your last nerve. What's that all about?"

Distance and time had happened to Denise and me. Dinners and lunches at our favorite Le Petit Poisson once scheduled with a simple phone call now required a reservation and a three-hour flight. So there was a lot I needed to tell her, but where should I start?

I hadn't told Denise too much about my rise with Jackson, which came as a result of my fall with Kelvin. And I wasn't going to mention hearing of Kelvin's plans to move back, though I wondered briefly what had happened with Kelvin's relationship with Lawrence. I hadn't mentioned the eerie phone calls that begun shortly after Jackson had settled into my life. Then there was Dexter. I didn't know how to tell her about the feelings for Dexter that had settled in the pit of my stomach; feelings I'd been trying to ignore and couldn't quite explain. I didn't want Denise to think news of Kelvin returning to the area, or that unexplained feelings for Dexter had thrown a curveball into what I had with Jackson. I was doing a good job making my relationship with Jackson work, even with all that was going on around me. I was through with my love for Kelvin, and as much as I could, I was showing Jackson just how much I loved him.

13

Ain't Nothing but Love

Trevor...

It seemed I had blinked and Thursday was here. Until tonight, I had no idea Natalie knew her way around the kitchen. Usually when my father suggested dinner, she was the first on the phone, pressing the numbers to one of her favorite restaurants. I think she had one or two of them on speed dial. She was keeping this talent hidden, but tonight she had definitely let her inner-chef work her magic in the kitchen.

Jackson had spent his third day at University Hospital in meetings, this time with the CEO and the board. Three days on the job and it seemed each day was already longer than the previous, but he wasn't complaining. He'd called earlier, a few minutes before five to say he had to work late, which was fine, since Natalie still had some time before dinner was placed on silver platters and brought to the table.

Apple avocado salad with tangerine dressing teased our taste buds in preparation for the main meal. The tomato and avocado salad with green empress dressing had become my father's favorite, so there was a colorful display of that, too. Grilled shrimp with garlic-red chile-thyme marinate satisfied the seafood lover in all of us. The Peking duck sat in the middle of the dining room table on a bed of greens and slices of oranges as if it were a succulent turkey on Thanksgiving. Natalie had everyone in mind when she began planning this dinner a few days ago. She was trying to please us all, which wasn't necessary. My father had already fallen in love with her, and, well, she had me when I saw him smile when he first mentioned her name.

An hour into dinner and Jackson still hadn't arrived. When my cell phone vibrated, I hoped it was him calling to say he was, at most, five minutes away. When I looked at the screen, Caela's asparagus-green eyes stared back at me. She sported a medium length short hairstyle. Her hair color fell somewhere between auburn and red, but I liked that color the most. This was my favorite picture of Caela, a glamour shot taken over a year ago when she entertained the idea of modeling. She would have been good, too.

"Hello," I answered, excusing myself from the table.

"Hey, are you busy?" Caela asked. That was a trick question. Even though I loved Caela, I hated being interrupted when having dinner with my family.

"What's going on, Caela?" I asked.

"I just saw Jackson at Java House. Didn't you say you two were having dinner with the family tonight?"

"I did. We are."

"Well, unless that's you sitting across from him at Java House, and you forgot to tell me your momma was Puerto Rican. Wait, let me look again." Caela paused. "Nope, that's not you."

"Are you sure?"

"That it's not you? Of course I'm sure."

"I know it's not me," I said, trying not to get loud. "I mean are you sure it's Jackson. Who is he with?" I asked, sounding like a detective firing questions like I was trying to solve a case.

"He's with some guy. And yes, I'm sure it's Jackson. Their interaction looked intense."

"What do you mean?" I asked.

"I mean they seemed to be discussing something important."

"Did he see you?"

"I doubt it."

"Look, Caela, I have to go. I'll call you later."

I hung up the phone and walked back to the dining table. I sat back in my chair and resumed eating in silence until my father broke in.

"Hey," he said. "Is everything ok?"

"That was Jackson. He should be here shortly." I didn't see any reason why I should share my conversation with Caela. If she said she had seen Jackson, she wasn't lying. Jackson wasn't a hard person to pick out from a crowd. We sat, ate, and talked about school, work, and trips my father was planning with Natalie.

"He better hurry up and get here," Adrian spoke. "I think my mom was trying to impress him. I hope he knows I'm packing a few to-go plates for later. He does know I'm a college student, right?"

Just as I was about to ask Adrian a question, the doorbell chimed.

"That's probably Jackson now," I said. I excused myself from the table again.

I walked to the door, looking at my watch. When I opened the door, Jackson stood with a wide smile across his face. He was looking good. He looked especially handsome in his grey solid Hugo Boss suit, white solid stretch fitted shirt, and textured stripe skinny tie. His suit jacket hung from the closest finger to his thumb, and he leaned against the door as if he expected me to answer.

He walked in, and after a long hug, said, "Sorry I'm late."

"No problem," I said, and closed the door behind him. "We're in the dining room. How was work?" I asked. I walked a few steps behind him.

"Long. Meetings."

I waited for Jackson to elaborate, but for now, that was all I got from him. He walked directly to the bathroom before making his way to the dining area.

My conversation with Caela came shooting back. Could she have been mistaking? Had she actually seen someone she thought was Jackson? I didn't want to think he had lied to me. Why would he? And if it was him, who was this person he was having this heated conversation with?

"Mr. Robert, Ms. Natalie, sorry I'm late," Jackson apologized as he removed a chair from the table and sat.

"You don't have to apologize. Things happen," my father responded. "Looks like you're going to have to get used to these long days. Just get you something to eat."

I looked at my father, and then at Jackson. Was he lying to my father, too?

I was able to push everything to the back of my mind during the next two-and-a-half hours as I sat having dinner and laughing with my family. Getting to know Adrian was fun. He had skipped his usual dining hall gathering with his roommate and campus buddies to spend the evening with us. I wouldn't exactly label him a momma's boy, but he definitely loved spending time with Natalie. His father was an undercover police officer who died in a drug deal gone wrong. Adrian was about six years old then. He wears his father's Medal of Valor he was given after foiling a teenager's suicide attempt from the bridge of a busy highway. Now a smart nineteen-year-old bio and chemistry major at the University of Pennsylvania, Adrian was already playing the role of my little brother, asking me questions about this female in his lab he had the hots for.

"I know you don't press for the ladies, but..." usually preceded his questions. He didn't care about my affection for Jackson. He was just glad to have an "older brother to chat it up with." I'm not sure how he took my advice, or what he did with them, but since his father wasn't around and my dad was now a part of his life, at least he now had two men to keep him grounded and walk the right path, though Natalie had already made sure he wasn't a nuisance.

I enjoyed getting more acquainted with Natalie, too. As she listened during our table conversations, debates, and disagreements, she kept her left hand pressed against the left side of her face, unintentionally displaying the white gold engagement ring my father presented her a year earlier.

"That's it," my father said when his eyes first met this perfect jewel.

I wondered if my dad had this much excitement when he chose the ring that represented the love he had for my mother. The diamonds that once sparkled under the fluorescent lights in the display case now gleamed from Natalie's perfectly manicured fingers under the lights above the dining room table.

Neither my father nor Natalie were in a rush to get married, but in the two years since they'd met, he was convinced this was the woman he wanted to spend the rest of his life with.

Adrian had his lab class early in the morning and was getting ready to go back to campus, but not before fixing a plate for himself and his roommate Brooks Clayman.

"He's going to see what real cooking tastes like," Adrian joked before leaving. Natalie and my father stayed in the dining room chitchatting over coffee. Since Natalie cooked, Jackson and I volunteered to clear the table and prepare the dishes for the dishwasher.

"I checked my schedule to see about dinner with Dexter," Jackson said, placing the last dinner plate in the dishwasher. He stood with his back towards the kitchen island, his palms pressed against the ceramic counter top.

Without turning to look at him I asked, "And?"

"I have to attend a conference." Suddenly thoughts of Kelvin and his conferences came rushing to the front of my brain. Half of those "conferences" were spent becoming familiar with Lawrence Cousins. Then I thought again back to the conversation I had with Caela. As much as I wanted to question Jackson about that, I held my tongue. I hoped I wasn't finding myself in a similar situation.

"When do you leave?"

"Sunday morning," Jackson said. "I'll be gone for a week."

"I guess when duty calls..." I said with sarcasm. "Guess I'll have to find a way to make it without you." I was joking.

"So tomorrow after work will you come stay with me?" Jackson asked. He walked over and stood beside me. Both of us stood facing the sink.

"If you weren't leaving for an entire week, would I still be spending the weekend?"

"Whatever, man." Jackson smiled, kissing me on my cheek. I loved it when he was affectionate like that. Even though we tried not to show too much of our love in the presence of my father and Natalie, I loved it when Jackson looked to the left, then to the right, and kissed me when he was sure they weren't looking.

14

Feel the Same Way I Do

Trevor...

"**S**o what did Jackson say?" Caela asked.

I was in the car driving to work. I knew she couldn't wait until morning came to find out if I had addressed her Jackson-sighting with him. But she wouldn't be Caela if I weren't hearing from her this early.

"It wouldn't hurt to say good morning. You know, use some of those manners that woman you call Mamma gave you."

"Oh, I'm sorry. Did I just hurt my chances of sitting at the royal table?"

"Girl, you didn't have a snowball's chance in hell, Adelaide, so you're not hurting anything."

Caela gasped. I knew how to take her breath away. That was the reaction I always got from her whenever I used her middle name, especially since it was unexpected. Her mother fell in love with the Australian city of the same name during a summer visit and insisted on the name for her oldest daughter. Like I always told Caela, she should consider herself lucky her mother hadn't fallen in love with the city of Cockburn or some other city that made the list of worst city names in the world.

"In that case, answer the question. What did Jackson say?

"I didn't give him a chance to deny or confirm?"

"What do you mean?"

"I mean I didn't ask him anything."

"Didn't you want to know?"

"Of course I did, but not at the cost of interrupting dinner." I was sitting in traffic a few feet from my exit. "He apologized to us and stuck to the story that he was working late."

It had started to drizzle lightly. I gazed out and up into the sky, watching gray clouds dominate. I don't remember the forecast calling for rain, but then again, I wasn't paying much attention to the TV while I dressed. The weather didn't surprise me anymore. I was just waiting for it to snow in June.

This was the usual exchange Caela and I enjoyed when we were out having lunch or dinner, or in my office, away from the watchful eyes of my other employees. I never hid from them we were like family, but I made sure she didn't receive any special treatment. Caela was reliable as an employee and as a friend. She was the friend with whom I shared my personal and business problems, 'cause I knew I would always hear the painful truth. Sometimes, even with Wesley around, I bounced business ventures and ideas off her. Wesley was my right hand man, but Caela had become my right hand woman, much like Camille, my former assistant.

"So, dinner was all right?" Caela asked.

"It was better than all right, but I'm not going to pretend I didn't think about your phone call from time to time."

"When I didn't hear back from you, I went to bed worrying my phone call had ruined your evening."

Caela was a natural worrier. "Well, you can rest your brain now, knowing the evening went on without a hitch. Oh! You didn't tell me where you were going last night."

"I was going to meet Jenilee, Kaitlyn, and Amadeus for dinner. They were already out and I didn't feel like cooking."

"That's nothing new. You never feel like cooking."

"You damn ass!" Caela yelled. "If you were in such a damn hurry, you do know a plane would get you there faster." It was raining, which meant her car windows were tightly shut and she was yelling at a man or woman who couldn't even hear her.

"I need you to get all that out your system before you even press the button to the fifth floor and step foot into the office."

"I'm sorry, but these people act like they are making monthly payments on their licenses."

I looked at the clock in the dash, which displayed 8:45. It was only 8:15. I had purposely set the clock ahead.

"I'm going to leave you and your road rage alone. I'm gonna stop at Daily Grind. You want something? No? Good," I said, smiling.

"Whatever! You know what I want."

"I do. Everything," I said, laughing at her. "I'll see you in a few. Hey," I said before hanging up. "Stop cursing at people who can't hear you."

I loved Fridays at work. Everyone was usually more relaxed, especially after feeling like Monday to Thursday was filled with accomplishments. And most, myself included, started their countdown to happy hour the moment they woke. Caela knew how I felt about Fridays, so meetings were never scheduled, and unless it's a must, meetings were never scheduled before 11:30 on Mondays.

There was a little bustle at Daily Grind. I walked up to the bar and ordered a Chai Latte and a Breakfast Bowl, and then a Mocha Espresso and a Monte Cristo for Caela. While I waited, I sent Wesley a text message asking if he wanted me to grab something for him.

I sat at a table and waited. When my cell phone rang, I answered thinking Wesley was calling to add his order. "You got my text?" I asked without looking at the phone.

"I'm guessing I'm not who you expected."

"You know the answer to that question," I responded, sounding perturbed. "What do you want?"

"Just keeping my promise. I said you would be hearing from me again."

"You're not doing me any favors. Hearing from you doesn't make my day any better. In fact, hearing from you does quite the opposite. So I'm going to ask you again. What the hell do you want?" I was trying to keep my voice down, but in this short time he had gotten on my last nerve.

"Chai Latte," the barrister called out.

I walked to the counter and picked up my order. I was planning on sitting down and enjoying my breakfast, but this call had changed my plans. I placed my Breakfast Bowl in the bag with Caela's Mocha Espresso and Monte Cristo and began walking towards the door. I hadn't checked my phone for a response from Wesley.

"I told you, you're not for Jackson."

"And you are?"

He laughed. "Oh, I don't want Jackson. But you don't either."

"And you know this because…"

"That's not important. What is important is that you understand Jackson isn't about to become your man-toy."

I was disgusted. Disgusted I was wasting my morning entertaining this fool, but even more disgusted he was talking about my plans for Jackson, and I didn't know who the hell he was. I pressed the remote to open the car door. I placed my order in the back on the floor and the cups in the cup holders in the front. I settled behind the steering wheel and turned on my blue tooth.

"Look," I said.

"No, you look," he snapped. "Leave Jackson alone. He's not about to be your guinea pig."

"Clearly you don't know what you're talking about."

"We'll see who doesn't know what. You just remember this conversation. You can't say I never warned you."

"Well, sir, you know what you and your warnings can do for me. Now, this is the last time I'm going to tell you to stop calling my fucking phone." I hung up and tossed the phone in the passenger seat.

I wasn't going to allow his phone call to disrupt an otherwise great morning so far. He was simply a wrinkle I wasn't going to spend too much time thinking about—or so I thought. I attempted to drive the few minutes from Daily Grind to work without trying to dissect the conversation I'd just had. I'd spoken to this man twice, and I still had no idea who he was or what connection he had to Jackson or me.

With my Daily Grind bag and cup in hand, I walked through the double doors to the agency and into Wesley.

"Oh, there better be something in that bag for me," he greeted.

"Didn't you get my message?"

"What message?"

"I sent a text asking if you wanted something." I checked my phone before continuing. "I never got a response from you."

"Good looking out, man." Wesley removed his phone from the clip. "That's my fault. I hadn't taken the phone off silent mode."

"No problem. You can't say I wasn't thinking about you."

"No, I can't," Wesley said. He placed his phone back in its holder and began walking towards his office. "Hey," he said, turning around. "Check with me before your lunch. I want something good."

"Will do." I walked over to Caela's desk, removed my breakfast bowl, handed her the bag and coffee, and started towards my office.

"How much do I owe you?" she asked.

"For just this order, or do I have time to add up all the other orders you haven't paid for?"

"Thank you, Trevor."

I walked into my office and over to my desk, ready to finally enjoy my breakfast. I sat in the chair and focused on the to-do list I started putting together for Caela yesterday. So far, it included only a few meetings I needed her to schedule, lunch with Mr. Millington, if he were available, and a staff meeting I'd been itching to have just to check-in on everyone. I picked up the receiver on the desk phone and dialed Caela's desk.

"Yes, Trevor," she answered.

"No rush, but when you're finished, may I see you for a few?"

"Of course."

I sat back in my chair. My cell phone buzzed. I looked at the phone screen before I answered.

"Hey you," I said.

"Good morning," Jackson replied. "I didn't hear you leave this morning."

"Probably 'cause you sleep like a darn rock. But I did say goodbye while you were changing position. You responded, but you were probably talking in your sleep."

"Probably." Jackson laughed.

"Shouldn't you be walking out the door now?" I asked looking at my watch.

"In a minute. Just wanted to check on you. I have a feeling this is going to be one of those Fridays."

"I'm sure it won't be that bad."

"You're probably right. So am I going to see you later?"

"Of course. Did you even have to ask?"

"Aiight, Trevor. Have a great day."

"Thanks. And you make sure you have one as well."

I had decided it wasn't a good idea to tell Jackson about the phone calls I'd been receiving. I wanted to do my own detective work before saying anything to him. Who was this stranger, and most importantly, where was he getting his information? I wasn't about to start walking around looking over my shoulders as if I had heard footsteps behind me, or driving and checking my rearview mirror like I was being followed. But that's how this man made me feel.

It was a smooth-sailing Friday. There was some business as usual happening, but nothing we needed to tighten our belts and roll up our shirtsleeves to get through. I sat with Caela for about an hour putting together my schedule for next week. Wesley and I treated the staff to lunch, ordering from a mom-and-pop restaurant a few blocks from the office. At exactly 12:15 I sent out a mass email calling for an emergency meeting to discuss our budget. I figured it would raise suspicion had it come from Caela.

We wanted to show our appreciation. Without everyone working together, this business, my vision, wouldn't thrive as well as it has.

The Harrison Agency was like one big happy family that had grown since we first started. Allessandra Dumarko now hyphenated her last name after last summer's nuptial to Bryson Starling. Asher Jones was now engaged to his high school sweetheart from Lake City, Florida, and was getting just as big a headache as she was planning the wedding she'd always dreamed about because she involved him in every detail. Xavier Mikkel and his fiancée of five years were expecting their first child. He was so excited. He had already picked out what he deemed "perfect names it can live up to": Richaud Jeron for a boy, and Chelsea Mackensie for a girl.

"You know you almost gave us a heart attack sending out a message like that," Jory joked. Besides Wesley and me, Jory had been here the longest. "You know what they say, first hired, first fired, and with this recession brewing, I was ready to count my losses."

"And now you know you have nothing to worry about." I lightly tapped him on his back and then stood next to Wesley and Caela, watching everyone.

It was good to see them relax without deadlines breathing down their backs. I left the crew in the conference room to return a few phone calls and tend to some personal business—how I sometimes spend my lunch hour on Fridays when I wasn't entertaining Caela's shenanigans.

The only thing I hated more than Monday morning traffic was Friday evening traffic. They drove as if it had been such a long week and the ability to obey traffic signals had disappeared the moment fatigue set it. They weren't driving any better on 395 either.

Before I left work, I called and left a message on Dexter's voicemail telling him I had to cancel dinner plans and that I was spending time with Jackson before his job took him away for a week. Dexter left his own voicemail with another dinner invitation on Tuesday, at his place. I don't know which devil was talking to me but I was considering telling Dexter yes.

My first conversation with Dexter was during our chance meeting at the Daily Grind. He was sitting in the corner enjoying a cold Cremosa. I was sitting in the same corner, a few tables over, my hands wrapped around a cup of Chai tea. Our encounter before that, Dexter was lying in a hospital bed in the PACU, leveled by the news that the man he thought needed his help had pulled one last selfish act out of his arsenal of selfish acts; as if he couldn't think of any other ways for Dexter to prove he still loved him. His scheme had also left Dexter's nephew, J.R., recovering in postoperative care with a broken hand and a sprained neck, minor injuries considering the scene I had come upon. As I approached the car, I swore whomever was inside couldn't have survived. Fortunately, I was wrong, although, according to Dexter, that night something inside him had died.

The business card Dexter handed me just before he walked out the doors of Daily Grind sat in my wallet unused, but as my taste buds watered at the thought of smelling honey and vanilla, I thought about cashing in on that offer Dexter made as he left. He was a man of his word, so when I called, he obliged.

While I spent nights constructing my relationship with Jackson, I spent days building my friendship with Dexter. We already had one thing in common: less-than-perfect circumstances with our then significant others we were able to get out of, though not unscathed. My relationship nearly cost me my sanity, and Dexter's relationship nearly cost him his life, but as the old adage goes, better late than never. Sometimes late just never comes soon enough.

On several Saturday mornings we found ourselves at Daily Grind in the same corner, sipping on cold cremosa and Chai tea. It became our ritual. We talked, not about the relationship he had with Patrick or the relationship I once had with Kelvin, but about *not* walking into our next relationship like carpenter bees.

Although I liked my interaction with Dexter, there were times I felt something else was stirring. Purposely, I would ignore his phone calls, his invitations, until I felt I had ignored him long enough.

There were moments when my two-year friendship with Dexter seemed like something more. Similarities had brought us up close and sometimes a little too personal. We playfully crossed that blurred line between friends and love-interest, but there was always that little annoying voice in my head reminding me about Jackson, keeping me from entertaining a potential relationship of convenience with Dexter because that's really all it would have been. That voice, of course, was my own, and although I listened, Dexter and I still flirted with trouble.

I liked the friendship that developed between us. We still fought to ignore the charge we felt whenever we met, especially when our meetings occurred in the privacy of his home or mine. Fighting eventually became easier. I had already convinced myself I was in total control. After all, we had the respect for our significant others, if not for self, to ignore everything and not act on impulses. I'm not sure if Dexter had the same pep talk with himself.

Chatter over savory stuffed chicken and salmon en papillote in the early evening sometimes led to an even quieter evening sipping on Semillon. Sometimes there were moments of uncomfortable silence. I could feel Dexter staring at me. When I turned around to look at him, he looked like temptation was killing him and he wasn't exactly sure what he should say or do. There were times I wrestled with really wanting to stay or really needing to go, especially when I thought me staying would put us in a predicament we would become too weakened to get ourselves out of. There were many parts of Dexter I wanted to explore and could have, but feelings I had for Jackson had tamed me. Although lust ran through our veins, there were many nights Dexter and I just sat and enjoyed intimate conversations.

One night we were supposed to have been watching *The Crazies*, an on-demand movie. I was watching *The Crazies*. *The Crazies* was watching Dexter, and Dexter was watching me.

"The craziest thing happened in court today," Dexter said, searching for something to fill the silence that had befallen us.

So often what he said happened was never really that crazy, but it was a conversation starter. But he did have some great stories.

"Sounds like half those people you come across need to sit with a psychologist and not stand before a judge," I joked. If I had a dime for the many moments of silence we've sat through, I'd be half way to rich by now.

"How about you tell me something about you I don't already know?" Dexter broke in.

"If there's something you want to know, why don't you just ask?" I said with authority.

"I think people are more forthcoming if given the opportunity to say anything. The conversation goes best if it's not guided by twenty questions that neither of us really want to answer."

"You think?" I asked.

"No. I know," Dexter said, and we fell silent again. I turned my attention back to the movie.

"I don't have anything to hide. Do you?"

"Ok," he broke in, sipping on wine and filling his glass again. A fresh bottle had sat beside him since we started our conversation. He offered me more but I had already decided I'd had enough. Plus I was tired of excusing myself to use the bathroom. "I'll go first," he continued.

I guess I'm going to have to watch this movie some other time...with Jackson, I thought.

I pulled up to the couch and leaned against it with my legs extended. I listened quietly, waiting for Dexter to lead the conversation. I didn't know much about the life of this man I had befriended, but did we have to choose tonight? Couldn't we just wait? I mean, what's the rush.

Dexter had moved on, or at least he was trying to, becoming more serious with Giovanni C. Dawkins, the handsome lawyer he had met just before a court hearing. After Dexter's father died, he finally decided to contact Giovanni. He knew Giovanni loved him. He hated that Giovanni had to split his free time between him and the lady in his life, his now sixteen-year-old daughter, Paisley. But how else did Dexter expect this man to treat his daughter? Dexter respected Giovanni for having always been a constant in Paisley's life. At least he wasn't sharing Giovanni with some other man.

"So, Giovanni is the world's greatest dad."

"And who bestowed him that title?" I had asked, looking at Dexter from the corner of my eyes.

"Definitely didn't come from me. Although he isn't that bad." Dexter laughed. "Paisley did, of course. I met her a couple weekends ago, at her sixteenth birthday dinner; finally. And Dexter had that conversation with her."

"What conversation? He finally told her where babies come from? I'm sure at sixteen she's already figured that out, if she hasn't been told already. Don't they have sex education in schools?"

"I'm sure they do, but that's not the conversation I'm talking about."

"Then what?"

"Apparently Giovanni had kept two promises he made to her, more to himself, since Paisley was a toddler running around in pampers and calling every dog she saw *"goddy"*. He promised he was going to tell her about the attraction he had to men on her sixteenth birthday and he would introduce her to the man in his life if he had one at the time."

"So…"

"He told Paisley about his alternative lifestyle, and introduced her to me."

"So this girl, for the rest of her life, is going to remember that on her sixteenth birthday she found out her father was gay, and met his lover. Oh fun!" I said, sarcastically. I learned less about Dexter and more about his relationship with Giovanni.

That conversation, like many Dexter and I have had before, was enlightening. I wondered what else I would learn about him, or Giovanni, or Paisely when Tuesday came. Maybe this time I could tell him more about me.

Since Jackson wasn't going to be in town, I already knew I wasn't going to tell Dexter no.

• • • • •

When I got to Jackson's I rang the bell instead of using the key he had given me. He answered the door wearing red plaid lounge pants, his bulging six-pack exposed to the world and the cool, late September breeze that swept in as the door opened. He smelled of pure vanilla. He had a few loose papers in his hand.

"What's that?" I asked, closing the door behind me.

"Just my travel itinerary and workshop schedules."

"You started packing already?"

"I looked in the closet at a few things I'll be taking, but that's the extent of my packing."

Jackson walked to the living room, sat in a chair, and continued to focus on the itinerary and schedule. I walked upstairs and dropped my overnight bag in a corner of his bedroom. I walked into the bathroom, turned on the shower and began to undress.

This was my warm water massage therapy. The water felt so soothing beating against my skin. I felt like I had waited all day for this. In my mind I had already escaped to the white sandy beach of the Vatulele Island resort in the Fiji's, lying with the sun from an almost perfect summer blue sky beating upon my face, listening to the sound of the pristine blue water. The week hadn't been stressful, just long. I was singing a few bars from Usher's "Moving Mountains" and lathering when I heard Jackson's voice.

"Hey, Trevor," he called out.

I pushed open the shower door slightly. Jackson was standing at the bathroom door with his feet crossed and his hands in his pockets. Is it possible to look good just standing there?

"How long have you been there?" I asked.

"Don't worry. I didn't hear you auditioning for your spot on *American Idol.*"

"I see you've got jokes."

"With that voice, I'm sure we both agree you're the one with the jokes," Jackson responded. "No, I'm kidding. You don't sound half bad."

I didn't have a good comeback, so I just laughed. "Boy, what do you want?"

"I...I think I'm gonna ask Colton to come see me while I'm in Miami."

"I'm sure he won't say no. When was the last time you spoke with him?" I stepped out the shower and stood in front of the mirror, allowing my body to air-dry. I turned and looked at Jackson. He was sitting in the doorway looking at me from head to toe.

"What?" I asked, smiling.

"Nothing." He stood up. "I'm going downstairs to get something to drink. Do you want anything?"

"Just some water. Oh, and bring up a movie." I began rubbing baby oil on my still wet skin. I walked into the bedroom pulling up my boxers and stepping into some gym shorts.

Jackson came back upstairs with a bottle water for me and a glass of wine for himself. He placed the DVD in the player, grabbed the remote, and slid up on the bed. He sat with his back against the wall.

"Have you seen this?" he asked.

"What's that?" I walked to the bathroom, dimmed the light to off, and was back in the bed, lying on my back.

"*Definitely, Maybe.*"

"Huh? Definitely, maybe, what?"

"That's the name of the movie. You know, with Ryan Reynolds."

I didn't respond. I propped my head on two pillows, tossed my legs over his, and settled into watching the movie until sleep found its way into my eyes.

"What time does your flight leave on Sunday?"

"7:15 a.m.," Jackson answered.

"So, how much are you going to miss me?"

"Do you want me to show you or tell you?" Jackson asked, grabbing and pulling my body closer to his.

Hmmm, I thought, but my mind was already made up.

"Do I really have to tell you?"

"You really don't."

That's the last thing I remember him saying to me. I was making love faces as he touched and stroked me like he knew how. I kept thoughts of not feeling his touch for a week out of my mind, and I allowed his lovemaking to take me to ecstasy. My body quivered and shivered as his tongue glided down the length of my spine. His fingertips dug deep into the small of my back. He felt weightless on top of me.

"I love you," Jackson whispered softly in the dark.

"I love you, too," I said. I relaxed and braced my body for his hard pleasure again.

15

Eyes Better Not Wonder

Jackson ...

I spent most of Saturday getting ready for Sunday. By 9:00 p.m. I was packed and ready to go on a trip I wasn't looking forward to. I placed my suit bag with the two suits I planned on wearing and a medium-size trolley garment bag by the front door. I packed a small bag of toiletries in the morning after I took my shower and was dressed. The attendant promised the Blue Van would be at the house between 3:45 a.m. and 5:00 a.m. to pick me up. Of course it was ten minutes to five before my phone rang, with an operator telling me they were outside. My flight, which was scheduled to depart at 7:15 a.m., didn't hit the runway until thirty minutes later after waiting for a connected flight from Philadelphia that was held on the runway until the dense fog had lifted. Since I was in Miami until Sunday, I called on Saturday and left a message for my best friend, Colton Merrick, asking if he would fly up for the weekend.

Colton Jamal Merrick was my straight-talking straight friend who loved the ladies and loved me like a brother. When we met, Colt, the name I had given him, lived in a house filled with women. I guess I was his escape from all that estrogen. He was a

Southern boy, an army brat who spent most of his teenage years in Fort Jackson, SC, off interstate 70. His father was an army officer. As soon as he was old enough to get away, Colt hopped on Interstate 20 to Georgia, settling in Atlanta and on the campus of Morris Brown College. It had been three days since I left that message, and here I was still waiting for him to call back. For now it looked like my plans to enjoy the weekend in his company weren't going to happen.

It was a sunny Sunday morning when I arrived in Miami at approximately 10:45. I made my way through baggage claim to my rental car. I was heading East on 836 towards the downtown area. The traffic on the 95 looked like normal Sunday morning traffic—church, or an early morning at the beach was my guess. I had reservations in the grand Epic Hotel on Biscayne Boulevard Way. My room overlooked Biscayne Bay and the Miami River and the picturesque Miami Skyline, something I don't get to see much of living in the District.

I stood staring at the sky and its color of cool orange and black, and the few stars I could see on this clear October night. Earlier, I had stood in this same place watching boaters make their way down the waterways and I could imagine a much busier Bay as shirtless men and women dressed in bikinis showcased their beach bodies and Miami Beach tans as they smooth-sailed on blazing hot summer days.

I had been able to get out on the town. I checked out the Heat/Pistons exhibition basketball game at the nearby American Airlines Arena, and dining at Lombardi's was enthralling. I enjoyed a striking conversation with a native brunette who offered to show me around the town if I weren't too busy. After telling her I only had a few days left, she said that was plenty of time for her to convince me. I never asked her about what I needed to be convinced.

I spent Tuesday morning listening to a panel on stem cell research and then Wednesday afternoon hearing about the latest advances in breast cancer research. I still hadn't heard from Colt and I wasn't sure I was going to be hearing from him before my week was over. There weren't any meetings or conference events scheduled the following day, so an early night sleep wasn't a must have. I sat front and center in the bed, browsing through the channels. I had spoken to Trevor since speaking with him during my slow walk to the Heat game, and then again during a lunch break on Wednesday. I reached back and stretched for my cell phone that was sitting on the bed close to the headboard.

"You're in beautiful Miami and you're sitting there thinking about me?" Trevor asked, teasing.

"It's never out of sight, out of mind when it comes to you," I said, and lay back in the bed, smiling.

"So what are you up to?"

"Lying here contemplating going downstairs to get a drink or two. I just wanted to call before I got too carried away."

"Carried away? Whatever! I think you got sharks beat."

"I'm not going to own that?"

"You don't have to. But who's going to tell, but you, if you don't show up to your seminar on time and sober?" Trevor said, laughing quietly at me.

"I may not like traveling, but I love what I do too much to even chance that happening," I paused. "Hey, this is definitely a room with a view, and I'm not talking about a ten-dollar view, either. Opulent doesn't even begin to describe it," I complimented, tilting my head towards the window, looking out into the night that stretched out as far as my eyes could see.

"Oh really? I remember when they started transforming that area. I wondered how they were going to survive the economic bust, but I guess they had a way."

"Don't they always." I removed the phone from my ear, looking at the clock displayed on the screen. It was 11 p.m. I had exactly one hour to quench this alcoholic thirst I was having. "So, how was work for you?"

"Work went well. It's Wednesday, two more days to the weekend. I went to happy hour with Wesley and Caela. Jory looked like he needed a middle-of-the-week pick me up, so he came along, too. I'll just say he was half past tipsy before we left, so I won't be surprised if his Thursday starts later than usual. He's probably lying in his bed now watching the room spin."

"I guess it always works in your favor to have it in good with the boss," I said, smiling at my remark.

"And I guess it's even better when you're sleeping with him," Trevor countered.

I wasn't expecting his comeback. His comment took my mind to a place I had avoided since getting on the phone with him.

I looked at my watch again. "I'm going to get that drink now," I said, adjusting the bulge that had formed in the front of my pants. All it took was the sound of Trevor's voice to get me exited.

"Don't drink too much," Trevor warned. "Love ya."

"Love ya back."

• • • • •

"What can I get for you, sir?" The waitress asked, looking at me.

I was standing at the bar lost in thought about that very question. I hadn't given much thought to what I wanted to drink. I wanted to ask the bartender, a gorgeous female with a close fade, to surprise me, but those words can be interpreted as "get me something that'll have me hung over when morning comes." I took my chance and ordered something I was sure she could mix, something that could get me close to nice.

"Sir," she called again.

"Huh?"

"What can I get you…to drink?" This time she smiled.

I smiled back. "I'll have a citrus smack," I requested, sounding as if I knew what I wanted all along.

While she busied herself with my request, I took the opportunity to scrutinize my surroundings. Besides the bartender and me, there were four other people who had the same craving for a nightcap. A man and his lady friend sat in the corner exchanging a little more than a few words and laughter. An older patron sat close by at a table by himself, frequently checking his wristwatch and cell phone. And then there he was, standing at the far end of the bar as if he were waiting for me to notice him, and even if I didn't want to, it was hard not to. He stood with one hand in his pocket and the other hand wrapped around the stem of his wine glass.

His presence demanded my attention. I tried looking at him from the corner of my eyes, but my second glance caught him with his eyes locked on mine, and I couldn't help but nod, acknowledging that I had noticed him noticing me noticing him. I wasn't sure if I was embarrassed that he had caught me staring at him. Surprisingly, he nodded in kind, and even added a smile.

His skin, the color of an evenly brown pear, looked as smooth as melted chocolate. Neatly dreaded hair was braided on top of his head, glistening under the hanging lights. His very thin sideburns extended down his face and under his chin. An even thinner manicured mustache extended across the top of lips that he never seemed to close completely. His face had a familiarity to it, and when I looked at him one last time, I realized who he was.

Dr. Tenerio Denard Beaumont was a keynote speaker at the Annual Forum and Childhood Obesity Congress earlier this year. His presentation, Childhood Obesity and the Future of America, held the audience's attention, and he even received an earsplitting round of applause that I definitely thought he deserved. I thought he had one of those unforgettable faces with an unforgettable voice to match.

"Late night pick me up?" he asked. I saw him walking over to me, but I purposely pretended to give him none of my attention during his approach.

I looked at him. "I guess you can call it that," I said. I acknowledged the waiter who was placing a coaster and my citrus smack in front of me. "But it's not that late," I said, looking at him again. I took a sip of my drink and took a peak at my watch. *This is good*, I thought.

"I hope I'm not intruding on your evening."

"Conversation is never an intrusion in my book, man."

"Cool. The name's Denard," he said, extending his hand.

"Nice to meet you," I said. Since we were never formally introduced before tonight, I decided to keep that I had seen him at least once before to myself. "Jackson Bradley." I shook the hand he extended to me. His hands were soft. His grip was firm. He stared into me.

"Are you here on business or pleasure?"

"Business," I said. "A conference for the job."

"At the Convention Center?"

"Yes. You too?"

"I am."

I enjoyed the conversation Denard and I had. Just like the time before, he was also a keynote speaker at this conference. He wasn't staying at the Epic, but had a small suite at the Marriott Hotel across the street, which allowed easy access to the Convention Center. Like me, he also had a clear schedule tomorrow. He spoke to me as if we were old friends who hadn't spoken in years and had some catching-up to do.

By the time my second glass of citrus smack arrived, I knew much more about Dr. Tenerio Denard Beaumont. He was an undergraduate at the University of California, Berkeley, a graduate at the University of Michigan, and earned his Doctorate from the Ohio State University. He was a Virgo two months removed from his thirty-second birthday and was between relationships. In summary, Dr. Beaumont was educated, not too much older than me, single, and according to his zodiac, modest and shy, meticulous and reliable, overcritical and harsh, perfectionist and conservative all rolled up in one fine-looking human being.

He placed his empty cocktail glass on the counter.

"Would you like another?" The waitress removed the glass and placed it in an under-counter washer. She removed the coaster and wiped where it was.

"No. I think I'm done."

"You think?" She paused, looking at him.

"I'm sure," he corrected. She turned and busied herself at the register behind her. Denard reached into his back pocket and removed his billfold. He placed a $20 bill and a credit card on the bar countertop. "Looks like my night's coming to an end." He looked at his watch and then at the waitress who was handing back his card and the receipt for his signature.

"It's not that late. Guess I'll have another one of these before heading back upstairs."

"Well, here," he said, handing me his business card. "Call me. We should do dinner or something before you leave."

I stared at his card, thinking over my response. "Dinner tomorrow, if you have nothing planned."

"Call me," he said, winking.

So I may not be spending my weekend with my best friend, Colt, but maybe my new friend, Dr. Tenerio Denard Beaumont, could entertain me while I'm here.

I spent the next thirty minutes at the bar being entertained by Nicolette Kerr. She's been in the area for four years now, moving to Miami after separating from her husband of two years. He asked for a divorce after deciding married life wasn't for him. She wished he had come to that conclusion before her long, slow ass walk down the aisle, smiling at people she hadn't seen in years who only came to see if she had lost the weight needed to fit perfectly in a dress she knew was two sizes too damn small when she bought it. She was young, ready to start over, and Miami was among the best places for single women.

"So, are you here tomorrow night, too?" I asked.

"I am. I get here around 3," Nicolette said, placing my bill in front of me.

"Maybe I'll come by and keep you company." I handed her my credit card.

"Before or after dinner?" she mumbled, turning around to the register.

"What was that?" We were the only two left in the restaurant.

"Nothing." She turned, handing me my receipt, a pen, and my credit card. I left her an impressive tip for making my drinks like she did and for sharing a few laughs with me.

16

Lately I

Trevor...

Would I still be complaining if every weekend were a three-day weekend? I didn't know where this weekend went. I spent Saturday morning with Jackson, the evening with my father, and Sunday evening having dinner with Caela and Kellen at her house. The kitchen had made my list of least favorite places, and since cooking was my least favorite activity, I happily accepted her invite. Plus I got to spend some time with my godson, which was icing on the red velvet cake Caela and I had for dessert. Late came early, and I still had my drive home. I still had to prepare for a week front-loaded with meetings. And of course, I had a few other things to get done before my private conversation with God before falling into deep sleep.

When the alarm on my cell phone first sounded at 6:10 a.m., I pressed the snooze button, giving myself thirty extra minutes of sleep. I wasn't tired. I just didn't feel like waking up or getting out of bed. I had decided a long time ago I wasn't a morning person and I wasn't going to start pretending to be one now.

On my way to work, I called and spoke briefly with Jackson before he had to rush off the phone and into his first scheduled seminar for the day.

It was like I lived with Caela, walking into the office and seeing her face, again, only a few hours after having dinner with her. She was standing behind her desk, her morning cup of coffee in one hand, her other hand dancing over the keyboard.

"Good morning," I said. I stood beside her desk.

She printed and handed me the day's schedule even though I had access to it on my desktop and cell phone. "I haven't gotten a call back from Mr. Millington," she said.

"I'll try reaching him myself today." I thanked Caela and began walking towards my office.

"Hey, Trevor," she called out. "Any plans for lunch?"

I looked at my watch. "Only greedy people think about lunch when breakfast isn't even over yet. You greedy?"

"Call me what you want as long as you call me to let me know what you're doing for lunch."

I walked into the office, sat behind my desk, and glanced at my schedule. I had a meeting immediately after lunch with Wesley. There was a 2:30 with Rory that was put on there by Caela. *I wonder what he wants to talk about*, I thought. I walked over to the coffee pot with a fresh brew Caela always started whenever she made it in the office before me, just in case I didn't have a chance or wasn't in the mood to stop at Daily Grind. I was stirring cream into my coffee when my cell phone buzzed.

"How's this Monday treating you?" I answered.

"I've had Mondays that have treated me better." It was Dexter. "Just trying to work through this hard case. This guy has to be the most noncompliant client I've ever worked for."

"What's he doing?"

"You know I can't tell you that."

"I know. I was just testing you."

"So listen, are we still on for dinner tomorrow?"

"It's Tuesday already?"

"Did you forget?"

"No, man. I'll see you tomorrow."

• • • • •

I didn't know what Dexter had on the dinner menu. When I entered the house, stepped inside the entryway, walked past his study to the left, and into the rotunda, something smelled heavenly. On each wall of the rotunda was an 18 x 24-inch picture of each member of his family, including his godson Sha'len. A picture of his father was missing. I remembered it being there the very first time I visited.

It seemed like I floated through the rotunda, allowing my nose and the scent to guide my entrance into the kitchen. There was a reproduction of Christian Vernet's *Jazz* hanging on a back wall separating his chef-style kitchen and dining area. I've admired the colorful painting since my first visit and tour of Dexter's home. I could tell then Dexter was a perfectionist.

Everything in his single-family house in his Georgetown neighborhood seemed to be in its exact place. His dark walnut oval dining table and chairs sat in the corner of the dining room on top of Makata Expresso hardwood floors. Four wall sconces in Olde Bronze finish on either side of the room created the perfect tone. His dining room was contemporary with a touch of antique elegance. His kitchen was just as inviting. A two-tier island was illuminated by recessed lighting and surrounded by a sea of stainless steel appliances and dark wood cabinets with frosted-glass doors. Twisted stairs vanishing behind a curved-glass partition brought you his bedroom on the second level and the three other bedrooms that, according him, are never occupied until his family visited or Sha'len visited, or his nephew J.R. stayed over during their summer vacation. But Sha'len was in his third year at the University of Connecticut and his time was now shared with his girlfriend Kimetra and his parents.

I stood in the kitchen watching Dexter put the finishing touches on braised cabbage with spicy croutons and balsamic rosemary pork loin with roasted potatoes. This was one of the better nights I'd had with Dexter.

"I think I just need a break from work, even if it's just for a couple of days," Dexter said.

"It's only Tuesday. Has your week really been that bad already?" I asked, putting a piece of pork loin in my mouth. "This is really good." The juices oozed from the piece of meat and wrapped around my tongue.

"I'm glad you like it. As for my week, it really has been that bad already. I'm defending this kid who's a major pain. Comparing him to a mule doesn't begin to describe how stubborn he is." He poured a glass of red wine for me, filled his own glass to the top, and then set the bottle of Burgess Cabernet Sauvignon to the side on the table.

"So this trip, where would you go?" I asked, taking a sip from my glass. The wine was delicate and elegant, and I allowed my tongue to take pleasure in the taste before swallowing. "Maybe Giovanni would enjoy such a trip." It was a mere suggestion.

"Hawaii is on my list of places I would love to visit, but I'll settle for Chicago. I don't necessarily need a beach, or white sand between my toes, or sun, just somewhere I could go and leave work behind."

The latter part of my question/statement got no response from Dexter. "But the work will still be here when you get back."

"You and I know that, but I'm sure I'll be more focused after. I haven't really taken a good break since…" Dexter paused.

"Since what?"

"It's not important. I just know I need a break."

We ate our meals in reverse order: the pork loin first, and then the roughage, topped with croutons, parsley, and lemon wedges. Before long, the bottle of Sauvignon was empty. Although I was enjoying Dexter's company, I needed to get home. It was getting late, and I wanted to work for about an hour on this project before showering and going to bed.

"Do you need any help with this?" I asked, placing my wine glass in the kitchen sink. Dexter had already prepped the dishes for the dishwasher, but he preferred washing his crystal wine glasses by hand.

"No, because I don't want you asking me to wash your dishes when I visit your house," he said, smiling.

"Don't worry. I have paper plates and plastic cups for people like you."

"I'll remember to say no when you extend your invite."

Dexter and I began walking towards the front door. This was one of the best times I'd spent with him. There were no interruptions. I didn't hear from Jackson and Dexter hadn't excused himself to entertain Giovanni in conversation.

"Don't you want to take some of that food with you?" Dexter asked.

"No. Thanks. It'll probably just sit in the fridge and eventually end up in the trash. And I hate to waste food."

"True."

"Look, I'll talk to you before the week is out," I said, waiting for Dexter to open the door. Dexter didn't respond. "Did you hear me?"

He stood with his hand on the doorknob. He paused in thought. "If you don't have plans this weekend, go with me?" he asked, turning around to face me.

I looked at him with perplexed eyes. "Go with you where?"

"That trip we were talking about...to Chicago. I'll take care of the reservations. Just say you'll go."

I wasn't sure if a trip with Dexter was a good idea. What about Giovanni? Where was he and why wasn't Dexter planning this trip with him?

"I don't have to give you an answer right now, do I?" I asked, quickly.

"I mean, if you need to think about it. It's only for the weekend."

"I'll call you. Thanks again for dinner." I walked out the door, through the gate, and into my car without looking back at him.

I slept on my decision for two nights, trying to decide if I really needed to be taking this trip with Dexter. I woke up Thursday morning, turned on the television and watched Presidential candidate Barack Obama deliver campaign promises at an early morning town hall meeting. I sat listening to him as if I were seeing or hearing him speak for the first time. This man was always impressive. Earlier in the year, I watched him with poise respond to skeptics who thought he might not be ready to lead our country in a time of war, growing debt, and a declining economy; what do they know? After Hillary's loss in the primaries, I wanted a Democratic ticket that would make history in more than one way—Presidential Candidate Barak Obama and Vice Presidential Candidate Hillary Clinton. Now that would have been something, but I was just as confident electing Barack with Mr. Joe Biden as his right-hand man.

I typed in my response in a text message to Dexter. I sat in contemplation, looking at the screen as if I were seeing a *Danger* or *Do Not Enter* sign flashing across the screen. I ignored those warnings and pressed the send button.

When I texted Dexter my response, my tickets were deliver-ed via messenger three hours after I arrived to work. I called Jackson but reached only his voicemail. I didn't want to leave a message about my weekend plans.

• • • • •

I didn't complain when I was stuck behind a family of six at the security checkpoint as every inch of their newly issued U.S. passports was scrutinized. Once on the escalator, a mother complimented her young girl-child for having successfully maneuvered her Dora the Explorer carry-on onto the moving stairs. At the departure gate, a father quickly consoled a young boy looking no more than three years old after he had tripped over his own over-stuffed carry-on, lightly bruising the side of his face on the carpeted floor. There was so much happening, and for whatever reason, I felt the need to process it all.

Another little boy, whose name was repeated several times by his grandmother as she instructed him to "stop," played tag by himself. He listened for a moment before continuing his child's play along the windows. Just when I thought I had seen everything, I noticed two young girls sitting. From their toes up, there was nothing out of the ordinary about them, but then I noticed them both dawning thick white shower caps, protecting whatever hairstyles they had especially for their trip.

Once on board, passengers rushed to complete flight confirmations with significant others and last minute business calls before the instructions to turn off all electronic devices were announced. Extremely dense fog had threatened to delay the flight. A flight attendant who had paced the length of the airplane searching for a man in uniform passed one last time with a soldier following closely behind her.

"You definitely deserve it," the flight attendant said as she made her way from coach to first class, an obvious upgrade for the soldier. Everyone erupted in applause as the captain announced the presence of military personnel amongst the plane's occupants, acknowledging the sacrifices they continue to make to protect countries from would-be attackers.

"Do you mind if I sit here?" a passenger asked as she removed the brown mini-duffle bag occupying the seat in question, as if her boarding pass hadn't given her the right to sit in the seat she was assigned. She needed no one else's permission.

"No, not at all," the dainty salt-and-pepper haired older passenger sitting in the middle seat beside me responded. She grabbed her bag and placed it under the seat in front of her.

"I saw you just before boarding and thought how gorgeous and how well coordinated you were," the younger passenger complimented.

"Thank you," the grandmother of two accepted. She spoke loudly as she sat, informing her new friend she was on her way to Chicago to visit her daughter, a trip she had taken every month for the past two years since the birth of her granddaughters, and to help plan her daughter's wedding. The only plan she had for this trip was to do nothing but sit and enjoy a wedding she was sure would turn out just right.

"She's marrying a fine young man," she said.

I sat staring out the window, looking down between clouds at the disappearing grounds as the airplane climbed steadily to cruising altitude.

I tried not to pay attention to the conversation between the two passengers occupying the row with me. Their conversation was without end. They had gone from politics to children and grandchildren with screwed up priorities. The women's constant chatter kept me from sleeping through the entire flight and I kicked myself for not accepting the first class ticket Dexter had offered me. I wouldn't have minded if their discussion didn't lack focus, but instead they rambled on mostly about things that didn't interest me.

Would you please shut up already? I thought as I tried to make myself comfortable in an otherwise uncomfortable seat. I couldn't wait to be removed from my torturous surroundings, and it was only the notion of seeing Dexter that made the torment worthwhile.

After the airplane's back wheels skidded along the runway pavement, everyone joined in applause, showing their appreciation of a successful flight.

"Could you believe this was his first flight?" a flight attendant announced moments later. I wished she had kept that bit of information to herself.

Chicago on this fall afternoon was beautiful. I was ready to stroll down North Lake Shore Drive, sit along the banks of Lake Michigan, and allow a light night breeze to whisper in my ear.

"So how was the flight?" Dexter asked as he threw my suitcase in the backseat of his black Sapphire X6.

"Besides the turbulence or the incessant rant between the women who sat beside me, it was fabulous," I replied, sounding more agitated than before. "I'm starving."

The coffee and lightly toasted bagel I had earlier this morning wore off long before I boarded my flight. And, unfortunately, my ten-minute in-flight sleep came at the expense of missing the mini bag of pretzels and soda that was served mid-flight, not that it would have satisfied the craving that now settled in the hollow of my stomach.

I sat in the car staring out the window as if this was my first time in Chicago. I thought about visiting so many places, starting with The Obamas' neighborhood on South Greenwood Ave in Hyde Park. I'd heard it had become a hot spot for vacationers, those who now had another proud reason to call Chicago home, and those poised to write one or two books about Obama's sudden rise to fame. Halfway between O'Hare International and Dexter's high-rise, I developed heavy eyelids, and suddenly my need for sleep had overtaken my tourist plans and eating.

• • • • •

I woke from my unplanned nap to find Dexter standing in the doorway staring into my face. Although I found it a bit strange that this grown man was standing there watching me sleep, it made me smile.

"So, how long have I been asleep?" I asked, feeling my wrist for my watch.

"It's on the nightstand," Dexter said, using his eyes and a quick nod, directing me to the corner of the large room.

"I would call you a thief-in-the-night, except that it's only…" I said, reaching for my watch and holding it close to my face.

"Four twenty five," Dexter added. "Listen, I was going to get in a quick workout. Would you like to go? If you'd rather eat, there's seafood in the kitchen I picked up from a quaint seafood restaurant a few blocks from here."

"I guess I was more tired than I thought," I said as I stretched and yawned, trying to find much needed energy.

"Don't worry, you didn't snore," Dexter joked.

Dexter was fully dressed in white and orange Adidas shorts and a white sleeveless crew. He had bulges everywhere, but one in particular brought a mischievous smile to my face. The shirt fell perfectly over his protruding pectoral muscles and I wondered if the white shorts made things look bigger than they were or if Dexter was really packing. I hoped my smile wasn't misinterpreted as intent to find out exactly how much packing there was.

I hadn't been thinking about it until then, and it was a good time to remind myself of our friendship. Still, I found myself thinking about just how intense it would be making love to Dexter. I shook my head in an attempt to shake away the impure thoughts infiltrating my mind.

My cell phone vibrated.

"What would it take to show you he's not worth it?" he questioned. The smile on my face disappeared. A part of me wanted to hang up, but my inquisitive side waited for him to go on. "Has he told you everything? Has he told you about…me? Of course he hasn't."

"Trevor," Dexter interrupted. "Is there someone on the other end? Aren't you going to say something?"

"What exactly did he tell you, Mr. Trevor Rene Harrison? That's right, I know all about you. The question is, what do you know about…me?" the caller asked.

"I'm waiting for you to tell me, and while you're at it, why don't you tell me who the hell you are," I finally spoke, but I was met with silence. I hung up without saying another word. I clasped my hands over the phone, bringing my fingertips just below the tip of my nose. I closed my eyes as if I were about to have a little talk with Jesus.

"What was that call about?" Dexter asked. He walked closer to me and leaned against a wall beside him. "You look like you've just received a call from death. What was that about?"

"Since Jackson moved in town, I've been getting these phone calls asking me these…questions," I began. I stood up, placing my hands in my pockets. "They're asking me if this man has told me everything about himself…about him, this stranger. Asking me if I think I can make him happy. Telling me that I am only…temporary. Only he won't tell me who he's talking about. He knows my name, but I know nothing about him. So, either someone out there is making assumptions about my friendship with you, or someone is trying desperately to put doubt in my relationship with Jackson. Now, what I need to figure out is who has anything to lose from our friendship, or who has anything to gain if my relationship with Jackson doesn't work out. Can you tell me, Dexter? Is there someone out there who stands to lose from our friendship?"

Dexter never responded. He stood there with his eyes locked on mine. His mind pondered responses to my questions.

What exactly are we doing here? I thought.

There was Patrick McKay, who had probably seen me at the hospital the day of Dexter's accident. There was Giovanni Dawkins, too, even though his daughter and his career didn't leave much time for anything else. But unless Dexter had hinted there was more to our friendship than what it actually is, Giovanni had nothing to worry about, unless he was paranoid and felt threatened by anyone who attempted to get too close to Dexter. He didn't strike me as that type, not that I knew him well enough to defend that.

Besides the disconcerting phone calls and the mounting questions, I had a great time with Dexter. We spent the evening at U.S. Cellular Field, sitting behind home plate watching the Chicago White Sox and Tampa Bay Rays in the American League Division Series playoff. The Cell, as Dexter and other fans called it, was stretched out before us. I didn't know too much about the White Sox, but Dexter had become a fan while attending Northwestern University Law School. At night, when he needed a break from studying, an impromptu trip to check out one of the night games usually provided the required mental break. That first game ended with the Rays on the wrong side of the win-loss column. Fortunately, they still had other opportunities to recover from that initial loss. Since the White Sox already had their supporter in Dexter, I cheered for the Rays. I knew just as much about them as I did about the Sox.

After dinner on Saturday, I concluded C-House restaurant in the Affinia Chicago had become one of my new favorite restaurants. The atmosphere was warm and inviting. The choice of color and deliberate use of lighting added an unparallel sexiness to the setting. Over Chablis and grilled salmon, Dexter's conversation remained light, airy, talking mostly about his family. *Together They Fall,* starring Dexter's twin brother, Dane, was scheduled for release early next year. I could tell he was anxiously anticipating seeing his brother in his first potential blockbuster.

He acknowledged how good an actor his brother was, but in an industry with other brilliant actors like Will Smith, Terrence Howard, and Idris Elba, and a barrage of male rappers and singers trying their hand in the movie business, landing a leading role in a good movie was hard. I admitted I hadn't seen any of the movies his brother starred in and promised to see *Together They Fall* when it arrived in theatres.

My grilled whole trout was cooked to perfection. I watched our reflection in the shiny copper light fixtures hanging above our table as I listened to Dexter talk proudly about the mother he lost and the woman who shaped his life. In all our talks I had never heard Dexter mention his father. I was curious and figured he wasn't going to tell me if I didn't ask.

I saw it on his face. I think I struck a nerve when I asked, "What about Mr. DeGregory?"

"Dead," Dexter responded, and I figured so was this conversation. That wasn't the response I expected. I was displeased. "I'll let you in on that part of my life later," he offered.

That part of my life, I thought. I couldn't imagine referring to my own father as "that part of my life," but I guess not everyone had a father like Robert Seymour Harrison, my very best friend, my confidant, and the only man I trust with my life.

After dinner, I was in the guest room where I had slept since arriving in Chicago. I lay in bed with my hands clasped behind my head, providing the perfect cradle. With my legs crossed at the ankles, I stared at the ceiling, unable to sleep. I wanted to call Jackson, but after looking at the time on my cell phone, I had already decided it was too late. I had spoken with him earlier after the baseball game. Though the conference was informative, he said he was ready to be back in his own bed and sleeping next to me. Hearing that made me smile. When he asked what I had done all weekend, I mentioned the baseball game and plans for dinner. I conveniently didn't tell him I had checked out the White Sox game and the dinner I had planned was with Dexter, in Chicago. I had kept my trip and the specifics to myself all week. Why mention it to him now?

I stood staring through the large windows that extended from one corner of the room to the other. I admired the Chicago skyline, forty-four stories up in the air. *How was Dexter affording this?* I thought. *He hadn't mentioned Giovanni all week. What if...?*

'Nice view isn't it," Dexter interrupted. He was standing in the door with two champagne flutes in one hand and a bottle in the other.

"Seriously, Dexter," I said, looking down at his possessions. "I think I've had enough wine for one night."

"Come on, man," he pleaded. "One for the road?"

Does he always sound like this when he begs? I thought. Dexter brought the bottle and glasses up to eye level, as if that action was supposed to convince me.

I smiled.

It had.

After pouring the glasses full, Dexter and I stood beside each other, leaning against the dresser. I looked at him, trying to figure out his intentions.

"To friendship," he toasted. He held up his glass and waited for me to follow suit.

"To friendship," I echoed, lightly tapping my glass against his. A fusion of papaya, guava, and sweet Cavaillon melon invaded my mouth. When I removed the glass from my lips, it was empty. I nodded at Dexter, instructing him to fill my glass again.

When the alarm sounded, I opened my eyes and stared across the room. I had a piercing headache. There were no signs of last night anywhere—no wine bottle, no wine glasses, no Dexter. I smiled at the obvious innocence in our nightcap.

After falling asleep I had missed just one phone call. I picked up my phone and proceeded to listen to my voicemail.

"You must think you're grown." It was Caela. "I haven't heard from you all weekend. Call me when you can," she instructed.

The next message rattled my nerves, but I tried to remain composed. "When the cat's away, he's going to play. And apparently, the mouse is doing a little playing of his own." I deleted the message without a second thought. This early in the morning and to think he had nothing better to do than to toy with me.

I still had four hours before my flight leaves for home. The aroma of rich Italian coffee had crept in my room and danced under my nose. Then Dexter appeared with two coffee mugs and a smile of satisfaction painted on his face. I knew what that smile meant. Last night, the innocence of our friendship disappeared. Now I wasn't sure if I was feeling the same hate towards him I was now feeling for myself.

17

When Can I See You Again?

Jackson...

There was only one imperfection in this otherwise perfect week. It was our first stop on our boys' night out when I was met with a not-so-lovely surprise. I hesitated when I saw him standing there, but I proceeded to the bar and stood beside him as if he were a total stranger.

"Jackson?" he asked, hearing my voice as I attempted to get the bartender's attention.

"Hey, Gavin," I greeted and turned my attention back to the bartender.

"What brought you to Miami?"

"Say what?"

"Are you here for business or pleasure?"

I wasn't interested in small talk with Gavin. My reasons for being in Miami were none of his business, but he was trying his hardest to make it so. I couldn't get away fast enough. The bartender took his time making the drinks, but I had no arguments when I tasted mine.

"Do you need some help?" Denard whispered in my ear. He stood behind me with his hand around my waist. I had left him on the dance floor with Colt. Colt had arrived 4 hours earlier. I was pleasanly surprised when I received Colt's phone call and his announcement that he had arrived in Miami and was in the lobby of my hotel waiting on me. My best friend hadn't let me down.

The look on Gavin's face when he saw Denard was priceless—a Kodak moment, if nothing else. I handed Denard two of the glasses the waiter had placed on the bar in front of me. I began walking away with my drink and bottled water in my hands when I felt someone's firm grip on my arm. I looked at the hand around my elbow and then into Gavin's face.

"So is that your new guy?" Gavin asked.

"Gavin, is who I'm with really any of your business?"

"I'll take that as a yes."

"I could care less how you take it." I stared at him as I spoke. "And please let me go," I said through gritted teeth, yanking my arm away from him. I continued my evening in the company of Denard and Colt, and although I felt Gavin's stares as the night progressed, I paid him no attention.

● ● ● ● ●

I had more fun with Colt and Denard than I intended—way too much fun. I had asked the concierge for a wake-up call at 4:30 a.m. since my flight was scheduled to leave at 6:20 a.m. It didn't help that our decision to get it in didn't end until 3:30 a.m. that morning. We should have just stayed awake when we made it back to the room, but our eyes had something else in mind.

So Colt and I had slept through the wake-up call, probably thought we were dreaming. I know I did. We slept through my phone alarm that was supposed to have given me only fifteen minutes of shut eye. I woke up to Colt tapping me on my feet.

"Jackson, man, get up," he said with urgency.

My head was pounding, and I could now admit I had one drink too many.

"What time is it?" I asked. A serious headache stretched across my forehead, a semi-serious hangover. When my eyes focused, Colt was pulling a fresh white t-shirt over his head. He sat on the bed and bent to lace his shoes.

"It's five-fifteen," he answered.

"Damn," I said and popped up like whole grain bread from a toaster. "I'm not going to make my flight." I lay back down.

"Not by lying there. Get your ass up," Colton said, slapping me on my ass cheek.

"Why didn't you wake me?"

"That's what that loud ass phone and that annoying alarm ring tone you have were supposed to do. Plus, you kept telling me 'five more minutes, five more minutes,' knowing damn well we didn't even have five more seconds.

"My bad, Colt."

"My bad," he teased. "Hell, get your ass up, dude." He knew I hated when he called me that, but I had no time to argue.

I rushed to the bathroom, hurriedly brushed my teeth and washed my face. I didn't care how much time was against me, I wasn't going to hop on anyone's plane with sleep in my eyes and last night's alcohol on my breath. I had already packed and placed my suitcase in the trunk of the car earlier. While I was in the bathroom, Colt left to get the car from the garage, leaving me to reminisce on the fun I had with him and Denard and the possibility of missing my flight home.

Sunday morning traffic on the 95 was as clear as the runway at Columbia Metropolitan Airport. I never thought bats came from hell, and I knew damn well they couldn't drive, but if they could, I imagined they would drive like Colt was driving.

"I'm not going to make this flight."

"Man, would you just be quiet," he begged. "Are you worried about getting home to Trevor? He's probably out there doing his thing," he said under his breath.

"What was that?"

"Nothing."

Colt nascared down the highway, pushing the 2009 midnight black Chevy Corvette coupe to its limits, looking through the rear and side view mirrors for a state trooper looking to fill his monthly quota for speeding tickets.

Colt obeyed the speed limit posted on the airport grounds. He pulled up to the Delta Airlines placard hanging from the rafters, threw the car in park, and told me to hurry. I hopped out the car, grabbed my suitcase from the trunk, and ran quickly up to the counter. I inserted the company credit card into the kiosk and typed in the first three letters of my destination.

"Good morning," the attendant standing behind the counter greeted with a warm smile.

"Good morning," I said without looking up at her.

"Long night?" she asked. I looked at her with an if-you-only-knew-the-half-of-it look in my eyes. *Until I'm sure I can make this flight, I'm not saying another word,* I thought and smiled. I wasn't going to give her attitude since she had nothing to do with the rush I was in this morning.

"What time does you flight leave?"

"6:20," I said.

"To Washington, DC?"

I didn't think I had native Washingtonian tattooed on my forehead, but I answered, "Yes."

She leaned closer to the counter. "There's a twenty minute delay. You can slow down." As she spoke, my boarding pass was spat out from the Kiosk.

I didn't ask for rhyme or reason. I just breathed in relief. This woman, Krystina Smythe, had just made my morning. I turned around, and looked at Colt who was still sitting in the car outside. I gave him the thumbs up. As I made my way to security checkpoint, I received a text. It was from Colt.

Lucky bastard. Glad you'll make your flight. Love you, playboy.
-Colt

Instead of texting back, I called Colt, thanked him for driving like my life depended on making this flight, gave him instructions to return the rental car, and told him to call me the moment he landed in Atlanta. I also thanked him for flying down to surprise me and ended our conversation with the same *I love you* he had included in his text message. As I walked up to gate 4, I called Trevor, leaving him a voicemail with my flight info.

Once onboard, I sat beside a male passenger who inquired about my fantasy football picks. When I told him I didn't have time to organize a football team, real or fantasy, he proceeded to share his theories in Virginia Tech's wins over Nebraska and Western Kentucky, and was prophesying the outcome of their upcoming game against Boston College Eagles. I thought both games were closely contested, and had nothing more to add.

While he continued, I felt the airplane reach maximum speed, going from zero to take-off in less than twenty-five seconds.

18

Could It Be?

Trevor...

When I walked through the double glass doors and into The Harrison Agency, I was expecting the usually cheerful voice that often greeted me during my early morning arrivals. Instead, an unmanned desk welcomed me. It was 7 a.m., two full hours before my usual arrival time. It was unlike Caela to arrive late to work. I walked steadily, scrolling through the emails on my phone, which actually could have waited until I reached my desk.

Before I could sit and ready myself for the morning, Caela appeared at the door.

"Good morning," she greeted with a mischievous smile on her face. She had two coffee mugs in her hands. She walked in and over to my desk, placed one of the cups in front of me, and then turned back slowly towards the door. As she walked, I smiled. Her pace slowed, and I knew exactly what she wanted.

"I went away with Dexter," I began, granting Caela a fragment of the information she sought. I walked and stood in front of the desk and leaned carefully against it. I reached for my coffee mug, and as I sipped, I lifted my eyes, staring at her.

"Tell me you told him you have to put space between you and him."

"I tried."

"You tried? I know that's not all you're giving me. I waited two weeks for this. I know there's more." Caela was tiptoeing over to my desk, her ears burning for more like some gossiping schoolgirl.

"Oh, there's more," I replied, smiling naughtily with my eyes. Caela walked behind the desk and sat gracefully, almost as if I had granted her an exclusive tell-all interview on some syndicated daytime talk show.

"I am all ears," she instructed, looking at her watch. "I'm not going to say anything, but because I'm listening doesn't mean I agree with what you're doing."

"Duly noted," I said, and continued. "Caela, he's perfect."

"Trevor, he's your friend. And if he were that perfect, he wouldn't be sharing his bed with you knowing you're with Jackson."

"Didn't you just say you weren't going to say anything?"

"Carry on," she directed.

"His lovemaking was nothing short of intoxicating. If I could lie in bed with him all day, I swear I would. His touch made me so weak, and even now, I wish I could see his face. I think about him at times when he shouldn't even be on my mind. And when I tell myself to focus, I find myself thinking about him even more."

"Are you listening to yourself?" Caela interrupted.

"What do you mean?"

"Listen to how you talk about him."

"I know, right. I'm so comfortable when I'm with him. There's just something about him." I licked my lips, smiled, and then took another sip of my coffee.

"And Jackson? Isn't there something about him, too?"

"There is something about Jackson. But..."

"I still think you need to distant yourself from Dexter."

"That's the problem, Caela. You think too much. Now, if you want to know more, you have to join me for lunch."

"Do you even have to ask? Where are we going?"

"Give me some time to think about it. I'm not sure what I feel like having. And you know how my appetite is dictated by my mood."

"Well, let me know. I'm thinking seafood."

"I'm thinking, see you later," I joked. I extended my hand and assisted Caela out of my chair. "And thanks for the coffee."

"And because you're feeding me, doesn't mean I condone," she reminded.

"Yes, Caela. I heard when you said it earlier."

"Before I forget, Morgan Frazier came looking for you early this morning. What does he want?"

"Nothing he couldn't have sent in an email, I'm sure," I responded.

Caela winked, flashed a girlish smiled, and then closed the door behind her as she exited the office.

• • • • •

A casual Eurasian restaurant a few blocks from the pavilion provided the backdrop for my conversation with Caela. Maybe she thought there were a ring and a proposal at the end. The interrogation continued over her Chilean Sea Bass and the Atlantic salmon I ordered.

"You better stop acting like you can't eat and talk. How long am I going to wait to get the details?" Caela asked, helping herself to a piece of my salmon.

"Be patient, heifer. Not too much to tell."

"Ok, look. Stop acting like you're the son of a preacher man. I know something went down," she said, pointing the empty fork at me.

I released a sigh and, as I spoke, I closed my eyes in an attempt to relive the moments. I told her about waking up in arms that held me all night, and how Dexter made love to me as if he felt like I needed his love.

"And how did that make you feel?" Caela interrupted.

"The weekend with him definitely made me think about many things. His loving brought tears to my eyes, and I found myself wondering, even in the moment, if I was giving him too much, too soon."

"Especially since you shouldn't be giving anything at all," Caela reminded. "How did you find yourself in Dexter's bed? Have you gotten that weak around him?"

"Being in his bed had nothing to do with weakness. And so you know, it was Dexter who found his way in my bed."

"Insignificant detail. Either way, you were wrong."

"I wasn't wrong, I was tired. We've been fighting this obvious attraction and urges for a long time. It was going to happen sooner or later. We've come close to messing around before, but something always stopped us."

"Maybe it was knowing you have Jackson."

"Whatever! At least we've gotten it out the way."

"What you've done was add another level of complication to your friendship with Dexter." She took a sip of water and stared at me with menacing eyes.

"Don't look at me like that."

"You're playing with fire, Trevor. Now, what about Jackson? What if he finds out?"

"You're not going to tell him. And I know I'm not going to tell him. Besides Giovanni, Savon is the only other person I've seen at Dexter's house, and I know I have never given him reasons to think something was going on between Dexter and me."

"Do you really think people need reason? This is no longer just between you and Dexter," Caela said, sounding as if she was warning me. "You think this is you and Dexter's little secret?"

"I don't know what Savon knows. Damn girl! You sure know how to ruin a moment," I retorted, and took a sip of my strawberry lemonade.

"What do you really know about this Dexter guy anyway? What if he falls for you and decides to tell Jackson everything when he realizes he can't have your love? Let me guess, 'He didn't seem like that type of person.' Certainly he hasn't revealed his true self in the little time you've known him. And what happened to this Giovanni person?"

"I don't know what happened to Giovanni. I didn't ask any questions and Dexter didn't volunteer any answers. If Giovanni retreated in the background while Dexter spent his weekend with me, that's his stupidity."

Caela sat back in her chair, allowing my last statement to float in her mind. Then she spoke out. "Trevor, I heard all about how the situation with you and Kelvin had unfolded before your eyes. And while it wasn't stupidity, love can blind you to certain things. You spent most of your time in the same house with Kelvin and you were clueless to his affairs. This situation is going to blow up in your face, not that I want to see it happen. You're not this person you're trying to be. Don't do this to Jackson. He doesn't deserve it. You don't deserve it."

"You know, I thought Kelvin wasn't that type of person either, and look what happened."

"Oh, so because you can't hurt Kelvin, you're going to hurt Jackson?"

"Before he hurts me."

Caela was quiet.

I sat looking at her and waited for her to respond. She was seething. "That's a rather selfish and reckless ass thing to say. Pardon my profanity, but what the hell makes you think it's Jackson's intention to hurt you?"

"It's never their intention, now is it? Isn't that what they say after it happens?" I paused and sat back in my chair.

"Trevor, in case you haven't noticed, he's not Kelvin." She gently placed her fork on the side of her plate. She removed a note from her skirt pocket. "By the way, I took this message for you this morning."

As I read, my eyes focused on a number I didn't recognize. "Does this person even have a name?" I asked, looking at the other side of the paper to see if anything was written on it.

"No," Caela responded. "He said you would know who it's from."

I removed my cell phone and dialed the mysterious number. I waited for someone to pick up, but instead, I listened absorbedly to the recording on the other end.

The man you see when you look at him today will not be the same man you see tomorrow. Whatever you do, don't give your heart to him.

I slowly moved the phone away from my ear and looked at Caela in disbelief.

"Trevor, what is it?" she asked, reaching across the table for the phone.

I pressed the number 4 button to repeat the message, and handed the phone to Caela. She listened with the same whodunit look on her face. She removed the phone from her ear and sat in silence, waiting for me to provide some verbal reaction.

"Someone obviously thought I needed to be warned," I finally broke.

"That's obvious. The million-dollar question is, why? And, what are you going to do?"

"Well...I can either ignore the warning of a possible bitter, heartbroken brother whose advances were dismissed by Jackson."

"Or Dexter," Caela added.

"Or," I continued, ignoring her comment, "I can heed the warning of someone who probably has a legitimate reason to find me."

"The choice is yours."

"True," I agreed.

"But can I tell you what I think you should do?"

"Why do you even ask? You're going to tell me anyway."

I listened cautiously. At the end, I still wasn't sure what I was going to do, if I was going to do anything at all. Caela's advice formed a cloud of uncertainty in my head. I had lost appetite for food and work, even though I had a half-day left. I tried not to let the phone call consume me, but for now, there was nothing I could do about it.

On our way back to the Pavilion, Caela and I walked in silence. A question, a suggestion every now and then from either of us broke in, trying to figure out the reason behind the phantom warnings. I tried to convince myself I had nothing to worry about, all the while wondering if I should even tell Caela about the other calls I had been receiving. I thought about my brief encounter with Savon while I visited Dexter, and then fixed my mind on the puzzled look on Dexter's face, almost as if he was warning him not to say something he knew he shouldn't.

"Are you ok?" Caela asked as we exited the elevator.

"I'm fine," I responded, and although she didn't believe me, she didn't press the issue. "I'm just going to finish up some prep work and then try to get out of here."

I spent the last few hours behind my desk unable to focus on much of anything. There was a long conversation with Jackson. I listened to him talk about Colt's surprise visit and about the fun time he had. I half-listened to his recount of meeting Denard, because I was too busy trying to figure things out in my own mind. None of what he was telling me mattered, but I think I did a pretty good job pretending.

I was ready for this day to be over. At five o'clock, I rushed out as if someone had just yelled "fire." I called my father hoping I could run a scenario by him, pretending I needed some advice for a friend, but he wasn't available. I drove to Ace of Spades and sat at the bar. I needed to drown my thoughts in a glass of something on the rocks. After two quick glasses of gin, I was in my car heading home. Although I didn't feel like talking, I answered my phone on the first ring.

"I'm just calling to check on you, Trevor," Caela began. "Are you ok?"

"I will be," I answered. "I stopped for a quick drink at Ace."

"Okay. Have you spoken to Jackson?"

"Yes, but not about what we discussed. I'm sure we'll talk again before the night is over."

"Look, Trevor. You went through your rough patch with Kelvin, and you know what, you just might be on a path to ruin your happy ending with Jackson."

"You're right. And just what do you suggest I do? This isn't the first phone call I've received. And they didn't start until Jackson moved here. Now this person is playing this game for a reason. It's not just for entertainment. Someone out there is doing all they can to get Jackson back. Or maybe that someone never really lost him."

"Or," Caela interrupted. "Maybe someone was hurt by Dexter and they don't want the same thing to happen to you. Why not just ask Jackson if there's someone else in his life."

"I'm not going to do that."

"Why not?"

"If there isn't, then sleeping with Dexter is no longer justified."

"You mean that was your justification?"

"Caela, I'm almost home. Why don't we talk about this tomorrow? Whatever is going on, I will figure it out. But I will bet money someone from Jackson's not-too-distant past is here to start up some shit. And whatever it is, I need to make sure I don't fall on my face like I did with Kelvin. I will talk with you later."

When I entered the house, I was greeted with silence, silence I needed. I loosened my tie enough to fit over my head. I removed my shirt from my slacks and begun unbuttoning it as I made my way to the kitchen. *Just what I needed,* I thought, removing a bottle of Merlot from the wine cooler and pouring a glass full. I walked upstairs and into the master suite, sat on the edge of the bed, turned on the television and began surfing through my recently recorded programs. Then I stared at a framed black and white photograph of my mother that sat across the room. I exhaled, and eventually fell asleep.

19

Truth Is

Jackson...

After parking my car in the garage and entering through the door into the foyer, I stopped facing the alarm pad, my fingers crisscrossing the keypad in a frenzied attempt to disarm the alarm system. I stopped in my office briefly, throwing my briefcase onto one of the Victorian style chairs along the wall. I began loosening my tie as I made my way up the stairs hastening over as many steps as I could for reasons I didn't even know. As I walked into the kitchen, I passed the pills, vitamins I had set out this morning. I turned, opened the refrigerator, and removed a cold bottle of Deer Park. One after the other I tossed the pills and capsules in my mouth, each being followed by a swallow of water to make sure it traveled smoothly down my throat.

You're such a health freak, I thought.

When I finally made my way to my master bedroom, which sat in the corner of the house facing a covered deck, my suitcase from my last trip sat almost in the center of the floor. I hadn't had the chance to unpack, and immediately, a feeling of exhaustion swept over me as the idea of the inevitable, somewhat tedious task, one I have avoided for the last two weeks, stared me in the face. I sat in a chair, which was cater-cornered on one side of the room. As I began unlacing my shoes, I smiled. One week before Thanksgiving, and unless I planned on bringing those same dirty clothes to my mother's house, I needed to start unpacking one t-shirt at a time.

Finally, the people I loved the most were going to meet the man I loved the most. I just wished my father was going to be there. As I pulled open the zippers to the suitcase, I remembered that, in my hurry, I hadn't picked up today's mail. I walked downstairs and headed towards the front door. I opened the door and removed the four pieces of mail from the silver mailbox.

Bills...bills... bills... I thought, putting each envelope to the back of the small pile.

Ocean View Condominiums, Chicago, Ill, I read, tearing open the cream-colored envelope. The note was written on a 7 by 5-inch notebook paper, the kind of paper found in a record book.

I began reading silently to myself. *Ask him a question you already know the answer to and see if he tells you the truth. Ask him about C-House and the White Sox, and let me know if the honesty you seek is the one you've found.*

The author had impressive penmanship.

There was no return address, no signature, nothing to help me identify the person this letter came from. The desire to unpack was gone. So too was the excitement I had about the upcoming Thanksgiving trip I had planned. If Trevor had done something and was keeping it from me, how could he accept an invitation to sit and smile in my family's face as if everything was all right?

• • • • •

I didn't mind spending another night watching an old episode of *Law and Order: SVU*. I picked up my cell phone several times to call Trevor, but I hadn't yet wrapped my mind around what I was going to say to him. I had nothing to prove he had done something wrong besides this letter, and I didn't think this was enough to accuse him. And who's to say someone wasn't out there trying to deliberately put doubt in my mind about this man.

When my cell phone rang, I answered with a bit of annoyance in my voice.

"I thought I would have heard from you by now." It was Gavin. He was the last person I needed to be talking to right now.

"What made you think calling you was on my list of priorities?" I thought after my cold reaction to him in Miami he would have tossed my number.

"What are you up to?"

"Gavin. What do you want?"

"Can't a brotha just call to talk?"

"Fine. Talk," I said. I paused.

"How's…" There was an awkward silence. "How's your new friend doing?"

"His name is Trevor. But something tells me you already knew that," I injected. "We both know you're not interested in him or his wellbeing, but if you must, he's doing quite well. Is there anything else?"

"Was that who you were with in Miami?"

"I gave you my answer to that question the first time you asked. I see you weren't satisfied."

Nothing could be odder about this night. First this letter, and now a call from Gavin. Was he really calling to "just talk" or was he trying to see if I had received his little present?

"Hey, Gavin," I began as I removed the letter once again from the envelope.

"Wassup, baby?" he asked.

I cringed as the word fell on my ear.

"Anyway, what do you know about Ocean View Condominiums?"

"What am I supposed to know? Sounds like a condo to me?" So, it wasn't the response I expected, but at least if he knew nothing, I could cross him off my short list of suspects. Or could I? Maybe he wanted me to think he knew nothing.

"And C-House?"

"And what?" Gavin asked. "Look, Jackson. Why don't you stop with the Final Jeopardy questions and tell me what's going on. What are you talking about?"

I'm not sure what came over me, but I spent the next hour talking with Gavin about the letter I received with directions to ask about C-House and the White Sox. Based on the letter, I told him I suspected Trevor must have taken a trip to Chicago, but I wasn't sure if he had gone alone. Why was it so important that I knew about this trip Trevor had taken? And if he had taken this trip alone, why didn't or hadn't he said anything about it to me? What or who was in Chicago, and was it best that I didn't know?

"You think this is much to do about nothing?" I asked. I was surprised at how attentive Gavin had been. Was he playing the role of a fool to catch wise?

"If you're over there mulling over the possibilities, then something isn't right. It doesn't make any sense to exist in doubt."

"You're right," I answered in agreement, surprising myself.

"Now that we've gotten that out of the way, let's talk about us," Gavin suggested.

It didn't take long for the Gavin I knew to return. And I was immediately reminded he was the same indecisive, self-centered Gavin I needed to get away from.

"Like I told you before, Gavin, there wasn't an 'us' to talk about when you attempted to do so over three weeks ago and there isn't an 'us' to talk about now.

"You'll change your mind," he said, sounding confident.

Something about his statement aroused a level of distrust in the pit of my stomach, and with that I bid him a good night. I guess Gavin didn't know what he had until I was gone. Something had gotten into him. I just didn't know what it was.

A cloud of regret hung over me. I was lying in bed, on my back, with my forearm resting on my forehead. I tried to suppress the avalanche of activities that went through my mind. All of my attempts were unsuccessful. In the back of my mind, everything I had hoped for in meeting Trevor, in moving here, now had the possibility of crumbling, falling like sandcastles in high tide. The idea that I didn't have to spend another New Year's Eve surfing the internet, again, alone, reading some daily horoscope with promises of things that might or might not come true, fizzled. The thought of another Valentine's Day that only found me draining the last drop of vodka into a half-glass of cranberry juice, wishing the day and the lonely night would just disappear, now seemed to be looming in the distant. All that had happened while I was with Gavin now threatened to return. Now I had let him into my relationship with Trevor, the one place he didn't belong.

Before I settled into sleep, I made one last phone call. My talk with Trevor was brief, and although I was tempted to question him, I resisted. I'm not sure if he saw through my attempt to sound normal, since he kept asking me if I was ok. He appeared satisfied with my response: "I had a long day, and tomorrow promised to be just the same." Work was keeping Trevor busy, too, but we did agree to meet for lunch later in the week.

20

Tell Me What You're Gonna do

Trevor...

After talking to Jackson last night, I went to sleep unable to shake the feeling something was troubling him. I spent a few minutes after our conversation conjuring convincing arguments that what was bothering him had nothing to do with me—that's what a big part of me wanted to believe. The dream I had when sleep finally came did nothing to ease the possibility that Jackson probably knew more than I thought he did, and was probably busy putting the pieces together before confronting me.

Even though it seemed I had just nestled my head in my pillow, I was glad when morning came. I was eager to get my day started. When my alarm sounded at 5:30 a.m., instead of walking across the room, pressing the snooze button, and then making my way back between the sheets, I walked unsteadily to my bathroom, opened the shower door, and turned on the shower. After removing my boxers, I stood under the shower, allowing the high-pressured water to beat against my body. There was a sharp pain on the side of my neck that I tried to massage away, but had no luck. It was a sign of stress, I guess, and I hoped it would soon disappear. A whiff of the citrus fragrance from my

Obsession hair and body shampoo had finally gotten me far away from sleep.

Hello morning.

I stayed longer in the shower than I would have on any other workday. When I closed my eyes, enjoying the soft feel of already smooth skin, I saw his face. I hadn't been thinking about him, so I couldn't explain how or why he appeared out of nowhere. We did have plans for lunch this afternoon, so maybe I was subconsciously anticipating seeing him again.

I had my own warped theory of friendships between gay men, why it works and why it doesn't. I'd always thought our friendships either worked because your friends were never men you were attracted to sexually, or because you had an attraction you worked extremely hard to ignore. This was my reason for keeping Denise and Caela close and all others farther away. I kept Wesley close, too, but he was as straight as a toothpick and was more attractive as my business partner than anything else, at least that was what I told myself. But here was Dexter, and the idea that I would be able to keep my urges for him at bay had been thrown out the window.

I drove like I owned the road, and for a good while, the road did belong to only me. I figured if I were a morning person, every morning commute to work could be like this. I expected to be the only one in the office when I walked in, but there he was waiting on me as if he had camped outside my office all night long.

"Good morning, Wesley," I greeted, opening the door to my office.

"Are you sure?" he asked with a worried look on his face. He stood leaning against the wall as if he were standing in front of a saloon with a straw in his mouth and a store-bought cowboy hat tilted halfway down his face, waiting for a country girl he had his eyes on to come out and entertain him.

"Is something on your mind?" I asked, stopping momentarily, making sure my eyes met his.

"I was gonna ask you the same question, but since you beat me to the punch..." I pushed the door open and walked across the room to my desk. Wesley entered behind me, checked his watch as if he were gauging the time he had with me, and then closed the door behind him.

He stood at the door with both hands in his pockets. I stood behind my desk. After searching his face, I waited for him to begin. There was definitely something on his mind, but he looked as if he was uncertain of my reaction that would follow. Maybe Wesley was just making sure his words would come out right.

"I'm listening," I said, giving his cue to begin.

"Lately you've seemed a little preoccupied. Is everything aiight?" Wesley asked in his big-brother tone. I gave him a what-the-hell-are-you-talking-about gaze, looking at him sideways.

"Besides work, everything is fine," I explained, staring at him, and I hoped my explanation had satisfied his concerns. I hoped he sensed this conversation was not on my list of topics I wanted to be discussing this early morning. I hadn't had my morning pick-me-up, and I could hear the poetry of Chai tea speaking to me in a whisper.

"Man, you're gonna have to come better than that if you expect me to believe you. I might not know what's bothering you, but I do know what it's not, and what it's not is work. Look, man, Trevor..." Wesley walked closer to me, pressed his palms against the desk, and continued speaking. "You had that same look on your face you had a couple years ago when you were you going through your dealings with Kelvin, that same look of distance, and the only person not aware of it was you."

I stood in front of Wesley with my eyes fixed on his, but when Kelvin's name was spoken, it broke my stare. I had no idea Wesley had been so observant before, and I wasn't aware he had been taking notice now.

"You don't know what you're talking about?" That was my only rebuttal.

"Oh, I don't? So, I guess you're not gonna tell me what's going on with you and Jackson?" His question stopped me in my tracks.

I stood there looking at him. Everything that had been happening came rushing through my mind, as if someone had pressed the rewind button on my love life and was playing them all over again. The faces of a handful of men, their distorted interpretation of love, and my short-lived involvement with them played like previews of a few poorly written, poorly acted movies. I wondered what Wesley would say if he knew what was going on had nothing to do with Jackson, at least not directly, or if he knew what he thought I was going through was a direct result of my own greed.

"You're one of the good guys, man," Wesley said. "Whatever it is shouldn't be happening to you."

I was glad Wesley had so much confidence in what I was and what I deserved. I, on the other hand, was starting to feel the opposite. I was even more relieved he couldn't read my mind.

I trusted Wesley and knew whatever I confided in him would stay between us, and within these four walls of brick and glass. He knew I shared a lot with Caela, but that I was sharing just as much of my world with him was unknown to her. I knew they would never compare notes in conversations.

So I spent the better half of my early morning in conversation with Wesley. Since he had already known about Kelvin and how I had met Jackson, I went straight to my now complicated friendship with Dexter.

"That trip I took to Chicago was a mistake," I began.

"A mistake? How so?"

"I went with Dexter?"

"And how does going with him make it a mistake?"

"Because…" I paused, quickly planning in my mind how I was going to tell what had transpired.

"Trevor," Wesley called out.

"What began as an innocent weekend turned out to be so much more. Nothing that happened was planned." I stood beside Wesley, leaning on my desk like he was, with my arms folded across my chest, protecting myself from my own inflicted hurt. "Things just went too far."

"In other words, you fucked up?" Though Wesley didn't ask what exactly went on between us, I was pretty sure he had a good idea.

"If you want to say that, but I don't think I'm the only one fucking up."

"What do you mean?"

"I have been getting these phone calls, only I haven't been able to figure out who's calling or why. They began over a month ago, just after Jackson moved here."

"And you think it's someone Jackson was involved with?"

"No. I think it's someone he *is* involved with."

"And you're sure about this?" Wesley asked, looking at me, but I kept my focus straight ahead.

"Come on, Wesley. What other explanation could there be?" I walked behind my desk and sat.

"So the idea that these calls could be connected to Dexter *never* crossed your mind?"

"I seriously doubt it."

"May I ask you a question?" Wesley asked. He turned to face me, leaned over and pressed his palms on the desk.

"Sure," I said.

"First I want you to look at me," he ordered.

I raised my head slowly, lifted my eyes, and then stared at him.

He stared back, without blinking, and then asked, "Do you love Jackson?"

Before I could respond, I felt my heart sink. "Yes," I responded, and for the first time since we started talking, my eyes were moist. "I'm just not sure how strong our love is."

"Does he know?"

"Yes," I said quickly.

"I'm not asking if Jackson knows the strength of your love for him." I looked at Wesley with puzzling eyes. "I mean does he know about you and Dexter, your trips, all of that?" Wesley said to clarify.

His question had taken words from me. The truth is I had no idea what Jackson knew, if he knew anything at all. He hadn't said anything yet.

"I don't know how it happened. I do know one morning I woke up and both Jackson and Dexter were on my mind, and sharing space in my heart. I knew how Jackson got there, but I don't remember letting Dexter in."

"I don't know why people complicate this beautiful thing call love."

I don't know why some of us go out of our way to complicate it either, I thought, looking at Wesley.

He got up from the desk and began walking towards the door. He stopped, raised his hand to his chin, and rubbed it pensively. He turned around slowly, held his arms wide, and summoned me over to him. When I got close, he drew me into him and into a warming embrace. "Man, I just thought my friend needed this," he said. "I'm sure you know what to do now."

And then I cried. I wouldn't have agreed with Wesley earlier, but he was right: a simple hug was exactly what I needed.

"I better get started on this day. The crew should be here any minute now," Wesley said, glancing at his watch.

I looked at my watch, too. It was about 8:45. "Yeah, you're right."

Wesley opened the door. Before he closed it behind him, I called out. "Wesley." He opened the door and stuck his head inside my office. "Thank you," I said, finally managing a smile.

"No big deal, man. I'm always here if you want some help figuring things out. Stay strong," he said and walked out.

21

Losing You

Jackson...

I couldn't explain the strange feeling I had when morning broke. It wasn't there when I fell asleep, but there it was, rising in the pit of my stomach. It resembled feelings I had before when I knew something just didn't feel right. It was that familiar feeling I had when I noticed smiles disappearing, and everything, including hearts, began to break. The feeling I had when I found myself trying to get to the heart of the matter, even after I knew nothing else mattered, at least not to him. I looked around only to find myself by myself, and finally I realized it was over. I didn't know what any of this meant, but I knew I didn't want to find myself in that place again, wondering what happened when I should have known all along.

I still hadn't figured out this letter, and it was giving me a headache I surely didn't need. So what if Trevor hasn't told me about his trip. I hadn't gone into details with him about Denard, either, and I figured his trip was just as innocent as my encounter with the doctor.

I was in the guest room sitting in the middle of my European Farmhouse Hampton Hill upholstered bed that was specifically bought for the room. I purposely fell asleep here, where I found myself sleeping most nights and awaking most mornings when I was in the house alone. I was giving Trevor the benefit of the doubt because I didn't know what else I should be giving him. If he had some secret he was keeping from me, I was sure it wouldn't be his secret for too long. I was willing to be patient, hoping when and if anything came to the fore I wouldn't be left with a shattered heart in my hand.

I wasn't going to get much accomplished by sitting here. I still had a day of work ahead of me and I hadn't even made it to the shower yet. With that in mind, I lay back in the bed, grabbed my cell phone and dialed my mother's work number. It had been a while since I left Mother a message to greet her as her morning began.

Mother, good morning. Hope your day has started out well. You know I love you, and will talk to you soon. Give my love to the husband if you talk to him before I do. Have a great day, and don't let those so-called crazy people cause my mother to stress. Love you.

- Jackson

It was a simple message I was sure would bring a smile to my mother's face. I tried to mask any anxiety in my voice because I knew how she was. All she needed was a hint and the phone calls and a myriad of questions were sure to follow.

I looked at the time on my cell phone. Just as the minutes ticked to 6:30, the television came on. I sat up for a moment listening to the weather. Well into November and fall was in full swing. I didn't mind the fall weather as long as it wasn't cold and raining, but that's exactly what was on the forecast, and not just for today, either. After convincing myself to get up and making my way to the bathroom, my cell phone rang.

"Hello," I answered. I hadn't checked the screen to see who was calling, but this early in the morning, the list of possible callers wasn't that long.

"What did you do with the information you received?" he asked in a deep, raspy voice. I wasn't sure if he was trying to sound incredibly sexy or if this was an attempt to conceal his true sound.

"And what information are you asking about?"

"Playing dumb is not going to get you anywhere. I'm trying to help you out."

"I don't know who told you I needed help." He had gotten my attention, as much as I didn't want to admit it.

"So you think you've really found love, don't you?" he asked.

"Assuming I had lost it, you tell me." I sat back in the bed and waited for this man to tell more of what he knew. I figured this phone call would come sooner or later since I did nothing with the letter I had received, besides sharing it with Gavin.

"Jackson, I know you want to be loved. I know you think Trevor has finally made you happy. It seems you've gone anywhere for love, but what if I tell you where you've gone is no different from where you've been, or where you just came from."

"I would say you don't know what you're talking about. And you don't know Trevor."

"I hate to disappoint you, Jackson, but I'm not interested in knowing him. But I do know you."

"You do?" I asked with a surprised look on my face. I sat on the bed trying to fit his voice to the Rolodex of faces that immediately came to mind.

No luck.

"Yes, I do. But you don't know Trevor. You think the person who knows hurt wouldn't hurt you. You think the person who has had his share of love gone wrong would know what to do when someone as real as you finally comes into his life. You, Jackson, have been searching for someone you want to just be yours, but if that's what you think you're getting from him, it's not."

"So let's say I believe just for a moment what you are saying is true. If you know what you're accusing Trevor of is true, why not just tell me? How do I know you're not just trying to start something?"

"You don't have to worry about me destroying this *love* you think you've found. Trevor is already doing what he needs to ruin whatever it is you have. And, I haven't come out and told you everything because I don't want to be the one to cause you hurt," the caller explained. "I figured the least Trevor could do is be truthful."

"And you know the truth?"

"Yes, and so do you."

"I don't suppose you're going to tell me who you are?"

"In time. Right now, my identity is not important. Like I said in the letter, ask him a question you already know the answer to, see if he lies." And then he hung up.

The conversation had left me with more questions than it

did answers, and I guess the only other person who had the answers I needed, since this man wasn't going to tell me anything, was Trevor.

My morning hadn't gone as planned. I usually mentally prepare for the day in the shower, but now I was standing there, the water from the spout beating against my face as I tried to think myself through approaching Trevor. All I did was convince myself it was best to say nothing at all, at least not now.

So many questions inundated my mind. My heart was racing, and nothing I thought helped to slow it down. I was starting to feel like the only kind of love I was ever going to know was the kind that only knew how to hurt. The faulty love that began with my father had somehow infiltrated every relationship I've had since he disappeared. When did I become such an attraction for this madness?

22

The Truth of it All

Trevor...

I spent the hours between my heart to heart with Wesley and lunch in my office, hidden from everyone. I had no meetings scheduled this morning so staying out of sight was practically easy. I pretended work was keeping me busy, when in fact it was those unsettling thoughts that kept my mind on everything but. When Caela arrived I gave her instructions to tell anyone who called I was in a conference until the afternoon. Since she scheduled most meetings, proposal, and demonstrations to clients, she knew I was not being the least bit truthful, and of course, she wanted to know why. I wasn't in the mood to explain. I didn't feel like giving her the answers to why. Though she had let me alone for the moment, I knew she would later return with her same inquisitions.

I had picked up my cell phone several times, but I couldn't decide whom to call. This decision should have been easy. It used to be so easy. I knew I should be calling the one I loved. His voice should have been the one I wanted to hear first. My fingers had a mind of their own and were already pressing buttons to call the man I lusted after.

"Mr. T. Harrison, what's going on?" Dexter answered as if he were hearing my voice for the first time in years.

"Sitting here thinking about you," I admitted, although that wasn't entirely true.

"Should you be over there doing that?"

"I don't know. Should I?" I asked. "Me thinking about you isn't going to hurt anyone, now is it?" The words fell from my mouth and part of me wished I could take them back.

"There's always that possibility of someone getting hurt, Trevor. Isn't Jackson still around?" he asked.

"Yes."

"I need to ask you something."

His statement sent my heart thumping as if he had said the worst thing in the world to me.

"What do you need to ask me?" I said when my heart was at a more controllable pulse.

"Are we going to talk about Chicago, or are we going to pretend it never happened?"

"I couldn't pretend if I wanted to. Maybe we can talk about it over lunch," I offered.

"When, today?"

"Yes, unless you've already made plans."

"No plans, at least not anything that can't be rearranged."

● ● ● ● ●

I managed to slip out of the office without Caela seeing me. It was exactly noon, which meant she was in the bathroom, leaning over the sink, carefully applying her Waterproof Microfiber mascara to extend and thicken already long and naturally curled lashes. Coming off the elevator, I ran into Morgan Frazier. He had taken an early lunch and was heading back into the office for a 12:30 conference call. This was only his second year with the company, but he had fit in as if he had been here as long as Jory or Xavier.

Like summer in D.C., fall had its perks, too. I had hoped for a repeat of the spectacular weather we had enjoyed in the beginning of October as November greeted us, but all hope had been lost. It was a cool sixty-degree day, cool enough to layer just a bit. There were moments of sun attempting to brighten the otherwise dreary day, but those stubborn clouds had been dominant.

My black cashmere v-neck sweater and gray tweed pants was appropriate attire. I forgot what traffic in the District was like on any given afternoon, but I was quickly reminded as I maneuvered my way down Connecticut Avenue in the northwest quadrant. As I did, I'm sure many people cursed purchasing a manual shift vehicle, especially when stuck in the 3rd Street tunnel, on Pennsylvania Ave, or on the 14th Street Bridge during the mass exodus at quitting time.

La Tomate Italian Bistro, a neighborhood bistro with affordable regional Italian cuisine, was Dexter's choice for lunch. Located on Connecticut Avenue in the heart of historic DuPont Circle, La Tomate was only a few blocks from Dexter's law firm, Abramson, DeGregory, and Dixon LLC, so travel was a breeze for him. A.D.D. LLC was nothing like its interesting abbreviation. They were a team of client-focused lawyers who committed to and believed in the innocence of those they defended. They sued for punitive damages that otherwise wouldn't have been sought after or rewarded. They always gave to charity and gave back to the community by establishing a paid summer internships to two law school students from any of the local colleges.

Dexter, too, was appropriately dressed for the fall weather. He wore black striped stretch wool pants, a marled half-zip gray mock-neck sweater, and an exposed white cotton crew. His tall physique made anything he wore look good, and he looked just as good covered up as he did with only his bare chest and underwear.

Dexter stood in a wide stance with both his thumbs in either pocket of his pants. His copper-color complexion glistened even under the blanket of autumn. His deep-set toast-brown eyes exuded sex. His lips were full, the kind you held on to at the end of a long passionate kiss. His face was hairless, just shapely sideburns that extended down his face and ended in line with the tip of his earlobes. He was a white man with soul and a very sexy swagger. He smiled as I neared him.

I figured Dexter had frequented this bistro on several occasions when the waiter welcomed him by name. He responded with that warm smile that melted hearts. We sat at a table for two, with Connecticut Ave and a handful of lunch-crowd pedestrians in plain sight through the many windows of LaTomate. The décor was simple elegance. Framed portraits, remnants of Italy, ornamented the eggshell-white walls. I could only imagine its ambiance at night. A few fall-loving patrons enjoyed asparagus, leek and potato puree, or the soup of the day on the patio. We perused our menus with unnecessary haste and selected our meals.

It wasn't easy sitting across from Dexter. I tried to avoid gazing into his eyes.

"What?" he asked, smiling.

"Nothing," I responded. Looking away, I smiled and acknowledged the waiter who had returned with lunch and a bottle of Pinot Grigio. I welcomed his interruption.

The ear-shaped pasta with diced mixed vegetables, chicken and pesto sauce made my mouth water in anticipation. I watched Dexter's eyes widen. The scent of his linguine pasta with cockle clams in white wine, garlic and parsley sauce opened up his insatiable appetite for seafood.

"You know I really had a great time in Chicago," Dexter began.

I had a great time in Chicago, too, but it didn't mean I wanted to talk about it every time I saw him or spoke to him. But since he had opened the door, there was something specific I wanted to ask him about the trip.

"Why wasn't Giovanni with you in Chicago?" I asked, and I was staring at him again.

"Because you were there?" he responded, jokingly. I didn't think my question was a punch line.

"Come on, Dexter. I mean, why was that invitation extended to me and not to Giovanni?"

"Well, he had court that Friday, and that was his weekend with Paisley, his daughter."

"So I was your second choice?"

"You didn't let me finish." He picked up his wine glass and took a quick sip. "Look at me," he instructed. "You and me, we were in Chicago because I wanted to be there with you. I asked not knowing what you would say and I was relieved when you said yes. I was aware of the sexual tension between us. I know you see how I look lasciviously at you at times, even when I'm not trying to."

"So the dinner, the wine afterwards, was part of your plan to get it done and over with?"

"No," he responded in a loud whisper. "It wasn't part of any plan. If you're not willing to admit it to me, Trevor, I will. I'm attracted to you. I have been since I ran into you at the Daily Grind. And for that long we've ignored it, trying to make a friendship work. But we can't ignore the obvious."

I waited until he finished speaking before looking up and acknowledging his sincerity.

"But there's Jackson and Giovanni," I said.

"I know. That complicates everything, doesn't it?" Dexter asked and turned his attention to finishing his lunch. I followed his lead until my cell phone vibrated. I wanted to ignore the vibration, thinking it might have been my stalker. I removed my cell phone and looked at the screen.

I knew better than to answer when Caela's picture and number appeared on the screen. I figured it was something important, but knowing her, this phone call had nosey written all over it and nothing to do with work.

I was right.

"You're having lunch with him, aren't you?" Caela asked when I answered.

"Are you spying on me?" I asked, turning around as I surveyed my surroundings. I tried to whisper, but I was sure Dexter could hear me.

"Answer the question, Trevor," she urged, but I remained silent, and that was all Caela needed to confirm her assumption. "Trevor, that's what got you in this mess in the first place. You said you were going to pull back from him. After what happened, that's what you need to do. This is not pulling back."

"Caela, it's only lunch. What harm could that do?"

"In case you have forgotten, the harm has already been done."

I sat listening to Caela. When I thought she had said all she needed to, or all I needed to hear, I ended the conversation and continued to lunch with Dexter.

"Someone doesn't think this is a good idea."

I ignored his comment. After some thought, I brought up an unfinished conversation with him. As we discussed his family over dinner in Chicago, Dexter had been reluctant to talk about his father. He promised to tell me about that part of his life later. And it was later. Why was he so apprehensive?

"So," I began.

"You're going to ask me about him, aren't you?" he presumed.

"Who? Your father?"

"Yes, Trevor. When I told you my father was dead, I wasn't lying. I thought when he died we had settled all the hatred I carried for him, and the disappointment I saw in his eyes every time he looked at me. He was on his deathbed unable to respond, so I did most of the talking. Lying there with his eyes closed was the first time I wasn't able to see in his eyes how much he despised what I was. But I used that moment as my opportunity to free my mind. I told him I purposely kept Patrick around to hurt him, even though I was being hurt just the same and worse. I told him about how I resented his existence after he walked out on my mother, Dane, and me, and blamed him for her suicide."

Dexter's eyes glistened with tears. I sat and listened. It was as if he had waited forever to say this to someone, but why hadn't he done so in Chicago?

"I told him that I visited him every day because I wanted to watch him die," Dexter continued, "just like Dane had to watch my mother die because she felt she couldn't go on without him."

"But…" I finally interrupted.

"We buried my father, Marvin, with a secret, one he forced my mother to keep. The same secret my mother was trying to tell me when I came home one day and he was gone, before she took her own life. But what did I do? I interrupted her."

"How did you find out about it?"

"A weak letter of apology written in my stepmother's handwriting, but it was definitely my father's voice. Apparently he did regain some speech after his heart attack, but only long enough to dictate the letter to Eleanor. But according to her, he had been nonresponsive since his fall."

"What did it say?"

"Look, Trevor. I can't."

I sat back looking disappointed. He stopped so abruptly. I could see the hurt in his eyes. I wanted to tell him it would hurt less once it was out of his system, but I held my tongue and left him alone.

We were ending lunch earlier than I had planned, an hour and a half from the time we sat down. After hugging Dexter goodbye, I was back in my car, heading down Connecticut Avenue to finish my afternoon at work.

23

What's a Man to Do?

Trevor...

I was somewhat distracted after lunch, trying to digest some of what Dexter had told me. What was this secret that had been revealed to him? I needed to talk to someone, and the only person I could think to call was Caela. I was almost sure Denise was busy. I wasn't as in-tuned with her schedule like I was when she was a stone's throw and less than a quarter tank of gas away. I could have called Jackson, but with these thoughts going through my head, he was the last person I needed to talk to. I wouldn't have been able to concentrate on any conversation with him, and a slip of the tongue could turn both our worlds upside down.

When Caela answered the phone, I could hear her fingers racing across the keyboard in a frenetic attempt to meet a self-imposed four o'clock deadline.

"Wow, slow down, Annabelle," I joked as the elevator doors closed. I stared at my reflection in the bronze-colored doors. A confused man stared back at me. When the doors opened, I entered the space occupied by the agency. I said a quick hello to Morgan, who was walking towards Wesley's office for a scheduled meeting. They had been working closely on the Copeland project.

"You have some explaining to do, Mister," Caela said, joking, but I knew she was serious. "I told you before, stop acting like you're grown."

"Meet me in my office," I continued almost in a sergeant-like tone.

She removed the wireless headset and placed it beside the telephone pad. Then she quickly saved the open file she had been working on.

"What's the rush? Is everything ok?" she asked in a quiet whisper. I did not respond. When I entered my office, Caela entered behind me.

"Close the door behind you, please," I ordered as I made my way to the miniature refrigerator and grabbed an ice-cold bottle of Deer Park.

"You haven't told him yet, have you?" Caela paused and waited for my answer. I wasn't looking at her. I kept the top of the bottle between my lips so words couldn't escape. "Trevor," she called out.

"No, Caela. No. I haven't told him yet." I walked over to my desk and sat in my chair, holding the bottled water in my hand.

"What are you waiting for?" Caela was standing in front of me, her hands folded across her chest.

"The right moment." Who was I kidding? Is there ever a right moment to share this kind of information?

"And you don't think the right moment has come and gone, and come and gone, again?"

"I get the point, Caela. You said you weren't going to argue with me about my decision again."

"Yeah, and you said you were going to tell him a while ago. What's stopping you?"

"What's stopping me? Every time my phone rings I think I had the right to do what I did. Every time I think about you calling me after seeing Jackson out with that guy, I convince myself I don't need to tell him a damn thing. And then I think about him lying to my father and Natalie about working late…" I paused. "Do you need me to continue? It only happened twice."

"And twice was two times too many. Next you're going to say it meant nothing, as if that is supposed to fix anything. Well, I could care less about it meaning nothing and more about how much it meant to you to have slept with him." She was incensed. "And then you went and had lunch with him today, and it will happen again." She pulled a chair from the conference table on the far side of the office, placed it in front of my desk and sat.

"You don't know that?"

"Then let's just call it my best guess."

"Whatever you say, Caela," I said, dismissing her statement. I stood behind the desk. "Why do I tell you anything?"

"Because you know I'm going to tell you the truth. And who else are you going to tell this mess?" She looked at her watch, crossed her legs, and then continued. "You still haven't figured out if those phone calls have anything to do with Jackson."

"Can you think of anyone else? How do I know he isn't out there doing his own thing? And now one of his flings has been interrupting my days and my nights with these brainless warnings."

"Trevor, you know as well as I do you can't use what you don't know to justify what you've done. You should have told him."

"Ok. Well, I didn't. Do you know how it feels to have carried this around for this long?"

"Carrying it around must not be feeling too bad, or else you wouldn't still be keeping your little secret," she said in a mumble.

"Are you saying something you want me to hear?"

"Look, I do know how it feels," Caela confirmed, thinking about her own confessions.

Caela was only supposed to have shared a cab ride with the tall, unsuspecting cocoa-brown skin man standing beside her. When she woke the next morning, she watched his naked muscle-filled masculinity as he stood in the bathroom relieving himself. She wanted to tell him again, she "doesn't usually do this," but she remembered her muted response during the night when he asked her, "What makes me so different?" She didn't want that question to come slapping her in the face again. The cab ride, the passionate kisses, and his boxers, which she then wore as her own undergarment, weren't all they shared.

Kellen Jimenez-Nisby introduced himself to the world nine months later. He came not kicking and screaming, but quiet as a church-mouse. While Caela wished she had taken the time to learn more about Kellen's father that unseasonably warm evening in January, she did learn his name before they made love.

His name was Tavaris Nisby, a computer-engineering student at Rice University. He looked and loved much older than his twenty-one years suggested. Even though she was only three years his senior, she was more ready for motherhood than he was to be a father, and this kept her from even reaching out to him. Unfortunately that was the first and last night she's seen or heard from him, and she only blamed herself that her son would never know his father.

"Look, I don't want to lose him," I admitted. "Telling him now after all this time jeopardizes everything."

"And if you don't tell him and he finds out, what do you think that's going to do? I can only imagine how it must feel to pretend you and Dexter are only friends, when in fact you are his..."

"Well, nothing in that is pretending," I interrupted.

"You know exactly what I mean, Trevor." Caela stood up, walked around my desk, and stood in front of me. "Look, babes, I have some work I'm trying to finish within the next half-hour, but we're not done here."

"I know we're not. I will tell him. I just have to figure out how, and when."

"Ok. You keep telling yourself that. I love you," Caela said, hugging me as tight as she could.

I kept my hands by my side knowing hugging her back would only bring tears to my eyes. When she finally let go, she turned and walked towards the door, leaving me a complete mute.

"Hey," I called out as she reached for the door, pulling it towards her, "I love you, too."

Caela winked, smiled, and continued her exit.

I was excited to have Caela Jimenez and my godson in my life again, the closest they have lived since moving back from Piedmont, Alabama, where she went to live with her parents to get help with Kellen. When she left, I had lost the sister I never had. I missed her closeness. Now I could kiss and tell Caela. If only Denise would move back, I would have both my girls around.

24

My Only Love Is You

Jackson...

I'm usually never reminded about the loneliness and difficulty of living far from home, far from family, until I'm back home. I felt this way when I left for school, too. I hated coming home on breaks 'cause I would have to get over being homesick all over again. Late night conversations with Devaan as Saturday nights became Sunday mornings were some of the best heart to heart conversations I've ever had with her.

"You know," Devaan had said years ago. "It's okay if you call him daddy."

She was referring to my mother's husband, Brodrick DeLeon Kirkwood. Devaan was a young woman and had been daddy's little girl for some time now, even though daddy wasn't the man whose blood ran through her veins. She sat on the floor snacking on a bag of unshelled roasted peanuts, her late night snack of choice. I was lying on her bed, looking over her shoulder at the television. I was 15 years old, still holding on to hopes my own father was coming back into my life. He was the only man I was going to call daddy. For now, calling my mother's husband Mr. Kirkwood was working well for the both of us.

I was 8 years old when my father, Demetrius Marquis Bradley, left. At the time, even though I was angry with him—and I remained that way for a long time—I made excuses, justified his departure, and defended his name against slander. But I knew better, and over time he became as sorry as the excuses I made, a failure afraid to face responsibilities. The only thing my father left me with, besides a handful of memories and dying hope, was that black and white self-portrait. I think he just forgot to take it with him, but he had taken everything else. He never planned on coming back, and I eventually had to accept that.

My mother woke early this Thanksgiving morning. Hearing her voice, I made my way downstairs and into the kitchen to keep her company. I loved having my mother to myself. Mr. Kirkwood was flying in later this afternoon from an assignment in Kansas, and was supposed to arrive in time for dinner. Devaan, who was never an early riser, was still asleep upstairs in her room down the hall from mine. Trevor was still asleep in the downstairs guestroom where he fell asleep last night while he, Devaan, and I watched *Nights in Rodanthe* late into the night, a romantic movie starring Richard Gere and Diane Lane.

"Have tea with me," I suggested. I walked into the kitchen and kissed my mother on her cheek.

"Same place?" Mother asked with a broad smile stretched across her face.

After the teakettle whistled, and our cups were filled, my mother and I sat on the back patio enjoying cups of honey lemon tea. This was one of my favorite times spent with her. It was a Thanksgiving morning ritual that never stopped even as I got older. This morning was no different.

Mother had a blanket thrown over her legs to block the light early morning breeze. I wore a button-down flannel shirt, old college sweat pants, wool socks and flip flops just to enjoy my mother's company and conversation. In the crisp November air, with December and winter lurking around the corner, Mother and I sat sometimes in silence with not more than the sound of us cooling our tea or taking a sip, the steam from for our cups visible in the outside air. I liked just looking at her, and I wondered sometimes why I didn't look like her. Her dark complexion was beautifully smooth. She always looked at you with warmth in her eyes. I loved to watch her laugh, loud, with her mouth wide open, and an open hand across her chest as if laughing might kill her.

"May I ask you a question?" she asked, looking serious. I rarely ever saw her without a smile. She stared into her cup as if the answer to her question would come somewhere between the sweet of honey or the sour of lemon.

"Sure, Mother," I said, and took a sip of my tea.

"Are you happy?"

I digested her question and thought carefully before responding. Why couldn't she have asked me whom I voted for in this month's election? "Work is going well," I answered. "The conferences and traveling can be a bit much at times, but I'm not complaining."

"That's not what I'm talking about, Junior. I meant with Trevor," she clarified. She sat up in her seat, turning to look at me. I saw the look of concern in her eyes. She had that same worried look the day I packed my car and moved away.

"If I were unhappy, Mother, I promise, you would be the first to know," I assured her. I don't know what would give her the idea I wasn't happy. For the most part, I had found my idea of happiness. No, I hadn't quite figured out the letter, or how to approach Trevor about it, but I hadn't led on that anything was going on that would make me unhappy.

"I hope so, Junior. I certainly hope so." She sat back in her chair and brought her cup to her mouth.

I looked at my mother through squinted eyes. If I knew her as well as I thought I did, I think she knew something. But what exactly did she know? Maybe she was just being my mother.

I took the last sip of tea. I got up and walked towards the patio doors. I slid one door open, and before I stepped into the breakfast area, I made one last request. "I'm sure you have your reasons, but you calling me Junior has bothered me since the day my father left. Can you please stop?"

She never responded.

Earlier in the year, my mother had decided this Thanksgiving was going to be just the family. Since Devaan was living on her own, I had finally moved out, and Mr. Kirkwood's job kept him gone most of the time, spending more time on the road than he was at home, she wanted her family together. Detrick Antone Kirkwood, Mr. Kirkwood's son from a previous marriage, had joined us from his studies at Wake Forest University. Telly, my sister's love interest, was there, too. And she was right, he did impress me, but from the look on Mr. Kirkwood's face, he needed more time to figure this guy out.

Here we were, one big happy extended family, enjoying a feast of a Thanksgiving meal that my mother, Devaan, Trevor, Detrick, and me had all lend a hand in preparing.

• • • • •

"Let's talk," Trevor began, breaking the thick shade of silence that existed between us. Trevor's eyes remained focused on the road before him.

I had my feet on the dashboard, my chair reclined all the way back, with an old issue of *Today's Black Woman* in my hand. A sexy, young Rihanna was featured on the cover wearing a black dress exposing sexy shoulders. Her mane was purposely swept across her face. *Damn! She looks good,* I thought. I had been thumbing through the magazine, quickly glancing over articles about Black Female Leaders changing the world, relationships between black men and black women, until I finally found interest in an article on one's love style.

"What exactly do you want to talk about?" I finally asked.

"Anything," Trevor answered.

"You know, we never did have that dinner with Dexter and Giovanni," I began. I kept my eyes on the pages of the magazine.

"No, we didn't. It's cool though. I'm sure they're just as busy as we've been."

"Yeah, I'm sure," I responded, sarcastically. Trevor shot me a look from the corner of his eyes.

"Are we having Christmas at your place or mine?"

"Mine, since I haven't hosted anything there yet." I looked at Trevor and smiled.

"Sounds like a plan."

"Oh, make sure you invite Dexter and Giovanni. That's if they aren't planning a Christmas of their own."

"I'll tell him. I'm not sure what they have planned, if anything."

And we were silent again.

It wasn't a long drive from the airport to my house, but we were caught in the Sunday evening traffic with everyone else who had decided to travel this Thanksgiving weekend. *Why didn't we take an earlier flight? We could have avoided all this,* I thought. The suitcases sat in the trunk and back seat, including two extra ones filled with a few things we had picked up from all the shopping we did early Friday morning, the craziest Black Friday ever. It cost an extra $50 to check-in those bags, but damn it, the savings were worth it.

"Did I tell you Denise was dating again?" Trevor asked.

"It didn't take her long at all," I said, closing the magazine and throwing it in the back seat. I opened the bottled water I had purchased at a busy deli across from an American Airline gate after we de-boarded the plane and took a long sip.

"Do they ever? I mean, life waits for no one. You might as well be happy and live."

I looked at Trevor and smiled again. I thought about the time it took him to move on from Kelvin. I guess he did learn something.

"What's that smile for?" he asked.

"Can't a man just smile?"

"Anyway, her name is Alaina Knowlton. They're supposed to be coming this way, either for Christmas or New Years. They're not sure yet."

"Bringing the new squeeze to meet the family and get your approval?" I asked, jokingly.

"Denise doesn't need my approval. Toni wasn't exactly a bad choice. She just chose someone else."

"I guess it's okay to be a little confused or unsure at times." I was playing with words, gauging how Trevor would react. I thought about how easy it was for him to discuss Denise and Alaina, but he couldn't bring himself to tell me about his trip to Chicago. He was definitely hiding something, but I wasn't going to make him any wiser.

Trevor answered his phone on the first ring, but remained silent. That he was disturbed by the call was apparent since his facial expression couldn't hide his annoyance. After he hung up, he still said nothing. Whoever it was, or whatever was said, had left him tight-faced and tight-lipped. I was wondering what he was thinking. I could bet my last dollar he wondered what I was wondering. He avoided eye contact and became even more focused on the road than he needed to be. Silence settled between us. After pulling into my driveway, I helped Trevor with his luggage, putting his suitcases in the trunk of his car.

"You know, I really enjoyed your folks," he said, slamming the trunk of his Athens blue Infiniti G37 Coupe. I loved seeing him in that car. "Your sister is crazy as hell."

"Yeah. Her overprotective self can be a jester sometimes. I love her though."

"How can you not?"

"We used to joke about her marrying a pastor so she could wear her big hat and sit in the front pew as women and men hung on to his every word. But you see Telly was no pastor."

"Oh, I saw the penetrating looks your father gave him. But he seems like a hard nut to crack."

"He's not my father," I corrected with some force.

Trevor shot me a look.

Inside the house, we sat on the couch looking at the TV screen, paying no particular attention to what was on. Trevor sat with his back towards the arm of the couch and his feet resting in my lap.

I felt exhausted.

He looked worst.

Five regular days with my family can wear you out. I held my head back, closed my eyes, and then let out a deep sigh.

"Hey," Trevor said, tapping his feet into my stomach.

"Huh," I answered, raising my head and looking at him.

"Are you ok?"

"A little tired, but yeah, I'm ok?" I brought his feet up to my lips and softly kissed his toes. Trevor looked at me, smiled, and then winked. He wanted me to continue, and since I didn't mind, I obliged. I loved Trevor's feet—soft, beautifully manicured, and they smelled good, too, even though they had spent the entire day wrapped in socks and stuffed in a pair of black and white Adidas sneakers.

I unzipped the fly of his slim straight 514 Levi's jeans. He lifted his pelvis and I slid the jeans under his ass. I tossed the jeans on the hardwood floor at the side of the couch and continued my sensual assault of Trevor's five-foot-eleven inch slender muscled physique, all one hundred and seventy-five pounds of him. I continued down his feet, around his ankles, making my way to that sensitive spot in the back on his knee. He sunk his body into the sofa.

"Hmmm," he moaned.

My lips kissed his groin. His body stiffened from pleasure, and I felt Trevor's man-piece slow growing against my face.

"Sit up," I ordered. I removed his winter-white v-neck sweater, and then his t-shirt and tank. He had a swimmer's build and the flexibility to match. I knelt on the floor in front of him between his legs.

"Ahhhh, yeah," Trevor let out.

I slid my lips over the mushroom-shaped head of his impressive penis. I looked in his eyes as he disappeared in my mouth. I was pleasing him like I always had. Although I was concentrating on this pleasure I was unleashing on him, it didn't stop a disquieting thought from entering my mind. *If he is giving his love to someone else, is he satisfied with me?* I thought.

I shook my head, attempting to dismiss the image of someone else making love to Trevor from my mind. With his eyes closed, he moaned in pleasure. I circled his dick head with my tongue, and then allowed his piece to disappear in my mouth again. He began to gyrate his pelvis.

"I'm close," Trevor warned.

I removed his piece from my mouth and allowed him to discharge the sexual tension he had been holding in all weekend.

25

What Do You Know?

Trevor...

When I walked outside this morning, I could smell winter approaching. It was getting darker earlier. Mornings now had a crisp start to it, and winter gears were in full swing, even though we were still a few weeks before winter's official start.

I pulled up to a parking space directly in front of Daily Grind. I inserted my credit card into the slot of the new parking kiosk, paying to park for the next hour and a half. I displayed the parking receipt on the dash and walked into Grind.

It wasn't unusual for Grind to be busy this early in the morning, and this Wednesday morning was no different. I walked up to the counter, placed my order, and grabbed a seat. I was sitting in my usual place, alone in the corner at a table for two. I removed my laptop from its case and carefully placed it on the table in front of me. I removed my cell phone from my waist and placed it next to the computer. I wasn't expecting any calls this early in the morning, but just in case. There was a text message from Jackson.

Good morning, handsome. Hope your morning has started off well. I woke this morning with you on my mind, as always. Hope you have an excellent day...talk to you later.

- JDB

I pressed my thumb against the screen to reply to Jackson's message, but then the phone rang. An unassigned number displayed on the screen. I held the phone against my ear and waited for the caller to speak.

"You don't deserve someone like him, and you know that. You don't know what to do with a good man. How does it feel?" he asked.

For the first time I realized these numbers displayed on my phone whenever he called were never the same, but his voice never changed. It was throat deep, filled with accusation and the occasional hatred that no matter what I had done or what he knew, I didn't deserve.

His phone call wasn't the first thing I wanted to deal with this early in the morning, or any other time, for that matter. I was hoping to enjoy my vanilla latte and cinnamon rolls, glance at a few stories in the morning's paper, and prepare a contract before my 9 a.m. meeting with Wesley and Morgan to get an update on the Copeland project. But damn it, here I was entertaining this fool who had decided, again, to interrupt my morning.

"And what exactly do you think these phone calls are doing to me?" I asked, hoping he would engage. "You think whoever you're talking about is going to come running back to you? Isn't that what you hope to accomplish?"

"It really doesn't matter to me who he runs to. But that does sound like something you should be concerned about."

"Right, but I don't seem concerned, now do I? Don't you see? Your phone calls are starting to lose credibility. First you warn me about him, now you're telling me how much of a good man he is and that I just don't know it. So which is it? I don't think you know who you're talking about."

"I see you've found your voice," he said calmly. "Usually you just sit on the phone like a church mouse." And then he was quiet.

"And I see you've lost yours. Caller, are you there?" I took a sip of my latte. It had dropped a few degrees since my first sip. This man was interrupting the flow of everything. "You're helpless and hopeless and wasting my damn time. Why don't you just walk away?"

"Did you tell him about your time in Chicago?" That was supposed to have been his dagger.

I wanted to see if he actually knew who he was talking about, or if he was just reaching for information, throwing a fishing line and waiting for me to fall for some life-like bait.

"Him?" I asked.

"Yes. Him. Jackson. I know you haven't forgotten his name. Did you tell him about Chicago…with Dexter? Or do you think he already knows?"

Now I was the church mouse he had just described. I acted as if I just couldn't find the words, as if the cat had my tongue. "Does he?" I finally asked.

"Does he what…know about Dexter? Why don't you ask him?" He paused, waiting for me to respond. "Oh that's right. You can't. See, for now, he only knows what you've told him. And what are you going to do when Dexter wants more. Whose heart are you going to break?"

"Who is this?"

"Trevor, what's most important, that you know my identity? Or is it important Jackson doesn't find out about your secret getaways with Dexter, or that the friendship you are playing up in his face goes far beyond your coffee-shop meetings?"

He had a point. "What do you want?"

He laughed. "You still think this has anything to do with me."

"Doesn't it?"

"I hate to disappoint you, man, but this isn't about me. This has everything to do with you, the foolish choices you've made, and the choice you need to make."

"Between Dexter and Jackson?" I asked as if I didn't already know. "But Dexter and I are only…"

"Friends?" he interrupted. "See, that's a lie you can only tell yourself and Jackson. You can't have your cake and eat it, too, Trevor. Look, I have to go. You will be hearing from me again. Something tells me you're not really listening to me."

"Wait," I called out. "You haven't told me your name."

He exhaled heavily. "It's Bran."

I was quite sure it was an alias he pulled out of nowhere. Then the phone went dead.

● ● ● ● ●

I was sitting in my office behind my desk, lazily tapping my pencil against the arm of the chair. I still hadn't responded to Jackson's text. My meeting with Wesley was less than ten minutes away, and the clarity and focus I had this morning was gone, thanks to Bran.

"Are you busy?" Caela was standing in the doorway.

I was deep in thought so I didn't respond immediately.

Does Jackson already know about my short vacation with Dexter? Was he just waiting for me to come clean? How could he even make love to me if he knew about the things I've done? How could I have allowed him to? What was Jackson up to, if he was up to anything at all? I thought. These questions are never going to end. Then I thought about him suggesting we invite Dexter and Gio for Christmas dinner.

"Helloooo," Caela called out, waving her hand in front of my face.

"Oh. Hey. Sorry," I said, snapping back to the present.

"What's got you so deep in thought? Nothing to do with your meeting with Wesley, is it?"

"No."

"Then what?"

"It's not important. Did you need something?" I asked, looking at my watch. "I have about seven minutes to kill before my meeting."

"It can wait." Caela started towards the door.

"Caela, you're already here. Just close the door." I looked at my watch again. "You now have six minutes, thirty seconds, and counting."

Caela closed the door, leaned against it, and began talking.

"Four years old, and now he wants to ask about his damn daddy." She was irritated.

"Who? Kellen?! Where did this come from?"

"When I asked him, he said, 'Kelsey has a daddy, and Jorden has a daddy, where's my daddy?' Trev, you should have seen the look on his little face. It killed my heart." She had her arms folded across her chest, her stare towards the floor.

"I'm sure it did." I walked over and gave Caela the hug she looked like she needed. She was starting to tear up. I held her shoulders with both hands and then asked, "Don't you think it's time he knows his father? Call Tavaris. I'm sure you know how to reach him."

"My God, he's going to hate me," she presumed.

"Well, maybe if he was ten or fifteen," I said, assuming she was talking about Kellen. "But he's only four. He's not going to hate you. But he's made his choice. He wants his daddy. You didn't grow up without your father, and I didn't grow up without mine. Regardless of the circumstances, why should he?"

I now had one minute before my briefing with Wesley and Morgan.

"Listen, Caela. Sorry to rush off, but I don't want Wes and Morgan waiting on me. You know how I hate walking into these meetings late. We'll finish this later. Deal?"

"Sure. Sure," she said, exiting my office.

When I walked out of my office behind Caela and looked down the hall, Morgan had just turned into the conference room. I wasn't sure if Wesley had entered ahead of him. When I walked into the conference room, Morgan was the only one seated around the mahogany boat-shaped conference table. Eight empty chairs and he chose the one to the far end of the room.

He sat reclined in the black leather conference chair, his left leg crossed over his right ankle to knee, his left elbow rested on the arm of the chair, and his hand pulling at the invisible hairs on his chin. For the first time since his hire, I paid attention to how handsome he actually was.

"Morgan, good morning," I greeted, and then opened my notebook in front of me. "Sorry I'm late."

"Good morning, Mr. Harrison," he responded in a voice much deeper than his age suggested. He kept his focus across the room. "It's all right. I'm sure you had other things to take care of this morning." I smiled at his assumption. What did he know that I didn't? I wasn't sure what other things Morgan was talking about, but I wasn't going to entertain his response.

Although I had told the staff I didn't mind if they addressed me using my first name, and most of them had followed my instruction, Morgan was adamant in using the formal Mr. Jackson. I stopped correcting him.

"Is Wesley on his way?" I asked, taking my seat in one of the chairs on the side. I hated sitting at the head of the table.

"He was finishing up a call when I stopped by his office," Morgan said. His face had an unusual seriousness about it.

"Morgan is everything okay?"

"Everything is fine," he responded. "Why do you ask?"

"Sorry I'm late, fellas," Wesley interrupted. He walked across the room and occupied one of the chairs across from me. "That was your boy, Copeland, I was just talking with."

"My boy?" I laughed. "What's the problem?" I asked, bracing myself for what might be. Lord knows I couldn't handle any other stressors right now. Dealing with Jackson, Dexter, and "Bran" was enough.

"Nah, no problem at all," Wesley said with coolness.

"Good."

"Well…" Wesley added.

"I knew it." I sat back in my chair and clasped my hands behind my head. "Lay it on me."

"Calm down. It's nothing major. He called to cancel the site visit we had planned two weeks from today. He says he's heading to Breckenridge Ski Resort for an early Christmas vacation with Mr. Flynn."

"He could have spared you the details," I said, smiling.

"Come on, man! This is Charney we're talking about. You know how it is with him."

Mr. Charney Copeland can be a little too transparent whenever he's comfortable with you. Turning to Morgan, I asked,

"Have you taken care of those invoices with Turner Construction?

"Those invoices, Mr. Harrison, have been taken care of."

Is it me or does Morgan sound like he has a big chip on his shoulders? I thought. Morgan was the epitome of formality, but this was a little much. "And…"

"And we are still operating under budget. We'll definitely be able to improve both our top and bottom lines once this project is completed."

"Which is exactly what we want," Wesley added.

"Anything else going on I should know about that hasn't been brought to my attention?" I asked, looking at Wesley, and then at Morgan.

"Janelle Glennon from Welsh Industries called this morning," Morgan explained. "She says you two have been playing phone tag all month."

"That's the understatement of the year. Were you able to confirm the meeting with Mr. Welch?"

"She says to have the proposal ready the first week of January," Morgan said, keeping his eyes on his leather bound planner where he kept all his notes. He was meticulously prepared.

"And is that something you can do?"

"It shouldn't be a problem, assuming I'm still going to be working with Ms. Dumarko and Mr. Jones."

I guess I'm not the only one he was being formal with. "Of course. Well…" I said as I got up and closed my notebook. "Yet another successful meeting. You gentlemen keep up the good work."

Wesley got up. "Yes, boss," he said, jokingly, and shook my hand. He exited the conference room, turning towards his office.

Morgan got up, closed his planner, and started towards the door. I interrupted his depart. "Morgan, may I speak with you for a minute?" He paused briefly, and then turned to face me. I closed the door and walked and stood closer to him. "Is something bothering you? Would you like to talk about it?"

"I'd rather not. It's kind of personal and I don't want to discuss my personal business on the job."

"Understand. But if you change your mind, you know where my office is," I said, and began to leave the room.

"I'm concerned about a buddy of mine," Morgan said when I neared the door. He placed his planner on the table and stood with his hands in his pockets. He looked guarded, disinclined. His voice had taken on an adolescent tone. He didn't sound like the confident, knowledgeable young man who had just sat in our meeting or the person Wesley and I had interviewed over a year ago.

"What's the concern?" I asked.

"My friend is in a situation I think she needs to get out of before she loses everything. I'm trying not to give advice, especially since she hasn't asked for any, but it's getting to where if she doesn't get out now, someone is going to get hurt."

"Don't you think she knows what she's doing?"

"I know she doesn't know what she's doing and she's going to lose the best thing she's ever had."

"What makes you so sure?" I asked, searching in his eyes.

"I don't know. A gut feeling, I guess," he said, looking away.

Then a disturbing thought entered my mind. *Could it be? No, it couldn't. Could Morgan and Bran be one and the same?*

"How old is she?"

"Huh?" I could tell my question caught him off guard. It made me wonder if Morgan was making up his story as he went along, doing what he needed to throw me off his trail. Maybe he figured I was on to him, and he had told me more than he needed to.

"The friend you're concerned about. How old is she?" I asked to clarify.

"That's not important," he said, grabbing his planner from the table and making his way towards the door. "I think I've said enough."

"Listen, I'm sure your friend will figure things out, but not until she is ready. So, cut her some slack. I'm sure she has the situation under control. If she is making a mistake, it's her mistake to make."

"You're right. I just don't think it's a mistake worth making. But I guess that's my opinion. I'll try to take what you said into consideration, but I'm not making any promises," he said, looking directly at me. He turned and walked out the door.

My heart leaped. "Fair enough," I said and walked out of the room behind him.

When I got back to my office and was seated behind my desk, I had several texts, messages, and missed phone calls.

Hey. I sent you an email with my itinerary. Alaina and I are coming on the 23rd, and I hope it's still ok we stay with you, in your guest room. Please text or email me later when you get this. Love you, Trev.

-Den K.

Wassup baby? Hit me back when you get this.

- Dex

I frowned after reading the last text, not at the message, but at the person it came from. Dexter hadn't said much to me since lunch at La Tomate. I'm not sure if I had crossed the line when I asked him about his father again. It's not like I held his head under water and forced him to speak. Realizing I still hadn't responded to Jackson's message he sent this morning, I decided to call him. After three rings, he answered.

"Hello," he said. I knew he hadn't looked at the screen since that wasn't his usual greeting whenever I called.

"Hello?" I said. "This is Trevor."

"I'm sorry, babe. What's going on?"

In the background I heard, "Table for two?" and a male voice responded, "Yes, please."

"Where are you?" I asked, looking at my watch. It was 10:45 am.

"I'm having a late breakfast," Jackson responded.

"Okay, but you didn't answer my question."

"Look, Trevor. I'll call you back." And the phone was silent.

Did Jackson just put me on pause? I thought aloud, but my phone screen was black.

I threw my cell phone on my desk, pressed the page button on my desk phone, and summoned Caela to my office. When she entered, I threw my question at her. "The evening Jackson and I had dinner at my dad's, where did you see him?"

"Java House, on the other side of town. Why?" Caela asked. She folded her hands and stood with attitude.

"Nothing. Thank you."

"Trevor, don't dismiss me like that," she said, closing my office door behind her. "What's going on?"

"I'm not sure. As soon as I find out, I'll let you know," I said, placing my phone in the case and grabbing my wallet from my desk drawer. "Can I use your car keys?"

"Not until you tell me what's going on."

"Fine! Suit yourself."

I rushed passed Caela, opened the door, and turned towards the exit.

"Wait a minute," she whispered. She walked swiftly over to her desk, fumbled through her black Dooney and Bourke Hobo, and then handed me her keys.

"Thank you," I said, heading towards the elevators. "Answer your phone in a few minutes."

"Okay."

26

Nothing, Nothing, Nothing

Jackson...

This meeting had regret written all over it. But, here I was sitting and talking with him. A caramel macchiato and a Canadian croissant with bacon and imported Swiss cheese sat in a plate in front of me.

"Didn't you get my message?" he asked, sticking the fork in his salmon salad. He still held the fork the same way. With his index finger extended down the handle, he placed the fork and its contents of salmon and greens in his mouth with the tines curving down. He closed his luscious lips together and slowly pulled the fork from his mouth. I tried not to stare at him, but my eyes temporarily had a mind of their own. I'd always loved his lips and that little mole on the left side of his nose was always so sexy to me. Nothing about Ethan Angelo Overstreet had changed. Not too much about me had changed, either, except over time I had developed an ability to resist him without even trying. Before, it took effort and a nice prayer.

"Are you asking me why I didn't respond? I told you. There's no need to tell me every time a meeting with one of your clients brings you to the area."

"Why is it such a big problem for you to see me?"

"I never said seeing you was a problem. You had your issues you had to deal with, and I have a relationship I need to focus on."

"So you just forgot about us?"

"I can't forget about something that never was. That was the cruel reality I had to come to terms with. See, 'us' was factual in my mind, but never existed in yours. I had broken an important rule, falling in love with someone who never loved me," I explained. "You can't ask about me forgetting about us when we never existed."

"So, you're happy?" Ethan asked, as if I had given him any reasons to think I wasn't.

"Weren't you? Your exact words, if I can remember correctly, were, 'I don't need any complications in my life. I'm happy the way things are'. Please correct me if I'm wrong. I didn't want to be anyone's complication, or the cause of anyone's unhappiness, so I left you alone. Was it hard? Yes, but what did you expect me to do?" I wasn't sure this was a conversation we should be having here, if at all, but here we were. I thought both our actions had made things crystal clear. He got what he wanted, and though it took me a little while, so did I.

"You didn't answer my question."

"Am I happy?" I repeated. "Yes, I'm happy," I said with confidence.

"So there's no chance for us?"

Between Ethan's questions and my answers, Angie Stone's "Here We Go Again" played through my mind:

> Oh oh, here we go again
> Trying to make it right
> When it don't make sense

"Now you're asking for the same chance I would have done anything for, that I did anything for? You can't be serious," I said as the chorus began to fade. But he was serious. "It was you who didn't give us a chance," I continued.

"What about Gavin?"

"What about him? You know damn well he had nothing to do with any of the decisions you made. You did spend some time convincing yourself I was still in love with him, didn't you? And with that in the back of your mind, you had to step back. Don't get me wrong, if that was how you felt, by all means, protect your heart."

"Then why are you...?" he interrupted.

"I'm not finished. Whatever feelings you thought I still had for Gavin weren't the issue. You wanted to be single and free. You wanted to entertain others while you entertained your clients, the ladies who threw themselves at you, and the men, too. You got what you wanted. So tell me again, Ethan, why are we here having this conversation when all I've done was allow you the happy, uncomplicated life you wanted?"

I began folding my sandwich. My caramel macchiato was almost ice cold, and I wouldn't be eating the croissant without first tossing it in a microwave. I stood up and grabbed my keys and cell phone.

"Why didn't you wait?"

My heart was laughing. My mind was smiling, but there was an absolute look of seriousness on my face. Ethan was serious, too. He sounded like he was pleading his case, and I didn't know how much more of it I could listen to. *He wanted me to wait*, I thought.

"How could I wait when you gave me nothing to wait for? All you knew was that I loved you, and I guess you thought as long as I loved you, I wasn't going anywhere. You know what happens when you're the only one loving, when the love you give is never given back to you?" He sat there staring up at me. "I stopped paying attention to what I felt for you, and started listening to how you made me feel, and what I heard didn't sound good."

"So that's it?" he asked as if he hadn't heard a word I've said.

"I'm done. And you should be, too," I suggested.

"You know nothing should come between us." He was still sitting. His slanted eyes stared at me with sadness. I hated seeing him like that: weak, vulnerable, and regretful. Then I remembered how many times I had that same feeling, that same look because of him.

I smiled. "It's funny. I once felt the same way about you. There were times when I felt I couldn't stop loving you. I didn't know what else to do. But as you can see, I figured it out. You, the person I loved, made me afraid to fall in love. You made me build up a wall no other love could break down. What makes you think I want to learn the same lesson twice?"

"I do love you, Jackson. I still love you," he said, whispering. His admission had fallen on ears that had waited to hear those words when they would have mattered.

"I'm sorry," I said, looking at him with painless eyes. "That's a tough place to be in all by yourself, isn't it?"

27

It Seems To Never Last

Trevor...

I hoped I hadn't missed what I had raced across town to see. I pulled into a parking space a few feet up from Java House. I adjusted the rearview mirror so I could see whomever would come out of the coffee shop. There I was slouched in my seat like I was on a stakeout, a hired Thomas Magnum, Private Investigator.

What the hell am I doing here? I thought to myself.

Was I here to confirm what I thought all along and wanted to match a face to those thoughts? Or was I here looking for a validation for my own actions?

After Jackson appeared outside Java, a man with remarkable stature followed behind him. While he talked, Jackson turned around to respond.

Damn. I wish I knew what they were saying.

I picked up my phone and quickly pressed the numbers to call Caela. "Come on, girl, please pick up," I mumbled.

Caela answered, "Trevor, where are you? What's going on?"

"I may be able to answer your questions in a few, but first I need you to do something for me."

"What?" she yells into the phone.

"The guy you saw with Jackson, can you describe him for me?"

"Gorgeous. That just about sums it up for me."

"Stop joking, please. Look, I need a little more than that."

"You know that guy who plays catch for the Redskins?" she continued.

"You mean, wide receiver," I corrected with an immediate smile. "Which one?"

"Number 23."

"DeAngelo Hall?"

"That's him."

"You know nothing about football. He plays cornerback," I corrected, injecting my limited knowledge.

"I don't need to know anything about football to know he's fine!" she said.

"Caela," I called out. "Focus, please."

"Anyway, he looked a lot like him. He looked a little over six feet tall. His skin was a light tan, the color of cinnamon. I wouldn't say he was muscular, but his clothes looked like they were tailor-made for him."

While she talked, I was looking at this man up and down, from the tip of his fresh-out-the-barbershop hair cut to the bottom of his black Kenneth Coles. "What about his hair. Did he have hair?"

"A close fade, I think, and a wide, bright smile." Then she paused. "Why?"

"Caela, I'm on my way back to the office," I said, and she could hear a changed tone in my voice. "My suspicion has been confirmed."

A part of me wished I hadn't witnessed this encounter between Jackson and this man, but at least I was no longer in the dark. I went searching for the evidence I needed, and there it was, and even if I wanted to, I couldn't ignore it. I stood there painting a picture of him in my mind.

"You think Jackson has this man on the side?" she asked.

"As we speak. So even with all these phone calls telling me about Jackson being a good man, it seems I'm not the only man he was sharing his goods with."

"Listen, Trevor, I don't think you should jump to conclusions. Seeing Jackson outside having a conversation with someone isn't exactly a smoking gun, you know."

"Right. It just so happens he's the same man you saw him with before. Whatever!" I said dismissively. "You loved that Jackson had come into my life at the time Kelvin and I were going through it. I didn't have one foot out of my relationship with Kelvin and you were already planning a life for me with Jackson. One step at a time didn't exist in your book, but that's exactly how I should have taken it. You and all your questions: When is he moving here? Are you moving there? And now this."

"Wait a minute. I know you're not blaming me for any of this. Yes, I was glad Jackson had come into your life when he did. You needed the distraction. It forced you to accept what was no longer between you and Kelvin. And I guess I need to remind you that while you had one foot in that relationship with Kelvin, he had both feet out and in his relationship with Lawrence. Now, before you go screwing up what you have with Jackson, ask yourself this: Why would he move here to be with you if he had someone else? That just doesn't make any sense. You know how small this place is."

"Yeah, but he doesn't."

Leave it to Caela to tell me exactly how she felt. She was holding nothing back. I knew she was not to blame for any of this. It was my choice to hang on to Kelvin for as long as I did. And I couldn't blame her for my getting involved with Jackson before I knew everything I could about him. He smiled and I fell in love. So when I was asking questions, trying to figure out if Jackson had a wife and child at home, what I should have asked was if there was a Mr. Jackson Bradley stashed away in some two-bedroom hillside condo while he ran around playing sexy lover-boy.

"Well, I didn't know Jackson. All I knew was what you told me. I thought I knew his type. I did put him in the too-good-to-be-true category, but sometimes we say they're too good to be true because we've only been with the ones who tasted like sour milk from a warm refrigerator. So now what? You think you rolling around in Dexter's bed has been justified?"

"You're damn right. Because guess what, buddy? While you were out there having your fun, so was I."

"You're not sixteen, Trevor. Leave the games to the kids," Caela said. "All you're doing is speculating. Maybe I shouldn't have called you that night I saw him."

"It's too late for maybes."

"If you want to know what's going on with Jackson and that man, lay your own cards on the table. Are you man enough to do that, Trevor?"

I was quiet.

"I didn't think so. See you when you get here."

28

And This Christmas

Jackson...

Besides my birthday, Christmas was my favorite holiday. I had more than enough reasons to erase this day from existence, except this was the same day they celebrate the birth of Christ. It was also the day my family, as I had known it, changed.

Christmas cards were mailed to my mother, Devaan, Detrick, and Mr. Kirkwood, and presents were sent by FedEx over two weeks early to avoid the holiday rush. An extra Christmas card was sent to the last known address of the man who had assisted in my creation. My messages to him were always a simple "Thank you." Like all the other Christmas and birthday cards, this one was returned with a bright red stamp that read "return to sender."

"What's that," Trevor asked. He walked into the kitchen pulling a white v-neck t-shirt over his head, over his chest and down his torso. He was a sexy man. He had stayed the night, leaving Denise and Alaina to themselves at his house.

"The letter I had sent to my father." I stood leaning over the breakfast island, staring at the envelope.

"It came back?" Trevor asked. He pulled a chair from the bar and sat.

"Just like I told you it would, but you told me to send it anyway."

"It was only a suggestion. I mean, you said you had been doing it all this time. I figured it wouldn't hurt. The worst that could happen is it being returned."

"And it was." I walked to the refrigerator and removed a pitcher of orange juice. I removed the raspberry pancakes that had been warming in the oven.

"You never told me the others were returned, too."

"I know."

I sat beside Trevor, pouring raspberry syrup over my light and fluffy pancakes. If there was one breakfast food I had perfected, it was making pancakes. Aunt Jemima had already done most of the work, and only a dummy would mess up just adding water and stirring. The fruit salad was easy to prepare as well.

"Jackson, I never hear you say too much about your father. Why is that?"

"There isn't too much I can say about someone I barely remember," I admitted. "And it's not like I haven't tried. But remembering didn't do anything but make me sad all over again. I was the little boy who still yearned for his father's affection that never came, because he wasn't there. So many times I felt I meant nothing to him because he never stayed around to help mold me into the man I would eventually become."

"So you know you didn't need him."

"By the looks of things, no, I didn't need him. But he didn't give me an option. I tried to tell myself I still loved him, and had even convinced myself a simple sorry would do if he ever made his way back into my life. I tried to find him, but he left and took his family with him, and by family I mean grandmother, grandfather, and everyone in between."

"Do you know why?"

"Of course I know why. My father was a smart man with money. He invested in Microsoft, Apple Inc., and women. He had friends in top positions in both companies. He thought his money gave him power and he tried to exert that self-given power over my mother with his outrageous demands and unconceivable requests. Only my mother wasn't having any of it. During the divorce she took him through the ringer, getting more than half of everything. The judge was a widow with a chip on her shoulder and a husband who died in a hotel room on top of a $500 dollar a night hooker. My mother called it Divine Intervention. Anyway, the letters didn't always come back."

"And you haven't seen him since?" Trevor asked.

The look I gave was the response he needed. How many times had Devaan and I been the topic of conversation at my father's new family's dinner table? How often had we been the thoughts that ran through his mind just before he fell asleep?

"I've seen him in dreams. Does that count?" I paused and looked at Trevor. "Can we please talk about something else?"

"Are you ready for this evening?" Trevor asked, changing the subject.

"Couldn't be more ready," I answered before putting two small triangular pieces of pancakes in my mouth.

A potluck dinner was a good idea. I had only promised to play host. I wasn't planning on spending my first Christmas with Trevor in the kitchen. The bottles of wine Mr. Harrison brought over two days ago had been chilling in the twelve-bottle wine cooler refrigerator under the counter in the kitchen. Although he and Natalie had planned a Christmas vacation on Brownes Beach in Barbados, her contribution of stuffed Cornish hens would be brought over when Adrian came later.

"You have any idea what Denise is going to prepare?"

Trevor laughed. "I've never seen that woman boil water. Whatever she makes is being made in your kitchen."

I gave him that how-dare-you-say-that-about-your-friend look, and then I joined him in laughter. "Maybe Alaina can throw down."

"Yeah, I guess we'll have to see," Trevor said before putting an apple slice in his mouth. "Aren't you gonna to get that?"

"What? Oh!" My cell phone had been ringing like nobody's business. I had left it in the living room area on the coffee table after talking with Colt. I hadn't spoken with him as often as I liked since moving here. I was glad he was able to make the trip. Since it was cheaper to fly from Atlanta on Christmas day, he had reserved a flight to leave after spending Christmas morning with his family. "Are Dexter and Giovanni coming?"

Trevor looked at his cell phone, which was sitting in a corner on the counter. "He said he would let me know by yesterday, but I haven't heard anything from him," he said.

I got off the chair and dashed down the hall to the living room.

"Merry Christmas," I answered without looking at the number on the screen. I began walking back towards the kitchen.

"Hey, handsome. Wassup? Merry Christmas to you, too." It was Ethan.

"Why are you calling me?" I asked in a whisper.

"You didn't tell me I couldn't."

"Which part of 'I'm done' didn't you understand?" I stood in the hallway trying to speak as softly as I could. "Listen, I don't want you to call me."

"I only called to wish you a Merry Christmas."

"And you have. Goodbye."

"Wait!" he insisted.

"What?" I shouted back, sounding a little louder than I wanted.

"I still love you."

I hung up.

My phone dinged to signal a text message. It was a message from Denard.

What's up, Jackson? Hope this Christmas finds you and your family well. I wanted to say Merry Christmas to you and yours before I got too busy with these folks. Hit me back later. Be good.

- Dr. TDB

When I walked back to the kitchen, Trevor was standing in front of the sink cleaning his breakfast plate before placing it in the dishwasher. I sat at the breakfast island to finish my breakfast. He turned around, wiped his hands in the paper towel and tossed it in the tall garbage can in the corner. He walked over and stood in front of me on the other side of the bar. He stared.

"Are you going to say something, or are you going to look at me as if the world just pissed you off?" I asked. I kept my eyes on my plate. *Had Trevor heard my conversation?* I thought. *No. I know I wasn't speaking that loud.*

"Who was that?"

"No one important."

"I didn't ask you if he or she was important, Jackson," he corrected. "I asked who it was."

"It was no one, Trevor. No one important."

I don't know why I didn't just come out and tell him. I guess before I knew it, I had decided Ethan really wasn't important, at least not to me. I thought about Ethan's admission a few minutes ago and smiled. I kept thinking to myself, *how does it feel?*

"Ok," Trevor said, and walked out the kitchen.

• • • • •

The dining room table looked like the last supper. Green salad with Posole and creamy cilantro-lime vinaigrette prepared the palate for the stuffed Cornish hens Natalie had labored over. I wished she were here so we could thank her personally. Alaina's baked Dijon salmon was finger-licking good, thumbs included, and she admitted all Denise did was watch. Needless to say, that comment had everyone at the dinner table laughing and holding their bellies or covering their mouths so food or wine couldn't escape. Attitude or not, Trevor's grated potato salad tasted as good as any potato salad I've had, and he had even garnished it with fresh basil. Colton came bearing only gifts.

Though they were meeting for the first time, Adrian, Denise, and Alaina hit it off well, as if they had known each other all his young life. He was full of compliments. I don't know if these two beauties were in love, but they were in something.

Dexter and Giovanni never made it. I couldn't determine if the look on Trevor's face spelled disappointment. Dinner was almost over and he had barely said four words to me. He only smiled or nodded in agreement when a compliment was given about how nicely decorated the house was or how flavorsome the grilled basil lemon turkey breasts tasted. I didn't entertain his displeasure with me because, after all, it was Christmas.

Caela had made a quick stop to drop off her gifts for Trevor and me and to pick up the gifts we had bought for her and Kellen. Trevor definitely showed just how happy he was now that Kellen was so close to him. She didn't stay too long, but packed a plate, making sure she included a piece of the much raved about turkey breast.

After dinner, Adrian demolished Colton in a friendly game of *Madden NFL* on the Wii. Then they sat in the living room with Denise and Alaina watching the classic *A Christmas Story*. Adrian had promised Colton a chance at redemption, challenging him in a game of tennis, a game Colton was much more skilled at. And everyone devoured a slice of the black forest cake I had baked from scratch. I might have been a little heavy-handed on the vodka, but no one complained.

Trevor and I had cleared the table and were loading the dishwasher when I finally decided to talk about him giving me the silent treatment.

"What are you so upset about? During dinner, you acted as if I wasn't even there," I said. I leaned against the kitchen counter, folding and unfolding a kitchen towel. Trevor remained silent, making me feel as if I were having this conversation with myself.

Looking stoic, Trevor said, "Something's going on, and you're going to tell me."

"What do you mean? Trevor, I told you earlier, it's nothing important, and I meant that. I've told you I have nothing to hide."

"Then why are you acting like you do?"

"How am I doing that?"

"I don't want to get into it," Trevor said. He poured the soap in the dispenser, closed the door to the dishwasher, and then pressed the start button.

"No, let's get into it." I wasn't going to allow him to shut down again. "You brought it up. Since you think I'm hiding something, since you think I've been acting suspicious, why don't you tell me what it is you think I'm hiding?"

"If you say you have nothing to hide, we're going to leave it at that," Trevor said. He walked out of the kitchen and headed towards the living room. I continued cleaning.

When Trevor's phone rang, I picked it up on the second ring. A number appeared on the screen, but no name. I held his phone to my ear and listened.

"This is Bran. I told you if you weren't going to tell him yourself, I would make sure he knows what you've been up to. I hope you're listening."

I didn't respond. I pressed my thumb on the red phone icon on the screen to end the call and then placed the phone back where it was.

"Was that my phone?" Trevor asked, standing in the doorway.

"It was," I confirmed. "They didn't say anything. I guess it was no one important." I never turned to look at him. I kept cleaning the kitchen counters just like I was when he first walked out.

29

If you're Reading This

Trevor...

It's probably a good idea to keep this short and to the point. I know I should be saying this face-to-face, but what I feel wouldn't let me. I've disappointed myself because I vowed I'd never be in this situation. I guess some things were just out of my control. I've been Jackson, and I've been Giovanni, but I've never been the one to cause anyone to feel like I made Giovanni feel. I have to accept that what has happened between us was what it was, but it can never happen again. I wish I could stay, but I know I can't—my past won't let me, my now won't let me. What happens now is up to you.

Dexter

Christmas and New Years came and went, and I hadn't heard from Dexter until now. My phone call a few days after Christmas and again on New Year's Eve went unanswered, and I didn't know if text and voice messages were received or deleted. Now three days after New Year's, I was holding this letter from him. I never saw this coming, but after all this time, I should have expected something. I wasn't sure what I felt or what I was supposed to be feeling.

I looked at the phone several times, and back to the letter, wondering what I really needed to say to him. His letter was clear, but I dialed his number anyway. If anything I should've been glad someone was unselfish enough to end this triangular affair.

"I didn't think I was going to hear from you," Dexter answered.

I guess this letter didn't mean he had totally erased me from his memory.

"I thought the same until I got your letter today."

"Listen, Trevor..."

"You mean you didn't already say all you had to say?"

"What do you think you were doing?" Dexter asked.

He asked that question as if he had no involvement in what we were doing. "What do you mean?" I asked.

"Your Christmas dinner invitation. You didn't think I was going to show up at this man's house, laughing and talking to him while scenes of us replayed in my mind? That would be a bit hypocritical, wouldn't you agree?"

"The invitation wasn't my idea," I explained. "Jackson asked me to invite you and Giovanni."

"He only did that because he has no knowledge of us. And Giovanni, he wasn't going to come."

"And why not?"

"Because I told him."

"You told him what? There's nothing to tell. It was just dinner."

"What I told him had nothing to do with dinner, or Jackson's invitation. I told him about us, Trevor. I told him about the feelings I have for you, and that I couldn't ignore them. I told him about Chicago, the game, dinner, and that night. He asked me if I had made love to you and I told him."

"Why didn't you lie?" I asked.

"You mean like you've been lying? That's not what you do to someone you love."

"Oh, and you haven't lied to Giovanni? So now that you've gotten what you wanted, you're all sanctimonious."

"I didn't make you do anything you didn't already want to do. But you've been lying, and you keep lying to yourself and to Jackson about our friends-with-benefits relationship. If you don't want the man, just tell him."

"But I do want him," I said, not knowing if I was convincing enough.

"Then while you do love him, while you still have him, do what you need to keep him." Dexter paused. "You know I ruined my Thanksgiving night with Gio. In our moment of passion, when I wanted to make his night beautiful, I called out your name."

Dexter's admission stunned me. "Why'd you do that?"

"What do you mean, 'Why'd I do that'? Why do we do so many of the things we do? I don't know. I hadn't planned it. You've been on my mind constantly. I tried to concentrate on him. Even in the moment I'm trying to remind myself I'm making love to this man I love, but that doesn't even work. I looked at him and saw your face, and then your name followed. I saw the hurt and disappointment in him. I felt his body shrivel under mine. I knew how he felt, and I hated how that made me feel."

"So you're blaming me."

"No, I'm blaming me. But you're being greedy and selfish, and I'm not going to perpetuate this greed and selfishness anymore."

"So what now?"

"Like I said in the letter, Trevor, where we go from here is up to you, but I have someone who I've hurt, someone I need to love, and love him like he deserves. And honestly, Jackson sounds like a good man. And you are, too. That's all I can offer you right now."

"Then I guess I should say thanks."

"For what?"

"I don't know yet, but thanks."

I was sitting in my living room, a glass of wine keeping me company. I wondered if I actually had the nerve to tell Jackson the truth. I wasn't sure I wanted to. Did I want to risk losing what I had, what I had wanted from Kelvin but never got? I guess I had some thinking to do, but at least Dexter had removed himself from the puzzling equation. I realized my suspicion that Jackson was out there doing his own thing didn't exactly excuse my own actions.

I tried keeping my mind from refocusing on the words in Dexter's letter. This wasn't going to happen by just sitting here. I picked up my cell phone and dialed Denise's number. When she didn't answer, I left her a message asking her to call me back. I tried to speak without a sense of urgency, but I wasn't sure I had done a good job pulling off that disguise. After I hung up, I dialed Caela's cell phone number.

"Hey, Caela, what are you doing?"

"Enjoying my week off with *The Plague of Doves*, this new novel by Louise Erdrich."

"How's it so far?"

"Are you kidding? I've waited years for a book from her. I finally get a chance to just sit and read. I said I wasn't going to start reading until I had time to finish it and I'm not putting down this book until I've turned the last page."

"You sound like a fiend," I said, jokingly.

"Call it what you may, you cheap trick."

"Where's my godson?"

"Trevor, you know he's in school. What's wrong? You're beating around the bush about something. Avoidance to the max."

"I don't know what you're talking about?" I asserted.

"Fine. I'll pretend right along with you."

Caela knew whether it took me two minutes or two hours, I was going to tell whatever was on my mind so she could chop and dissect it without any objection from me. I loved my working relationship with her. But what I loved most was the relationship we had after my shirt and tie and her black stilettos and pencil skirt came off. If I could ever have a sister, I would want her to be just like Caela—serious when I wanted her to be, crazy as hell when I needed her to be, and never afraid to tell me when I was being naive, gullible, or just dead wrong.

"So what chapter are you on?" I asked, stalling again. How bad was what I had to tell her anyway?

"You're doing it again."

I told Caela about the letter I received from Dexter. I remembered her asking me what was I going to do if Dexter wanted more than the romp between the sheets, but I guess now I didn't have to contemplate doing anything, since his letter and his revelation had taken that away from me. I sat and waited to hear her say, "I told you so," those four words I hated so much. And even though she hadn't said it yet, I was sure she was just holding back. I knew her that well. It was on the tip of her tongue. I could sense it.

"Aren't you going to say anything?"

"Like what? I don't know what you want me to say besides I told you so."

"You wouldn't be you if you didn't say that."

"And you know I can't be anyone else. But, friend, I warned you about this thing you got going on with Dexter. And the scary thing about this is, whether or not you want to admit it, you feel something for him, too."

"What are you talking about?" I said defensively.

"Come on, Trev. You know, sometimes I think I know you better than you know yourself. Some people can have affairs and not get emotionally attached, but you're not one of those people. And you know damn well that's why you don't do it. You invest in one person, that's it. That's you. You don't like to share the person you love, and you don't want to share the love you have for him, either."

It wasn't that Caela knew me better than I knew my own self. I went to sleep and woke up with me every morning. It was simple. What she was saying I just didn't want to admit, and as long as I didn't admit it, it wasn't true.

"So you were right."

"You don't have to admit that to me. I already knew it. I was hoping I wasn't," Caela said, and I knew she was sincere.

"Now what am I going to do?"

"Trevor. Trevor. Trevor." I heard her the first time she called my name. "Are you hearing yourself? I don't think what you have to do is too hard to figure out. Dexter has separated himself from you. Leave it at that. If he hasn't done so emotionally, he has physically. Concentrate on what you have with Jackson." She paused like she always did when she wanted to make sure she was about to ask the right question or make the right statement. "What has Kelvin done to you?"

What has Kelvin done to you? Her question replayed in my mind like echoes. Until then I hadn't thought Kelvin had done anything to me. Besides making me question my worthiness of love, and taking away the trust I had for love, I didn't think he had done anything to me.

30

Why Should I Care?

Trevor ...

This January weather is so damn unpredictable, I thought, opening the back door and staring at the rain that had been falling all week. It was the middle of winter and nothing in the form of snow had fallen.

"Chance of a late day thunderstorms my ass," I said out loud, closing the door. "Meteorologists and politicians are the only people I know who can lie and still keep their jobs."

I walked to the closet near the front entrance, grabbed my midnight black leather Aaron Barak umbrella and proceeded again towards the back door. I walked swiftly down the walkway towards the car, turning around only to push the away button on the remote control, setting the alarm on the house. I stopped for a moment and listened for the four continuous beeps that always followed. My umbrella was wide enough to protect my suit and briefcase from the morning's element, but my shoes were shown no mercy. After pressing another remote to unlock the car door,

I opened the back door, threw my briefcase and umbrella in the back seat, pressed my foot against the gas pedal, gently pressing it to the floor, and reversed my Range down the long driveway.

Until the highway, I had been making good on time. The traffic signals on the neighborhood streets worked in my favor, almost as if my Range had some controlling device installed somewhere between the V-8 engine and the front grill. As I drove, throwback sounds of songstress Whitney Houston calmed my nerves, distracting my mind from the slower-than-normal traffic and the bad news that overwhelmed the NBC TV station while I readied for work: Iraq, President-elect Obama, troop withdrawal, Iran and their nuclear power plant, the economy, job loss and unemployment, and foreclosures.

Apparently, everyone sharing the road with me had the same bright idea pop into their heads: leave early to avoid the Monday morning traffic only to get caught in it. Sitting in traffic wasn't my idea of a great start to my workweek.

As I neared my downtown exit, the rain that had been falling my entire thirty-minute drive came to an abrupt end. I continued my drive to work without incident or further interruption. I thought I was home free, but as I turned right into the driveway to the underground parking garage and waved my badge against the keypad, my cell phone rang, interrupting a text message that was coming in from Jackson at the same time.

"I said you would be hearing from me again," Bran began when I answered. "I know you haven't told him about your disloyalty."

"How do you know that?"

"'Cause you're stubborn, and like most stubborn people, you don't act until it's too late," he explained. "And it's almost too late."

"You seem to know a lot about me and Jackson. So, I'm going to presume you know what he's been doing?"

"What he's been doing?" Bran chuckled. "If you think Jackson is being unfaithful then you really don't know the man who loves you. But since it's something you believe, please, do tell." He laughed.

I told Bran about seeing Jackson at Java House and the man I saw with him. I gave him a full description of this person, and although Bran listened, he didn't say too much about me suspecting Jackson was sneaking around. After each admission, he just laughed. Here I was feeding my enemy arsenal he could use to destroy me.

"This is what I mean when I say you don't deserve him. You don't even know him."

"Right. And you do. I know what I saw."

"Are you sure you didn't see what you wanted to see? You know people in your situation do that quite often."

People in my situation? Ok, this man, whoever he is, has some nerve. I drove up the ramp to the second floor and assumed my parking space. I put the gear in park and since I had a few minutes to kill, I sat in the truck going back and forth with Bran. I wasn't sure what I was going to accomplish, if anything, by talking to him, but I entertained him anyway.

"People in my situation?" I finally asked.

"Yes. You're running out of time, Trevor. Before you no longer have a say in what happens to your relationship with Jackson, end this friendship you have with Dexter."

I wasn't going to tell him Dexter had already ended whatever we had. "Why are you so invested in my situation?" I asked, adjusting the volume on the radio.

"Trevor, you are no stranger to unhappiness or heartbreak. You do remember what that felt like, don't you? You remember how many times you went to sleep alone, crying, hurting, and feeling no one understood your pain?"

"Yes, but…?" He was talking to me as if he were a best friend I shared everything with.

"And the only person you wanted to hear the words 'I'm sorry' from was so busy involved with himself you swore he didn't care? Remember when all you wanted was for someone, him, to love the hurt away? You knew love wasn't supposed to make you feel the way you felt, but that was how it made you feel, and there was nothing you could do. You sleep but don't remember sleeping, you dream but can't remember what you dreamed about, you laughed but don't remember laughing because everything was blurred by the pain that enveloped your heart."

"Yes, but…"

"Stop interrupting. I'm not interested in your explanations." He paused. "Don't think you're going to put Jackson through that. He doesn't deserve to feel that way. Don't you know love, Trevor?"

"Don't I know love?" I repeated his question, buying time until I had a response. I thought I knew love.

That simple question brought back a flood of memories of those I had pushed out of or to the back of my mind. There was the love Kelvin Phillip Patterson alleged before he was with Lawrence professing the same. There was Landry Carlisle who loved me Monday, Wednesday, and Thursday nights, but never on weekends, which were reserved for his wife, and never on Sundays since that was his family day with the twins and the older Landry, Jr. And how could I forget Teric Keron Hunter. He was a star basketball and all-America football player, a receiver on our high school team. I loved the way his dreads dangled from underneath his helmet as he raced down the sideline, running forty, fifty, sixty yards to a touchdown, increasing his yards-after-reception stats. I was too busy watching his body move before my eyes. "I love you," he said, just before he took my virginity the weekend his parents left him home alone. That next Monday morning at school, he looked at me like I was the new boy, as he stood at his locker staring into the eyes of Sienna McLean, my best friend. Though Sienna and I shared everything, I kept what happened between Teric and me to myself. That was the last time Teric ever spoke to me, even though we sat beside each other in Trig class.

Bran knew I was stalling.

"Yet those tears still came at night," he continued. "And now, look what you got."

So all I knew about this man was the name he gave me, an alias. He was either closer to me than he was telling me, or closer to Jackson. I still hadn't figured that out. He was doing an excellent job keeping his identity under wraps. As much as he didn't want me to hurt Jackson, he didn't want to hurt him, either, or else he would have disclosed all this information to him a long time ago. I could always call his bluff except I wasn't sure he was bluffing. For someone on the outside, he sure did know a lot. He knew the right questions to ask and something about him told me he already knew my answers.

I looked at the clock on the dash. It was almost 9 o'clock and I had a full day ahead of me. "Look, Bran. I have to go."

"Remember what I said. You're running out of time," he warned.

"Goodbye, Bran. And I won't be answering your calls again."

"If you come clean with Jackson, or end your so-called platonic friendship with Dexter, you won't have to worry about ever hearing from me. But until then, you have no choice. You're a curious one, and your curiosity won't stop you from answering. Like I told you on Christmas, if you don't tell him, I'm going to make sure he knows what you've been doing."

"Say what?"

"Enjoy your day, Trevor," Bran said and hung up.

On the elevator, I sent a text to Jackson wishing him a good day. It seems we've been texting more and talking less, but I guess it was better than no communication at all. I wanted to call him since I hadn't spoken to him at all yesterday, but knowing how much he hated to be late for anything, I figure he was already in his 9 o'clock meeting. When I came off the elevator, Morgan was entering the Agency. This was his late day.

"Hey, Morgan, hold up a second."

"Good morning, Mr. Harrison," he said, holding the straps dangling from his black Columbia bag.

"Question."

"Answer," he said, smiling. His pearly whites glistened.

"That friend you told me about in that meeting. How is she? Did she work out her situation?"

"She's trying to figure it out. I've kind of followed your advice."

"I forgot. What advice was that?" I lied.

"I've cut her some slack," he said, opening the door. "Have a good day, Mr. Harrison."

"And you do the same, Morgan." As I turned down the hall, heading to my office, I called out, "Morgan."

"Yes." He stopped.

"Won't you join me for lunch, if you don't already have plans?"

"Well, I brought a brown bag, but I guess I can save it for tomorrow. Sure."

I tried to focus. No luck. What had Bran done to me? I didn't think what I did was wrong, because I had good reasons. Yet my conversation with Bran developed a feeling of guilt in the pit of my stomach. His "don't I know love" question really jolted me. Whatever happened to Landry Carlisle? And the last time I saw Sienna McLean, she was ending her reign as Ms. New York. I still catch a glimpse of Teric Hunter during a Sunday or Monday night football game. He hadn't changed much, except he was now a millionaire. He still looked sexy in his winter-white football pants, his ass lifted by his jock straps and his helmet in his left hand, just as he did on the sidelines during our high school football games. The last time I Googled him, there was still no mention of a Mrs. Hunter or kids.

I lounged in my chair behind my desk, rocking back and forth as if I was lulling myself to sleep. When my phone buzzed, I answered without thinking. With the luck I'd had, I figured it was none other than Bran.

"Yes," I said, sitting up and placing my elbows on my desk. I hadn't heard his voice and yet I had an immediate headache.

"Yes?" he questioned. "Is that any way to greet your old man?"

"Oh. What's up, pops," I said with a quick grin. It was good to hear my father's familiar voice. I hadn't been able to speak to him as often as I would like. With Jackson, Dexter, and Bran and his confusing, menacing phone calls, I hadn't been able to make time. I wasn't making excuses. Yet how could I not have time to speak to the only man who had been in my life all my life?

"What's up pops?" he mocked. "Feels like I haven't spoken to you in ages."

"Yeah. I have to remind myself you have Natalie in your life now."

"Don't say things like that. You know that means nothing."

"I'm kidding."

"Okay, but don't joke like that." He paused. "So, how you been?"

In the years I've known myself, I can't remember ever not being truthful with my father. I'd never lied about my sexual preference. I'd never lied about Kelvin and how he made me almost hate life and love. I thought about how disappointed he would be if I spoke this truth. Even if Jackson was sharing his bed with this man, I wasn't making things any better if I were doing the same. I could hear my father now: "You can't right a wrong by doing wrong yourself."

"I'm great." I lied to my father.

"How's Jackson?"

"He's fine. I think we're due for a happy hour. Speaking of which, I got an invitation from Sidney."

"An invitation to what?"

"Her wedding… to Jamel. They finally set a date. The wedding is in June." I hadn't spoken to Sidney so often since she finished school and moved back to Florida, but I was glad she hadn't left me off the guest list.

My father and I had some catching up to do. He hadn't given any details about their Christmas trip to the Bahamas or their New Years trip to Las Vegas. I do know he and Natalie were close to setting their own wedding date. My father, married again. I was already looking forward to the day.

"Mr. Harrison…" Caela's voice sounded over the intercom.

"One second, Dad." I lowered the cell phone from my mouth. "Yes, Caela," I said, pressing the intercom button.

"Mr. DeGregory is holding on the line for you."

"Thanks, Caela. Listen, Dad. I have to take this."

"Drinks on Wednesday," he said. "At my spot." I had no idea where his spot was. I said, "Ok," and then hung up.

31

And I Love You

Jackson...

I loved my mother and sister, but sometimes I do think they can be a little over protective. Sometimes I think, in their eyes, I will never be old enough to take care of myself. Besides the hurting love had put on me, I think I had done a decent job taking care of me for some time now.

"All I've heard from you so far this year is 'Happy New Year.' Is that any way to treat your sister?" Devaan asked.

"Or your mother?" my mother broke in. She and Devaan were a ruthless tag-team. I'd seen them in action.

"My two favorite ladies. How are you doing?"

"We're fine," they answered in unison. "The question is, how are you?" my mother asked.

I could see my mother now, sitting at her desk with her legs crossed, reading an email from a fellow supervisor that made no sense. She's always said she worked in an organization full of fools, and sometimes I believed her.

"Work is going well. Trevor and I are...fine."

Why did I hesitate? I thought.

"What's going on, Jackson? You know you can talk to us,"

my mother said with assurance.

"I hope this isn't another Gavin situation." I wished Devaan hadn't said that. She had opened the floodgates and the questions poured in.

"What situation? What did Gavin do?" my mother began.

"I'm sorry, Jackson," Devaan pleaded. "I thought she knew."

"You thought I knew what?"

"No, she doesn't know. I never told her."

"Stop acting like I'm not on this phone. Can someone tell me what's going on," my mother whispered.

My mother hated feeling out of the loop when it came to Devaan and me. But she was the same one who taught us to try and solve issues on our own. And now she hated that we practiced what she preached.

I told my mother the same story about Gavin I had told Devaan. I told her how I went to sleep and woke up wondering if he ever loved me. He never understood the way he made me feel because he never took the time to. I thought loving him completed me, but as much as I loved him, there was still an emptiness that was never filled.

"There was nothing left to do but walk away. Mom, he's part of the reason I left."

"And the other part?"

"My job." I paused. "And Trevor."

"And you're sure Trevor isn't going to do to you what Gavin did?"

"I'm sure. He's nothing like Gavin." I reassured her. Now wasn't the time to tell them about Ethan, or the letter I received, or the phone call that came for Trevor on Christmas Day. Those were three cans of worms I didn't feel like opening.

Why hadn't I told my mother about Gavin earlier? "So, to answer your question, this isn't another Gavin situation."

I felt a tear in the corner of my eye. I felt that tickling feeling as it moved down the right side of my nose. I had to remind myself I was at work.

"I didn't know you had all this going on with Gavin. I thought he was such a nice man."

"Guess he played that role well, just like he played all the other roles. There's an Oscar out there with his name on it. Trust me."

"Like Rihanna said, 'and the award for the best liar goes to you,' Mr. Gavin what's-his-name," Devaan said, almost in a song. We all laughed.

"Look ladies," I said, getting up from behind my desk.

"Mom, I love you. Thanks for listening."

"I love you, too, sweetheart. Tell Trevor hello for me and I'm looking forward to seeing him again."

"And sis, thanks for making me laugh. I love you, too."

"And I love you, too. Take care and remember I'm only a phone call away if you ever want to talk."

"Thanks," I said, and hung up.

32

There's Nothing

Trevor...

The rain that fell was nothing but a nuisance. The temperature had been falling steadily, and it was finally starting to feel like January again. The threat of snow mentioned on this morning's news finally looked as if it would actually happen. The rain did nothing to diminish the crowd that busied themselves up and down 7th street, most either rushing back to work after a long lunch hour or scrambling to find a place to just escape from their usual day at the office.

When I told Caela I would be having lunch with Morgan, she suggested I take him somewhere I hadn't been in a long time and some place she was almost certain he hadn't been either. Ping Pong Dim Sum on the corner of 7th and I streets in the Chinatown section of DC was definitely a good choice. Since I had extended the lunch invite and had never seen Morgan drive, I decided to drive. Morgan wasn't the talkative type during the fifteen minutes it took to drive across town. He paid more attention to the various satellite radio stations than to me or my attempts at a conversation, and I didn't mind since I welcomed the music to drown the sometimes-deafening silence between us.

Once in Ping Pong, we sat on the side closest to the street, watching women dodge raindrops they thought should have stopped falling by now. Morgan stared at the menu before settling on pork puffs. As I've done on my previous visits, I ordered the scallops and king prawns with shitake. Morgan picked up the chopsticks, cradled them between his fingers, and grabbed a pork puff from his plate.

"You know Trevor, I know I've never told you this, but I one day want to be like you," he said, bringing the chopsticks to his mouth. He chewed quietly on the pork puff. He kept his eyes gazed at the table and I could sense a level of nervousness rising within him.

Did he just call me Trevor? I thought. "Be like me? In what way?" I asked, and smiled to put him at ease.

"In every way. Even with the threat of a recession, your business continues to do well. The banks are lending money so contractors are building condos atop of condos and I have no idea who's going be living in them. And you and your partner are still going strong." He grabbed his glass of water. "And I respect you."

"Thanks. But don't you think you're limiting yourself by settling to just want to be like me?" I took a taste of my exotic mix of pineapple juice, coconut purée and fresh lime.

"It's not settling if it's more than I have right now."

I'm not sure what Morgan was talking about. He didn't look like someone who didn't have all of what he needed, and if he didn't have all, he, at least, had most. Needless to say, I was not prepared for his comment. I didn't expect he would be wearing his inadequacies on his sleeve next to his Gautier watch and diamond square cuff links.

"More than you have right now?"

"I don't mean to get personal with you," Morgan said, loosening his tie and unbuttoning the top three buttons on his shirt.

There on the base of the left side of his neck was that word, the one thing that can hurt you and save you. I looked at his tattoo and smiled to myself. "Love?" I asked.

"Oh," he said, slowly covering his neck as if some dark secret had been revealed. "It's nothing."

"And how long have you been convincing yourself it's nothing. You don't just tattoo such a powerful word on your body and say *it's nothing.*"

"Let me know if you gentlemen need anything else," the waiter said, his Chinese accent infiltrating his otherwise perfect American English. When the waiter excused himself again, Morgan continued to answer.

"That was his name, but the only persons who knows this now is me and you."

"He doesn't know you have his name, or the name you gave him, permanently etched in your skin?"

"No. I liked that I had this little secret to myself. That's the best decision I ever made."

Already, outside of our meetings, this is the most I had ever spoken to Morgan. He had already heightened my level of curiosity.

"If you don't mind me asking, what happened?" There, I asked the burning question that had been on the tip of my tongue.

"I'll give you the short version now and the long version over some strong drinks. Trust me, I'm going to need it." Morgan paused as if he were organizing his story in his head. "The last time he said he loved me was the night after his bachelor party ended. The next day, as his best man, I had to watch him lie to this woman about forsaking all others. I guess he meant after the rings were on both their fingers. I couldn't say anything then because I was just as big a hypocrite as he was standing there smiling at her, our love scene on repeat mode in my mind. In her mind she's thinking she's about to marry the one man she had been saving her love for."

"And the last time you saw him?"

"He went running from our hotel room like he had wheels for feet. I had given Ms. Tyesa Maynard all the clues and information she needed to catch his lying ass in the act. She wasn't the only one he was giving his tender kisses to. And even though he was giving her great sex, she wasn't the only one he was sexing like that. She thanked me, grabbed her Burberry printed tote and left as calmly as she walked in."

"And what did you do?"

"I laid there with my hands behind my head, my legs spread apart, and contentment flowing through my veins. I enjoyed the last night on his dime and waited for his loser-ass to show up." The smile Morgan wore now, I figured, mimicked the smile he wore then.

"You don't think that bordered on cruelty?" I asked.

"Greed, Trevor, is never an excuse to hurt, or lie," he began, staring at me as if he were giving me my final warning. "When everything you need is staring you in your face, you need to do one of two things: Accept the man or woman who, before God or in heart, had promised to love you, or just let them go."

"So he lied to…?"

"To me? No," Morgan interrupted. Now he was reading my thoughts, finishing my sentences. "I wouldn't let him. He was lying only to himself, and Tyesa."

Morgan spoke with an obvious disdain, only now I couldn't discern if this was directed towards me or if it was remnants of the scorn he once had for this unspecified man. Unknowingly, Morgan had storied his way onto my short list of suspects. So, is this what he sees when he looks at me? Since running into Morgan this morning after getting off the elevator, I'd agonized over exactly how I was going to ask him about his potential involvement in my personal life. I wasn't going to dance around the issue any longer than I already had.

The waiter returned and placed my order of satay squid on the table in front of me, and proceeded to set Morgan's dish of lemon chicken in front of him.

"Gentlemen, would that be all?" he asked.

"Yes, thank you," Morgan and I answered, sounding like one voice.

When the waiter had distanced himself from the table, I decided to ask my question before we were interrupted again.

"Who's Bran?" I asked without a blink.

"I have no idea, but I assume you're going to tell me." Morgan sat back in his chair and waited for me to divulge more information about Bran.

I told him about the phone calls I had been receiving from someone who introduced himself as "Bran." I told him I was quite sure Bran was some alias he probably picked out from a daily newspaper.

"I just need to know if you have anything to do with it."

"Why would I…?" He paused and stared out the glass window. "So is this what this lunch is about, to see if somehow your life and your involvement with whomever had made it to my list of priorities?" He still hadn't looked at me.

"When you mentioned your friend after that meeting we had,

I just assumed…"

Morgan laughed. "I mentioned Neyvada and her situation because you asked. You thought I was making her up? Did you think I was replacing pronouns to keep you from figuring me out?"

"I just thought…" and the words I wanted to come out had disappeared. Apparently, what I thought was wrong.

"Look Trevor, when I said I wanted to be like you, it wasn't to hear myself talk. I don't know what you have going on in your personal life, and I don't care to know, but professionally, I think you have your stuff together. How many times have you asked me to call you Trevor?" Morgan asked. I shrugged my shoulders in response. "And I don't because I respect you. Anyway, who has that much time on their hands to sit around making I-see-you phone calls? Isn't that like a second job?"

"That's what I'm trying to figure out."

"Well, I'm glad we've cleared the air with that question. Don't want you walking around the office thinking I'm running around spying on you."

"I'm glad you took the accusation well."

"Like you said, man, you're just trying to figure things out."

I could tell a part of Morgan really wanted me to go into details about the phone calls. They say a drunken man tells no tale. Maybe under the influence of cranberry juice and vodka, he would get all his questions answered.

"So, you still have to tell me the long version of your story over drinks."

"Don't worry, we're still on."

Although it was only lunch, Morgan made sure he saved room for dessert and enjoyed the pineapple and mango puff I suggested. There was a lot more conversation on the drive back to the office. I don't know how many times I apologized to him. I had gotten to know my young coworker a little better and I had a new friend. Morgan admitted he still had so much to learn, and thanked me for taking the chance of hiring someone with no experience fresh out of graduate school. He was surprised to learn almost everyone on staff had just about as much experience as him when they started.

33

Once You've Heard the Truth

Jackson...

I was sitting in my office watching the day transform from sunny and bright to dark and overcast. The thunder whispered, then boom, it rumbled across the sky. It sounded so near. A car alarm sounded in the distant, then quiet. I walked over to the window and lifted it open. It smelled like rain. The sky was grey, and white, and grey. Then it began. A light drizzle turned the dry asphalt wet. The thunder rumbled across the sky again. The lightning flashed in the distance, and there stood my father. It flashed again, but this time I saw Trevor's face illuminated. I struggled to see the face of the figure that stood in front of him. I never did. The lightning flashed again, and I jumped, startled. It was expected, yet it was unexpected.

That's how my dream ended. I hated when my dreams were incomplete, and I spent the rest of my morning, the day, trying to figure out what all this really meant. I knew it meant something. A glimpse into what really is, pieces of puzzles that needed to be put together to reveal an image, except now I could never figure out what was the bigger picture.

I've sat here going half crazy, agonizing over the little bit of information that had been given to me. Not having quite figured out what I should do, I had kept what I knew to myself. It was clear Trevor wasn't going to say anything unless I confronted him. Until answering his phone on Christmas Day and hearing that warning meant for Trevor, I hadn't given much credence to the letter. I went back and forth over how much of it was truth and how much of it was Gavin, or Ethan, trying to use their brain all in an attempt to get me back.

But I wasn't going to find out what truth existed by sitting on my hands, swinging my feet, and not doing anything. I had been questioning myself and still couldn't find the answers. I didn't want to accuse Trevor, so I had purposely given him time. *Ask him a question you already know the answer to and see if he lies.* That line kept playing over and over in my head, and no matter what I did, I couldn't think it away. But I had a plan.

I picked up my cell phone and hastily dialed Trevor's number.

"Hey," I spoke when he answered.

"Good morning to you, sir. Shouldn't you be making your way to the shower, getting ready for work?"

"The shower isn't going anywhere," I said. "Listen, do you have any plans after work?"

"Nope. Well, I had planned on calling and chatting with Denise. We have some catching up to do, and you know how long those can last."

"Well, like my shower, she can wait, right?"

"Yeah. There's always tomorrow. What's going on?"

I told Trevor it seemed we hadn't had an evening with just the two of us in some time. I shared the blame, blaming work for keeping us busy. We agreed on 7:30 for dinner, but he said he would come right after work. I left it at that, not bothering to ask what time was right after work.

I spent the day working from home, catching up on Obama news and getting dinner ready. DC was bracing itself for the biggest inauguration crowd ever in the next couple days, and it was expected to be very cold. Official and unofficial inauguration balls were planned to celebrate the historic moment. It still brings tears to my eyes every time I think about waking early election morning and going with Trevor to the polling station. We listened to women as old as our grandmothers who've always voted admitting to never seeing the line as long as it was. That night I stayed up late with Trevor, Natalie, and Mr. Harrison, watching the results as they came in.

I took some time thinking about a special menu. I remembered the steak I had marinating in the refrigerator in a blend of olive oil, light brown sugar, red wine, soy sauce, onion powder, honey, green onions, garlic and garlic vinegar, ground ginger, and garlic powder. My mouth watered just thinking about the aftertaste. I added baked garlic potatoes and a bottle of Cabernet Franc I had chilling in the wine cooler—it was a gift from Mr. Harrison. They say the best way to a man's heart was through his stomach, but today, Trevor's stomach was going to be my best way to the truth. Hopefully.

When I opened the door, Trevor stood leaning to one side with a wide smile on his face. He probably went home and changed since he showed up wearing black Levi's cords and a black and white crewneck cashmere sweater, replacing his usual slacks, dress shirt and tie. I leaned in and kissed him, and then turned and walked away. I headed back towards the kitchen.

"So that's it? You're not going to invite me in?"

"Stand out there if you think you need an invitation." I didn't even turn around.

"Smells good," he complimented, walking behind me. "What are we having? Whatever it is, I hope you made a lot of it." He walked into the dining area and sat.

"Hungry or greedy?" I asked, laughing.

"Whatever. I skipped out on lunch after your invitation. I wanted to save room for whatever is in that kitchen and whatever comes after."

I looked at Trevor and smiled, thinking, *if this letter has some truth in it, dinner is all you're going to get.*

After placing our dinners on the table and pouring the two glasses full of red wine, Trevor and I talked about work. Every now and then silence interrupted. The sounds and words of Patti, Toni, and an occasional song from Eric Benet played in the background. Eric's "You're the Only One" echoed sentiments I was beginning to question.

"This is good," Trevor said, as if I needed his approval. "You should cook like this every day."

"Only if it means you'll be here every day eating, 'cause I definitely don't need to cook like this for just me."

"Sure. Just as long as I don't have to clean up afterwards."

"You do know that's not fair, right?" I was waiting for the best opening. I was drinking wine to settle my nerves.

"You cook, I'll eat. You don't think that's fair?"

"Ok, Trevor."

"I'm joking. Stop looking so serious."

I was sitting on the letter I had placed in my seat earlier. I wouldn't need it if he were going to be honest. But just in case, it was right there.

As Chantay Savage's "This Time" began, I looked across the table at Trevor and I saw the faces of Ethan, Landry, Teric, and

Gavin staring back at me. Like the end of Michael Jackson's "Black or White" music video, Trevor seemed to morph into one and then the other. Everything I felt for them and after them came rushing back. Everything they never gave me and all I wished from them were vivid flashbacks, and I couldn't hold my tongue anymore. *Here we go again!* I thought. I knew I wasn't about to head down this familiar road again, not if I could help it.

"I haven't heard you say too much about Dexter. How's he doing?"

"Not much to say about him. I haven't spoken to him in a while."

"How often have you spoken to him?" I paused.

"I haven't…" Trevor began.

"Since Chicago?" I added. My question surprised him. I surprised myself, too. Trevor had just cut a cube of steak and was about to place it in his mouth. He stopped with his fork mid-air and looked at me with his eyes wide open.

"When was I in Chicago?" he asked.

"I was hoping you could answer that question, and while you're giving answers you can tell me who went with you." I hadn't looked at Trevor because I didn't want him to see the disappointment in my eyes.

"I was never in Chicago."

Trevor had just lied to me.

I sat back in the chair and stared at him. My pulse increased, and I felt a quiver in the side of my top lip. He stopped eating, and stared back, not blinking.

"So maybe you can explain this." I sat up and removed the letter, slowly opened it and placed it in front of him, setting it in his plate, on top of his steak and potatoes.

"Why did you do that?"

I picked up my plate, walked into the kitchen and over to the trash can. I had lost my appetite. "'Cause you're lying to me, Trevor." I scraped the remaining steak and potatoes into the trash. "I thought I was done dealing with liars, and here you come again. Why is it so hard for people to tell the truth?" I wasn't expecting him to respond, but he did.

Hook.

Line.

Sinker.

I watched him squirm in his seat. I stood in the kitchen, waiting for his confession.

"And are you going to tell your truth?" he asked. I didn't know when I had lied to him. I walked back over to him and picked up the letter. I ignored his question.

"I got this in the mail over a month ago. I didn't say anything because I thought there was nothing to be said."

"No, you said nothing because you had no proof."

"But then I got the phone call telling me to ask you a question I already knew the answer to and see if you were going to lie. Then, on Christmas, when I answered your phone, the caller, Bran, said he told you if you weren't going to tell him yourself, he would make sure he knows what you've been up to. Now if the 'he' he's talking about in that call isn't me, then your trip to Chicago isn't the only thing you have to explain."

"You spoke to Bran?"

"What's going on Trevor? What are you not telling me?"

He stood up. "You want to know about Chicago?"

"Everything." I walked back into the kitchen, stood against the counter and listened.

Trevor followed.

"Dexter," he said. "I went to Chicago with Dexter. It wasn't a trip I planned. Since you were away at your conference, I didn't see anything wrong."

"So when I asked you that same weekend what you were doing you told me everything, but you never told me where you were or who you were with. Why didn't you?"

"Because…"

"You're lying," I interrupted. "What happened in Chicago, Trevor?"

"I slept with him." He walked back to the table and sat staring out the window. "If you wanted me to love only you, you should have loved only me. I had my justifications. Caela told me she saw you. I saw you."

I thought I had prepared myself for the worst, but here I was hearing the worst and it had taken my legs from under me. I watched my heart being torn to pieces and scattered over the dining room floor.

"You slept with Dexter?" I didn't know if I was asking a question or confirming what I heard. Then I thought about Trevor's questions, his accusations. "And what do you mean you and Caela saw me?" I was still leaning against the counter.

"Yes," Trevor said adamantly.

"Is that what you do? So, not knowing if what you saw, or thought you saw was true, you decided in order to right my supposed wrong you had to do wrong yourself. Tell me this, Trevor, are you satisfied? Did it make you feel better that you were doing to me what you thought I was doing to you?"

"It wasn't supposed to happen like that?"

"How exactly was it supposed to happen?" I asked, knowing no explanation would satisfy my curiosity.

"I don't…"

"And please don't tell me you don't know," I quickly interrupted. "Were you supposed to just sit there beside him, feeling hurt and vulnerable, and Dexter was supposed to just stroke your back and send you on your way? Do you always seek comfort in another man's arms when you think the man you're with is seeking comfort, too?"

"You have some damn nerve," Trevor shot back. "If I remember correctly, it was you who waltzed your way into my space that night we met. I wasn't looking for anything, and I wasn't looking for you. Why didn't you just tell me everything?"

I stood with my eyes wide in disbelief. "Is that how you feel?"

"Had you just been honest with me, none of this would have happened."

"Oh get the hell outta here! Don't sit there trying to convince me things or people in my life you think I left out..."

"Conveniently," Trevor broke in.

"Regardless, that didn't give you reasons to sleep with him. If you went to him to be comforted about what you thought I was doing, you should have settled for his shoulders. But what do you do? Have sex with him after your first tear."

"It wasn't after..."

"Spare me the fucking details. Now is not the time to indulge me with intimate particulars," I warned.

"So I guess this means you don't love me anymore?" Trevor asked. I didn't know if he was ready to hear my response.

"I'm not going to say I love you any less," I paused. I stared at Trevor with the disappointment I tried to hide earlier etched in my face. "But I can't exactly say I can love you anymore. Tell me this. Did it at least make you feel better? I hope it was an amazing time for you." I finally walked over to him and stood with my face inches from his. My eyes were dry because, unfortunately, I had been here before. "I'm curious. What did you do with me while he made love to you? Did I not matter as long as you were getting your fix?"

"Is that what you want me to say?" Trevor questioned.

"How about you continue telling the truth, or have you forgotten what the truth sounds like? It's what you say so you won't have to keep track of lies." I walked back into the kitchen and stood leaning against the island. Trevor followed behind me.

As much as Trevor was willing to accept his wrong in what he did, he obviously wasn't going to sit there and pretend I didn't have my faults in all that had happened. He wasn't going to sit there on the chair and be chastised by me. He needed me to see my own reflection in the mirror I was holding up to his face.

"Since we're handing out accusations and telling our truths, you can tell me who you were with at Java House the day…"

"The day I ran late to dinner with your father and Natalie?" I offered.

"Yes."

"The day Caela saw me?"

"Yes. The day Cae…" I guess Trevor wasn't expecting that either. I had defused the bomb he thought he was going to drop on me. "The truth is, you lied, too, Jackson. You lied when you didn't tell me about the man Caela saw you with, the same man I saw you having a mid-afternoon heart to heart with in front of Java House." Trevor paused. He poured his glass full of wine and emptied it in what seemed like one swallow. "What was I supposed to think? You running around having these secret meetings with this man didn't exactly leave me with many options. Right! Now the question is why did you feel the need to leave out such information? What or who else are you hiding? And let's start with Bran."

"I don't know anyone name Bran. I have nothing to hide. I saw Caela, and I knew she saw me. I also knew she wouldn't think twice about telling you. I didn't say anything to you because I thought you knew me better than that. I waited for you to ask. I could've told you who I was with."

Trevor was quiet.

"Why didn't you tell me without me asking?"

"It's complicated," I explained.

"Simplify it, like you've simplified everything else you've told me. Whatever! But you need to tell me something."

"You wouldn't..."

"Don't tell me I wouldn't understand. The brain has a way of figuring things out. What you need to figure out is where you want to start this story." Trevor sat in the chair by the window and waited for me to begin.

I began telling him about Ethan. I wanted to tell him this soon after we met, but I was too busy listening to his own story of the heartache Kelvin was putting him through.

● ● ● ● ●

The only person important to Ethan Angelo Overstreet was Ethan Angelo Overstreet. I saw intimations of Ethan's selfishness, but against my better judgment, I ignored them. The morning I met Ethan, I had carpooled with a friend, Seth Crandall, something we often did when I didn't feel like driving. Seth was an older respectful sportscaster. To the ladies, he was sexy and sweet, and for whatever reason, his cavalier attitude towards their advances kept their interest. To me, Seth was the best friend who only visited when an arctic wind blew him out of Ohio, where he now calls home, continuing to earn the respect of other sportscasters on WLWT – TV, an NBC affiliate.

When Ethan stepped from his silver Lexus IS 350, I wasn't supposed to give him the attention I did. I wasn't supposed to notice those black custom calf Allen-Edmonds shoes he carefully placed on the sidewalk, avoiding the makeshift stream skillfully making its way to a nearby drain. He was supposed to just walk by, smelling as good as he did, looking as good as he did, and I wasn't supposed to be affected by him, not in the least bit.

His suit jacket was swung over his left shoulder and a leather attaché case was held firmly in his right hand. He was suave and had a rhythm to his walk. He must have felt my eyes piercing him in his back, since he paused, looked in my direction with intent, and then continued his climb up the steps at Eighty Two Waltham Avenue.

When he reached the first platform that separated the two long flights of stairs leading up to the Pavilion, he stopped as if someone had interrupted his ascent and stared at his silver watch that sat tightly on his left wrist. I walked by him, resisting all temptation to look this man over one last time. We'd crossed path several times before, but I never gave Ethan the attention I was giving him now.

Mr. Ethan Angelo Overstreet, Marketing Management. His name and title displayed in bold black letters on gold brass. Mr. Overstreet was a reputable sports agent, gracing the pages of *Essence* magazine as one of America's most eligible bachelors. But who was he eligible to? The jury hadn't rendered a verdict on that. He was partner, agent, and majority owner of Starpower Sports and Entertainment Agency, which he started five years earlier with Alena Mallory. He was in the area orchestrating a contract deal for basketball power-forward Kenyon Anthony.

Ethan entered the Pavilion and stared at the elevators busied by the morning rush. Business men and women filled the elevators seemingly to capacity, eager to start their morning, hopefully quickly making their way to the office breakfast room, avoiding the morning charge to freshly brewed coffee. To avoid the chaos, the wrinkled business suits and scuffed Horatio oxfords, I turned left and headed up the marble stairs that curled upwards along the interior architecture of glass and steel.

My cell phone was already an active hotbox that morning. As I answered, I glanced over my right shoulder only to notice Ethan giving me the once-over. He was bold. I smiled innocently, acknowledging his examination. Ethan nodded as he stepped on the elevator, his image disappearing behind the closing doors.

When I walked into the office and greeted McKenzie, she gave me a look wrapped in mystery. She had become one of my best friends since my first day as an intern. After I walked a few steps passed her desk, she demanded my attention. McKenzie handed me a pink message slip.

I unfolded the message and read as I walked. Surprised by the details, I stopped and turned, looking back at McKenzie and thought, *He actually asked you to take this message?* McKenzie shrugged her shoulders and smiled, as if she knew exactly what I was thinking. It was a lunch invitation with none other than Mr. Overstreet. Before I knew it, I was in a restaurant waiting to have lunch with him.

"So, let me get this straight," Trevor interrupted. "This man winked at you, left you a message, and you were already waiting to have lunch with him?"

"Don't judge me. You wanted me to tell you about him, and that's what I'm doing. If you don't like what you're hearing, I can stop. This wasn't my idea."

When I saw him, something told me I was never going to be the same. I eventually fell in love with the man I met that morning. He fell in love with everyone else. While he was setting my heart on fire with his pretentious affections and broken promises, he was also sharing himself with men and women who never bothered to listen to how his heart beat. It took me a while to realize that the Ethan I met was nothing but an avatar, a misrepresentation of his true self. He wasn't ready for love, and the kind of love he was ready for wasn't mine.

"And you expect me to believe that story?"

"Honestly, Trevor, I love you, but I don't care what you believe." I smiled. "I met Ethan at Java because he had to see in my eyes that I had moved on. All the other times me leaving him were just words, but he knew what was in my heart. I needed him to see that the only person in my heart this time around was you. Caela should have told you that while you were busy with Dexter, I was sitting across from Ethan convincing him I had finally found happiness, and professing your love for me, because he already knew how I love."

"That's it?"

"What more did you want? You wanted something, anything, to justify your irresponsible choices. So what are you going to do now that your theory no longer has one good leg to stand on?" I walked towards the stairs and headed towards the front door.

"Where are you going?" Trevor asked following behind me.

"I'm not going anywhere, Trevor. You are," I responded, not even turning around to look at him. I opened the door and leaned against it. My body had grown cold.

"I made a mistake, Jackson, a bad decision in moments of weakness, a lapse in judgment. Call it whatever you want, but I didn't do it hurt you." Trevor stood at the bottom of the steps looking at me.

"You think your reason is supposed to dictate how I feel? You make mistakes when you're young and still trying to figure out your place in this world. You're a grown ass man, Trevor, and you should've learned by now that mistakes have consequences. And unfortunately, yours is losing me."

"That's it?"

"Goodnight, Trevor."

He walked towards the door, stopped, and then looked at me with a dead stare. He walked through the door, and as he turned around, I slammed the door shut in his face.

This was such a familiar scene. I walked back upstairs and into the dining area. I stood at the table and poured my glass full with the last bit of wine. I walked into the living room, picked up my cell phone and began to dial.

"Hello," he answered.

"Hey Colt." My voice was soft. "Can you talk?"

34

To The Arms of the One

Trevor...

I stood on the other side of Jackson's door waiting for my *Love and Basketball* moment, my second chance, but it never came. I contemplated ringing the doorbell, but I found no strength in my finger.

As I walked towards my truck, my cell phone buzzed. I looked at the screen but purposely ignored the phone call. I dialed Denise's number.

"Hello love," she answered.

"Hey, Den. I need a favor."

"Anything for you."

"I need you to tell me whatever you can about a Mr. Ethan Angelo Overstreet. He's affiliated with Starpower, but I want to know how deep is his affiliation with Jackson."

"What's the matter, sweetie?"

"I can't go into details now, but I will tell you everything soon. Can you do that for me?"

"Sure. I hope everything is ok."

"If it isn't right now, it will be. I'll call you later."

"Wait a minute. I think you'll want to hear this."

"Ok." I opened the car and sat listening to Denise.

"There isn't going to be a wedding." I couldn't tell if she was disappointed.

"What did you do?"

"I didn't have to do anything. Didn't I tell you someone was going to show their ass before the veil was lifted?"

"I'm sitting."

"But of course you are." She laughed.

"Let me guess. Cold feet?"

"No. Cold heart."

"You have to tell me more, but let me know what you find out about Mr. Overstreet."

"I'll do my best research, love."

"Love you, Den."

"Love you, too, Trevor."

My conversation with Denise had given me a quick reprieve. After hanging up, I dialed into my voicemail. I wished I had ignored this message just like I had ignored the call. Even if I wanted to, my curiosity wouldn't let me. Just as I suspected. It was Bran telling me my time was up. Little did he know, my time being up had nothing to do with him.

I deleted the message and dialed Dexter.

"Are you busy?" I asked when he answered. He was the only other person I wanted to talk to right now.

"Trevor, hey. You okay?"

"I'm not. Are you busy? I need to talk."

"Phone, or in person?" Dexter asked.

"In person, if you don't mind."

I wondered if I was making another mistake running to Dexter in my time of crisis, but besides Denise and Caela, who better to run to. There was nothing to fear since this time, unlike the last times, what I had to lose had already been lost.

When I reached Dexter's house, I stood in the living room leaning against a back wall with my legs crossed at my feet, my hands in my pockets and my shoulders shrugged forward. Dexter sat in the couch, his legs extended, his hands clasped behind his head.

"What's going on with you, Trevor?" he asked

"Jackson knows."

"Oh, man. I'm sorry. I guess it didn't turn out well."

"You guessed right."

"Come on, Trevor. Have a seat."

I was fine standing, but I obliged.

When I sat down I didn't look at Dexter. He was partially to blame. I was staring at the picture that sat on the coffee table in front of us.

"Who's that?" I asked, pointing at the 8 x 10 silver picture frame.

"That's my ex, Patrick."

"Why do you still have pictures of him? How does Giovanni feel about that?

"It's only one picture, and that's the picture I look good in." He smiled. He ignored my last question and I took that as my cue to suppress any further questions about Giovanni. But I did have one last question.

"How is Giovanni?"

"He's fine. He's away with Paisley. We're taking things one

step at a time, but we're fine."

I wanted to comment on what Dexter said, but I had an epiphany. "Wait, did you say his name is Patrick, as in the man from the hospital?"

"That's him."

"He looks familiar. Does Patrick have a last name?" I picked up the picture and examined it closely.

"McCay," Dexter responded.

I didn't think it was possible, but my breath had been taken away. "I know him?"

"From the hospital?"

"No. I never really got a good look at him that day. I know him from Jackson."

"Jackson?" Dexter asked. "You're confusing me."

"No. When we went to Jackson's folks for Thanksgiving, his sister, Devaan, introduced him as Telly, the man she's dating,"

"His name is Patrick Telly McCay," Dexter offered.

"So Devaan only knew his middle name. He never said too much to me, but I think I know why."

"God, I hope you're going to tell me. "

"That phone call I got while I was in Chicago and the ones I have been getting since Jackson moved here, since our friendship began, they're all from him. Patrick is Telly. Telly is Bran." I got up and paced around Dexter's living room like a detective who had just figured out a cold case. "Telly, or Patrick, was trying to keep his past a secret. Your ex, Patrick, is involved with Jackson's sister. His past was getting too close to his present and he had to do something to make sure one never meets the other. So what does he do? He threatens me to either end my friendship with you so this doesn't happen." I pointed back and forth between Dexter and me, "or end my relationship with Jackson so I would never meet him, thinking I might know who he is from your accident. I guess he thought I would have seen him and then say something to Jackson. But how did he know me?"

"I can answer that." Dexter finally spoke. I looked over at him. "A couple weeks after you and I met at Daily Grind, I got a call from Patrick, which I reluctantly accepted after ignoring so many of his previous calls and messages. He wanted to know who I was dating. I was so pleased to rub his face in my relationship with Giovanni. I didn't bother to ask this man whom I cared nothing for why who I was dating mattered to him. Then he asked about the man I sipped coffee with at Daily Grind. All I gave him was your name. How he got your number, knew about our involvement or your relationship with Jackson, I can't tell you."

"Oh, I'm sure he has his ways."

"I'm sure he does," Dexter agreed.

As I talked with Dexter, my phone vibrated. When I looked at the screen, it was a number similar to those usually displayed whenever Bran called. With the information I had just found, I was more than willing to talk to him.

"Hello," I answered.

"I'm done playing with you," he said. The familiar voice was Bran's.

I decided to play stupid. "Who is this?"

"It's Bran," he confirmed.

"I'm just making sure, because I'm done playing this game with you, too. I've saved you some trouble. You don't have to worry about hurting Jackson by telling him about me and Dexter and Chicago. He already knows. So now that you have nothing to threaten me with, I don't expect to hear from you again."

"You think I'm going away that easily? I know you're not going to let Jackson walk out of your life just like that. I know you, and as long as you remain friends with Dexter, you will find yourself in his bed again."

"As for what happens with Jackson and me after tonight, we won't know now will we? But since you say you know me, you should also know that I don't plan on ending my friendship with Dexter either. But I do want you to do something for me. Bran, is it?" I loved this feeling of control.

"What's that?"

"When this conversation ends, I want you to call Devaan and tell her you like to play with boys. Tell her about the special fondness you have for men. Make sure you tell her about Dexter and how he almost died proving his love for you. Oh, and make sure you tell her about any other man that came before him. See, I know who you are, Patrick Telly McCay. We just need to make sure Devaan does, too. I know what you were trying to do with your phone calls and your threats. Now that your threats mean nothing to me, how long can you keep your secret?" There was silence. "I hope this silence means I've gotten your attention. I remember you telling me about men like me, but it's men like you I can't figure out. Men like you who keep running back. Remember you told me I didn't deserve Jackson? Well, you damn sure don't deserve Devaan."

I stood with the phone to my ear, but I heard nothing. Dexter remained in the couch, his face covered in disbelief as he listened.

The phone went dead.

• • • • •

I left Dexter's house feeling a little better than I did when I got there. I found some satisfaction in my conversation with Mr. McKay. I'm sure wherever he was I had him sweating bullets, wondering what else I knew, what else Dexter had told me, and thinking of ways to keep me quiet. But I wasn't worried about Patrick and his wondering.

I hadn't heard from Jackson, and I didn't think I would be hearing from him before morning came. I wanted to call him. I wanted to tell him how sorry I was, but calling him and not getting a response would make me feel even worse. I had hurt someone I really loved. I wished I could take it all back.

When I reached the house, I dialed my voicemail and listened to a message I received while I talked to Patrick. I was praying it was from Jackson.

"Hey, Trevor, this is Caela. I did it. Call me." Her voice had an unusual excitement.

I hung up the phone and walked upstairs. I lay across my bed with my arms stretched above my head and my feet hanging close to the floor. I closed my eyes, squeezing tears that finally fell to the sides of my face. Where I lay was where I slept.

35

That Same Old Feeling

Jackson...

"Is love really that important to you, Jackson?" Colt asked. It was 2:30 in the morning and we hadn't yet run out of words. "You keep waiting for these sorry ass brothas to love you, and you can't yet see that, in the end, all they do is hurt you."

I sat in silence and listened to Colt beat me with words.

"After Gavin, what did I tell you? Love yourself. After Ethan, what did I tell you? Love yourself. And guess what I'm gonna tell you now that Trevor has followed in their footsteps? Love your damn self, man."

"I thought he was different."

"He's not different, he's hurt. And he's already told himself before any man hurts him again, he was going to do the hurting first. Just like there are some scorned women out there, there are some men out there who are scorned as hell, too. They make even the man who loves them pay for the hurt the previous man inflicted on them."

"But why me?"

"Damn, man. You love asking that question. It's you because you make it you. You put yourself in the situation for it to be you. You keep searching for love expecting it to end differently all the time. You keep telling yourself, *this time it's gonna to be different, this time it's gonna be different.* Because you settled for less the last time, you tell yourself this time you want it all, so you go searching for all, and still you fall short. And still, you keep going back. I love love, and I love optimism, but man, ain't that much optimism in the world."

"So you expect me to just give up?"

"No, Jackson. I expect you to give in."

"What?"

Our conversation was intense. My mouth was dry, and I was becoming furious with myself. My heart began to race as Trevor's admission played in my mind. *How could he?* I thought. *When all I did was love him, how could he?*

"Give in to the idea that you're not gonna find your father's love in these men. That's right, 'cause if I don't say it, you're not gonna admit it. Seems you don't get it. You're always going to find those who love you and leave you, or those who never even bother to love you at all, because that's what your father did. You try to find him in them and the only part of him that exists is the kind of hurt you're feeling now. And I know it feels familiar. This didn't start with Gavin, or Ethan, but with Kynard, and if your reason for love doesn't change, it's not going to end with Trevor."

"You know what kills me, Colt? He expected to fix everything by telling me he's sorry."

"That wasn't for you. That was for him. He had nothing else to say, so he said the next best thing, hoping he had fixed everything. My question to you is, has he?"

I never answered Colton. I had some figuring out to do.

After finally hanging up, I went to sleep with thoughts I couldn't get rid of. My mind traveled down some familiar roads, with familiar signs I never paid attention to. I painted my own disturbing pictures of Trevor and Dexter, and the more I told myself to stop thinking, the more I thought. Was Colt right? When will I stop looking for my father's love and begin loving myself?

36

If You Ask Me To

Trevor...

Patrick's phone calls had stopped. I guess my last conversation with him gave him some things to think about, and if I were in his shoes, I'd be doing some thinking, too. I wanted to know if he'd had his talk with Devaan. Jackson hadn't called, so I didn't have anyone to get information from. I didn't speak to Dexter as often since he was cementing the cracks in his relationship with Giovanni. The last time we spoke, he hadn't mentioned hearing from Patrick.

But the joy of not getting one of Patrick's annoying phone calls was short-lived.

"It's you again," I answered. "Nice to hear your voice."

"Just be quiet and listen."

"I don't think you're in the position to be giving out orders. In case you forgot, you no longer have the upper hand. But guess what? I'm going to let you think you're still in control and I'm going to listen. Now, what the hell do you want?"

"I'm making reservations at Teatro Goldini for 8 p.m. tomorrow night. I think we need to talk."

"The person you need to be talking to is Devaan Bradley, the woman you have kept your past from. See, this is what you didn't want to happen, but you know what, sometimes you can't stop or control the inevitable. You should have just quit while you were ahead."

"Feels good, doesn't it?" Patrick asked.

"You got what you wanted, didn't you? You wanted me to tell Jackson the truth. Now the challenge is can you tell Devaan your truth? Do you need my help?"

"What I need you to do is meet me tomorrow at 8, and please don't be late."

"I told you, you're not in the position to tell me what to do. Now I'll think about it." I said nothing for a few seconds.

"And please don't mention this to Dexter."

"And why not? Don't you tell him everything? He seems to have forgiven you for almost killing him and his nephew."

Patrick was quiet. "Just please don't say anything to him. Or Jackson."

"You don't have to worry about Jackson. We aren't on speaking terms right now."

• • • • •

I was supposed to follow Patrick's instructions when I arrived at Teatro Goldini. I was supposed to tell the headwaiter who I was there to have dinner with and everything would be taken care of.

At exactly twenty minutes before 8, I entered the peculiarly opulent interior of Teatro Goldini. I had a troubling afterthought, which I ignored. I had dismissed the childhood lessons my father taught me: *Never talk to strangers.*

"Good evening, sir." I was greeted by the headwaiter in a profound Italian accent. "Will you be dining alone?"

"No. I'm meeting a Mr. Patrick McKay."

"Oh, yes. Mr. McKay. Right this way, please."

I followed the waiter upstairs to what I assumed was Patrick's usual table. I was surrounded by etched glass windows, which gave clientele privacy should they need it. As I sat in a carrot-orange velvet Vittoria sidechair, the waiter, who had yet to introduce himself, unfolded a menu and placed it before me. He placed another on the table in front of the empty chair soon to be occupied by Patrick and then excused himself. Lighted tea candles in frosted crystal on each table illuminated the cozy ambiance. Calming Italian music played at a whispering level, adding to the mood. The walls boasted black and white portraits of famous Italians, from famed actresses Anne Bancroft and Alessa Marcuzzi to prominent painters Raphael and Michelangelo Buonarroti, smiling as if they owned a piece of the brick wall behind them.

"Excuse me sir, but I have a message from Lomax," the waiter interjected.

Like I'm supposed to know who Lomax is, I thought, but I kept my thoughts private.

"Yes. What is the message?" I asked, giving my attention to the unusually tall figure standing in front of me. His name was Andreas. His medium copper brown hair fell to either side of his head. His facial hair seemed only two days removed from a fresh shave, and until his return to the table, I hadn't noticed his thin pink lips and intense azure blue eyes.

"Mr. Patrick McKay has asked that you be informed his business meeting is running a few minutes late and he should arrive shortly," Andreas repeated.

I sat thwarted, not by the news that had just been delivered, but at the barefaced gentleman who had been paying more attention to me than to the Chicken Scaloppine that sat on a white square dinner plate since it was brought to him—undoubtedly chilled by the cooling air flowing from the vents above. When I acknowledged the attention, this stranger, with his stoic demeanor, quickly interrupted his gaze, reached for his dinner fork, and toyed nervously with the cuisine before him. I took a quick glance at my watch. When I looked up again, my admirer had invited himself, not only to my space, but to an unsolicited conversation as well. He welcomed himself to the chair, which should have already been occupied by Patrick.

"I should apologize for my gaze as it was not my attempt to make you uncomfortable," he offered. "I couldn't help but overhear the message. I don't think this is my place, but just a quick warning about Mr. McKay. He's a man with an indecisive ego. He thinks he should have you and anyone else he wants. If your relationship with him is anything but business, I suggest you reconsider. You don't want a man like that in your life, unless you're ready for the hurt that comes with it."

I was surprised at his assumption. Why would my relationship with Patrick be anything but business? He's audacious. I wasn't going to feed into this conversation. It seemed Patrick had left a bad taste in the mouths of a few people.

"My meeting with Mr. McKay is all business, trust me," I said with a serious face.

"Well, even in business we find time for a little pleasure. Here." He slid his card across the table. "Call me. If you want to know anything about this man you're about to do business with, I'm your man."

He excused himself. As he left, he walked with his eyes toward his feet. He did not return to his seat, but turned and headed downstairs. As he descended the stairs, the confidence with which he spoke while he sat across from me seemed to disappear from his body.

I looked at the name across the top of the card. *Travis Price,* I thought. He was an agent from De Nouveaux Visages Modeling Agency—at least that was the information on his business card. *Could it be?* I thought. *The same Travis Price that Jackson said approached him about modeling. This world can't be that small.*

"This is Mr. McKay's favorite," the waiter interrupted. He poured a glass of Fuligini Brunello. I reached for the wine glass. The passionate bouquet of blackberries and cherries danced at my nose, and then wrapped around every taste bud in my mouth. I nodded, giving the waiter my approval.

As I waited for Patrick, I began to peruse the menu, searching for the first entrée description that watered my mouth. Mr. McKay seemed to be a popular man around here. I was sitting at his usual table, drinking his favorite wine, and I wondered what else was in store for me.

"He's sampled just about everything on the menu, and everything is a must have." Her voice was soft and sexy. At first I paid it no attention, but it did sound familiar. "The Linguine Fra Diavolo with lobster, shrimp, calamari and clams is his favorite, but I'd suggest the Risotto with lobster, crab, and roasted sweet red peppers. That sounds even better," she suggested, reciting the dishes and their contents from memory.

I lowered the menu. My eyes widened in disbelief. I expected Patrick McKay, but instead Devaan Bradley stood before me.

I looked at her from head to toe.

She wore brown Michael Kors Veronica boots, rocker denim jeans and a toggle leather jacket. She stood with her hand to her side and a mocha shoulder tote hanging from one hand. The curly charcoal-black hair she sported during Thanksgiving had been cut short and lightly colored. Her short hair blew lightly in the air flowing from the vent above her.

"I wish I knew Patrick as well as I knew the menu," she said. She opened her jacket and sat. She placed her tote on the floor in front of her and crossed her leg one over the other. She leaned forward with her elbows on the table and rested her chin on top of clasped hands.

"I thought Mr. McKay was running late?" I asked, looking at her.

"Trevor, you've never spoken to Mr. McKay, or Bran, for that matter." I looked at her and waited for her to clarify. "It was me the whole time."

"What are you talking about?"

She reached down into her tote and placed a black box on the table. "It's a voice alteration device."

"So you're not here because Patrick..."

"Told me about his past?" She laughed. "No. That was a bomb you dropped. Everything I know about that side of him, so far, I've learned from you."

"Hmmm. Aren't you going to ask how Jackson is doing, or do you already know."

"All I know is what you told me the last time we spoke."

"You mean the last time I spoke to Bran." I sat back and smiled.

"I have spoken to Jackson, but my brother tends to keep relationship problems to himself."

"I see." I stared at Devaan. "Why did it take you so long to call? I thought I wasn't going to hear from you again, not that I looked forward to any of your calls. Though I must say, our last two conversations were a delight. Wouldn't you agree?"

"Trevor, all I was doing was looking out for my little brother."

"Your little brother isn't little anymore. And what makes you think he isn't capable of looking out for himself? I'm curious. You had opportunities to tell him everything, the letter, Thanksgiving, the phone call on Christmas, but yet you didn't. Why did you prolong this?"

"Like I told you. I didn't want to be the one to hurt him."

"But you could have used your voice alternation device and he wouldn't have known it was you."

"But I'd know it was me. Besides, when I met you I liked you. I liked how you interacted with him. I know my brother, and I knew that it'd be easier to forgive you if you told him about Dexter. That's what I tried to get you to do. Jackson has a good heart, and I know you do, too. But you don't deserve him if this is how you're going to treat him."

"How'd you do it? How did you know about Chicago and anything that happened with Dexter?"

"You'll be surprised how many people Telly knows?"

"You mean Patrick."

"You know some people can't keep their mouths shut. Dexter is one of those people. He told Patrick about the trip. As for knowing what happened in Chicago, that was just pure luck. I relied on your conscience and what I thought I knew about relationships between attractive men like you and Dexter. Obvious attraction equals sexual tension, and you have to get the sexual tension out of the way before you can work on a true friendship. I know I can't say that for everyone, but in your case, I was right. Patrick knew I didn't want to see Jackson hurt again. But I can see now he had his own reasons for feeding me the information."

"You never wondered why this man, Dexter, was telling Patrick so much?"

"I wondered, and I had my suspicions. But what are suspicions without proof? The only way I was going to get proof was to play his game. These days you have to do your research. I acted naive and allowed him to lead me to the sources."

"It wasn't my intention to hurt Jackson."

"A lot of times hurt isn't intentional, but our actions usually are."

"Aren't you going to say anything to Patrick?"

"I've heard stories about women finding out the man they love having shared their beds with other men, and I wondered how they deal with it. You asked yourself how could they not know. There had to have been some sign, something. Then I realize you can't really question how people handle situations 'til it happens to you. So, no, I'm not going to say anything to Patrick yet. I need to know what else you know."

"I think you just missed someone who would be more than willing to give you the information you're looking for." I removed Travis's business card from my wallet and handed it to Devaan. "His name is Travis Price. I'm not sure what he knows, but he just gave me a warning when he heard I was meeting with Patrick. He left immediately after his warning. He didn't even finish his dinner."

"Thanks. And what about Dexter?"

"I'm not sure what he's going to tell you, but I'll see what I can do. I didn't know he and Patrick were talking like they do, so he might not tell you anything at all."

"Thank you, Trevor," Devaan said.

"Don't thank me yet. I haven't made you any promises."

The waiter returned, poured Devaan a glass of wine, and then asked if we would be eating. Devaan looked at me, and I nodded to confirm.

She admired the wine. "Hmmm," she responded, giving the waiter her approval.

I decided on Lobster panzerotti in spicy lobster brodo with diavolicchio, which was enjoyed mostly in silence. Devaan savored her British Columbia King Salmon with fresh cranberry and garden beans, and salsa verde.

"So what made you think I would show up here?" I asked, bringing my wine glass to my lips.

"It wasn't a matter of thinking. I was told you're a curious one. Plus you said you had already told Jackson everything, so you had nothing to lose."

"I have nothing to gain, either."

"You don't know that," Devaan smiled. "Help me get the details I need on Mr. McKay, I'll help you get my brother back."

"How are you going to do that?"

"Remember, he's my brother." She took a sip of her wine and then looked at me. "Can I ask you a question?"

"Sure."

"Why'd you do it?"

"I thought I had my reasons figured out. I thought he was cheating 'til I found out I was wrong."

"Then I was right. You really don't know the man who loves you."

37

Friday, February 13th

Trevor...

The message I wrote in Jackson's Valentine's Day Card was simple. *Meet me halfway*, I wrote, and included the name and address of my favorite restaurant. I was taking a big chance, asking to meet him, and on Valentine's Day. What if he doesn't show? What if he does?

Like new Easter dresses in church on Easter Sunday, Halloween costumes on Halloween, and Christmas sweaters on Christmas Day, there were many in the office wearing red and white in observance of Valentine's Day.

Caela had an oversized bouquet of red and white roses she received, and it came from none other than Tavaris Nisby, Kellen's father. According to Caela, the reconciliation went better than expected. He had made plans to visit and spend some time getting to know Kellen—and her.

Morgan stopped by my office a few times, and on one of his visits, he offered to return the favor, inviting me to lunch, his treat. Unfortunately, I had to decline since I had planned on leaving early. I did ask him to pencil me in for a later date.

I was sitting behind my desk, getting ready to call Denise when there was a tap on my door. Before I invited my visitor in, the door swung open.

"Please tell me you're not busy," Wesley said. He stood in the door in one of his best fitting suits.

"For you? Nope," I said, hanging up the phone.

Wesley walked over to my desk and stood. "I need your opinion on something." He removed two small black boxes from his pockets, opened one and then the other, and placed them on my desk. "What do you think? Which one?"

I looked at the rings and then up at Wesley. "Shouldn't you be asking Caela or one of the other ladies for their opinions on these?"

"Come on, man. Which one of these would you give your lady?"

I took each engagement ring and examined it carefully. Both were sparklingly beautiful. One was a diamond three-stone platinum, the other was a white gold diamond twisty ring, which I thought would look sexy on Erin's finger. I could understand why Wesley was having a hard time choosing just one.

"When do you plan on taking the knee?"

"Tomorrow night," Wesley answered quickly. "I'm really feeling this girl, Trevor. I'm just hoping she says yes."

"I'm sure she will." I picked up the second ring again, the white gold twisty ring. "I think she will love this one."

"I think she will, too." Wesley agreed. He picked up both boxes and began walking towards the door. "Oh," he said, turning around. "I forgot to ask you how are things with Jackson."

I think I was more nervous about tomorrow night, even

though Wesley was about to take his relationship with Erin further with his planned proposal. "There's nothing to say about me and Jackson right now. I have plans for dinner tomorrow." Wesley stood in silence looking at me.

"What?" I asked.

"You said 'I have plans for dinner tomorrow'."

"Yeah."

"Don't you mean we?"

"No. I mean I made reservations for dinner and sent Jackson an invitation. Now whether or not he shows up..."

"My guess is he won't stand you up like that. Doesn't seem his style."

I hope you know him better than I do, I thought.

· · · · ·

I sat on the couch in the living room bringing a long Friday to a close. Since morning, I had sat in one staff meeting after conference and hadn't had time to lunch, and the idea of doing this all over again next week had me looking forward to a work-free weekend. I felt like I had completed a work-week in one day and I knew if I kept this up, it was going to have an adverse affect on some aspect of my personal life.

After work, I spent the rest of the evening doing the chores I knew I didn't want taking up much of my Saturday. With Jackson still not speaking to me. I had so much free time on my hands. I had dropped off clothes at the drycleaners, giving them my usual instructions: No seam in my flat front pants. I had completed my grocery shopping without a grocery list, which meant I had probably picked up a few things I didn't need and might have left off a few items I would be need sooner or later. The reviled task of folding laundry hidden in the laundry room was still ahead of me, but for now, I just wanted to relax.

I wanted to wake up next to Jackson. I wished tonight included dinner for two at one of my favorite restaurants with him, but for now, it was a quiet evening, and I was by myself.

I had just sat on the couch with one leg crossed in front of me. I had the remote in my hand searching through a list of free on-demand movies. February came in like it had a death warrant. It should be against the law to be this cold. The day before Valentine's Day and here I was, alone. Before tonight it hadn't dawned on me, but the possibility of spending Valentine's Day alone was looming, and I had no one to blame but myself. I was preparing to drink myself to oblivion. It seemed every movie had something to do with love—just what I needed. As I settled into the movie *The Good Night*, my cell phone rang. I hoped it was Jackson. I still hadn't heard from him. He hadn't answered my calls and I wondered what he did with messages I left him. I had apologized so many times—I was running out of ways to say I'm sorry. I had even spoken to Dexter more than I ever had, having conversations with him that I wished I were having with Jackson.

Earlier in the week, on his way home from work, Dexter decided to explain his letter and the real reason for telling Giovanni the truth. Dexter had learned how lying hurts and how secrets divided.

Dexter had always lived his life as the product of a biracial relationship, but the letter he received imploded that world he knew. In a letter from his father, the one his stepmother finally decided to share with him, Dexter learned the truth. Connie Mears, the Black woman he and his brother Dane had called Mom wasn't their birth mother. She was forced to carry his father's secret to her grave. Dexter's mother, Elizabeth Stallings was still alive. Now he just had to find her and find out why they had kept his real identify from him. Dexter was devastated that he didn't belong to the family that had loved and accepted him and his brother, and wondered how much of the secret the woman he called Grandma Stoney knew.

My phone rang again, and again.

"How's my man doing?" My father asked when I answered. "What are you doing home on a Friday night?"

"It's cold."

"That's never stopped you before."

"True. It's been a long, stressful week." I reached for the remote and paused the movie. "I just wanted to come home and relax."

"Work?"

"Yeah, work." I didn't want to tell my father about my fallout with Jackson, so I bent the truth just a little.

"Well, son, take some time off, get some rest."

"That's exactly what I planned on doing."

"Hey, how's Jackson? We need to do dinner soon."

"I'll tell him you asked about him. And we'll do dinner soon. I love you, Dad."

"Love you, too."

I sat back in the couch and continued watching the movie. How long was Jackson going to pretend I no longer exist? I couldn't get him off my mind, and I wondered if he was having just as hard a time trying not to think about me. Patrick, or should I say Devaan, was right. I wasn't going to just let Jackson walk out of my life. She had become my ally, promising to help me get Jackson back. I didn't know what backdoor deals she was making with him, but I had my own thinking to do. I had to get Jackson back into my life.

38

Decisions, Decision

Jackson...

Saturday, February 14th was a cold brisk day. It had snowed two days earlier, but the only remnants of the one-and-a-half inches we received were a few patches on grass that rarely saw the sun. The sun was shining bright, and I thought the day couldn't look more perfect, from inside the house.

I spent the first part of the day calling my mother and sister. I wondered if Mr. Kirkwood had given Mother another charm for a bracelet she rarely wore, or maybe he'd replaced those pearl earrings she wore to my Aunt Delaney's wedding to Uncle Talbert Dawson, the ones she lost when he dipped her on the dance floor. She wasn't home. When I called Devaan, I was only able to leave a message since her phone went straight to voicemail.

I spent the other part of the day convincing myself what to do about tonight's dinner with Trevor. I was telling myself go...go, but sometimes the mouth says things the heart doesn't understand.

I sat in the chair in the corner of the room, tying my shoelace. I had placed the card from Trevor on the corner of the bed after reading it one last time. *Meet me halfway,* I thought. It hadn't been an easy couple of weeks. These weeks I felt more alone than I had ever felt since moving, and I was reminded more often than I needed to be that I had no one here. Every night I was talking to someone else. On some nights, I talked to my mother, though I hadn't told her anything, but just like that morning on the patio on Thanksgiving Day when she asked me if everything was ok, she again, sensed something was wrong. My conversations with Devaan came with unusual rhetoric.

"Maybe this guy Dexter caught him in a rare moment of weakness, and he just couldn't help it," Devaan said. "You did say he thought you were doing your own thing, right?"

"Yes," I responded "But that doesn't excuse anything."

"Ask yourself this. Do you think he would have done it otherwise?"

I didn't know how to respond to her last question. Part of me hoped he wouldn't have, but another part of me simply just didn't know. All I knew was what happened. There's no telling what he would have done if things were different. I must say, Devaan had me thinking, and for a minute, I was ready to give in. After all, aren't people allowed one mistake? I thought about the many mistakes Gavin and Ethan made and I remembered how easily I found it to forgive them, because I loved them. What did that say about me? I didn't love Trevor any less, so why was forgiving him so difficult. Could it be that I expected more from him, a different level of respect?

I searched for my cell phone, which was hidden under my sweater, shirt and, tie. It was 7:15 p.m. I had forty-five minutes to finish getting dressed and drive across town to meet Trevor. But something in my head clicked, putting all my questions together and finding one clear answer. I dialed Trevor's number, sat back in the chair and waited for him to answer.

"You on your way?" he asked. "I'm leaving out now."

"Trevor," I called out quietly. He was silent.

"You're going tell me you're not coming, aren't you?"

"I didn't want you sitting at the restaurant looking at your watch, wondering why I hadn't gotten there yet, or checking your cell phone for a vibration that never comes. I'm sitting here in dress slacks and shoes with my shirt, sweater and tie laid out on the bed.

"But Jackson..." Trevor began.

"No, Trevor. What have I done since I've met you? I waited for you. I distanced myself, giving you space and time to figure out your emotions and your feelings for Kelvin, and since then, the only thing I've done was love you. Why couldn't you do the same? If you were tempted, why couldn't you resist? I know that feeling you got with Dexter. The excitement of new. This high you get every time you see him. You know what? I still get those feelings with you. But look what happens when the new is old and the excitement has died. We find ourselves here, wanting the same person you've hurt."

"I told you I was..."

"I know. You told me you were sorry—I heard you," I added. I stood up and began pacing. "But sorry doesn't fix everything. So am I supposed to put what you did and my hurt aside and we celebrate tonight like nothing ever happened. And then what, I give you another chance to fuck me over again because forgiveness came so easily?"

"Isn't that what you do when you love someone?"

"What you do when you love someone is not hurt them."

"So we're spending Valentine's Day alone?"

"I suggest you call and cancel your reservation." I sat back in my chair thinking about what I had just done. Knowing Trevor, I knew how much he wanted tonight to happen. The fairytale ending he was attempting to orchestrate had just been spoiled. This wasn't a movie where he could do whatever he wanted to me and then write the ending he wanted. It doesn't work that way.

• • • • •

"Say it isn't so," Denard spoke when I answered my phone.

"Hey, Denard. Shouldn't you be out entertaining?" He was the last person I expected to speak to tonight.

"Sure. Are you coming, or are you sending someone over?"

"I'll see what I can come up with."

"What are you doing home? Waiting for the manfriend to come over?"

"There's nothing happening between me and Trevor tonight." I laughed, thinking about Denard's use of the word manfriend.

"Is that what you want?"

"I don't think what I want matters."

"What you want should always matter, Jackson, and not just to you. I'm not even going to ask what happened, but it's Valentine's Day, man. You know you love Trevor. Call the guy."

"I've already called him."

"Then go and be wherever he is."

"Thanks, Denard. But I think where I am is where I need to be right now."

"Are you?"

I hesitated. "Yes."

"Hey, Jackson. Happy Valentine's Day, my friend." Denard hung up before I could respond in kind.

39
Only You

Jackson...

Happy wasn't how I would describe any of what I felt. Valentine's Day had turned into a regular Saturday night. Denard was right. What I want should always matter, but for a long time, it never mattered to the person it should. I picked up my cell phone, placed it in my pocket, and walked downstairs to the kitchen. I was ready to pour my glass of wine, sit on the couch and eventually fall asleep to a basketball game because I surely didn't want to watch any movie about love. But whoever was calling me now had a different plan.

I removed the phone from my pocket.

"Hello Mother," I answered.

"Thought I would have gotten your voicemail. Happy Valentine's Day! How are you?"

"I'm ok."

"You don't sound ok," she speculated. "How's Trevor? Is he there? Tell him I said hello. Did you boys end your night...?"

"Mother." I paused.

"Yes."

I hesitated. "I didn't have a night with Trevor, Mother."

"What happened?"

I removed a bottle of wine from the cooler and poured a glass full. I leaned against the refrigerator and drank the wine as if it were water. "The same thing that always happens. Trevor turned out to be not so different," I said, and poured another glass full.

"No different from whom?"

"You name him," I suggested. "No different from Gavin, from Ethan, from D…"

"From Demetrius?"

"That wasn't what I was going to say."

"And who are you trying to convince, me or yourself?"

"They came into my life or brought me into theirs only to do what, prove to me that love's only purpose, as far as I'm concern, is to hurt me."

"So now you're through with Trevor? And what do you do now? Are you going to just move on to the next? Is it always one and done with you?"

"Mother, nothing gives you the right to say that."

"Besides being your mother and loving you, you're right."

"Love has been one big disappointment after the other."

"And there's no second chance?"

"What about my second chance? Did I ever get one? I'm waiting for a reason that never came. And I have forgotten how it feels to have his love. Why couldn't he have left before I had gotten to know him? Then his love wouldn't have mattered."

"Jackson, sweetheart. You do realize you're no longer talking about Trevor. Your relationships are never going to work if you keep looking for your father in these men you love. They don't owe you his love. You are no longer the little boy he left."

"He gave me no choice."

"You're right. He didn't. But not being here to see the man you've become is his lost. I hate to sound harsh, but baby, get over it. Your father has, I'm sure."

"Happy Valentine's Day, Mother. I have to go."

"I love you, Jackson. And remember, love doesn't end because you choose not to forgive."

"I love you, too, Mrs. Kirkwood."

• • • • •

I usually don't question my decisions. Each exit I passed, I tried to convince myself to take the next one, and then the next, but here I was turning onto Willow Crest Court, still wondering if it were too late to turn around.

"What are you doing?" I asked Trevor when he answered his phone. He sounded as if my call was the last thing he expected.

"Sitting at the table, thinking?"

"About?"

"You. What else?" Trevor asked.

"Come outside."

"What am I coming outside for?"

"Stop asking questions. Are you coming or not?"

I sat in Trevor's driveway, playing with the radio dial. It's funny how a song can summarize exactly what you were feeling.

John Legend bellowed with his passion wrapped around his voice. *"You love, you love, you love, though you've been burn, you still return."*

I wasn't ready for what his words were doing to me. My heart sank as I thought of Trevor, his love for me, and the love I had for him. I thought about how much I had grown because of loving, and because of losing love.

I reclined my seat, closed my eyes momentarily, and smiled, ignoring the tears that created their own path down the side of my face. I smiled again. When I finally opened my eyes, Trevor was standing there looking at me. He looked at me like he was seeing my face again for the first time. His look appeased me.

"Are you okay?" he asked. His arms were folded and rested on the top of the car. He was staring down at me. He licked his lips as I answered.

"Oh, I'm fine." I was still in my reclined position, looking at Trevor from the corners of my eyes.

"You're going to have to try harder than that to convince me."

I returned the chair back to its upright position, folded my arms on the car door, and rested my chin on them. Trevor stooped. We were now looking into each other's eyes.

"No, seriously, I'm fine." I turned my head and smiled.

We both sat there in silence. As we sat, I thought. The thoughts came and went. The smiles came in between thoughts. I did nothing to interrupt.

My search for love had always been one constant in my life. I tried to picture myself with someone else, but even when I closed my eyes, squeezing them tighter than my muscles would allow, the only face I saw was Trevor's. Love was telling me not to let go, but it couldn't tell me how to stop hurting if I held on.

I wanted something.

I wanted someone to ask me what I was doing on New Year's Eve, though it was only the Fourth of July. The part of my heart I thought I would never get back was mine again. Many things never happened for me, but I'm glad Trevor did. And to think I almost lost him. I did everything I could to keep my father, Gavin, and then Ethan, in my life, but here I was, doing everything I could to shut Trevor out.

"So how much longer are you going to stay out here?" Trevor asked. "As much as I like looking at you, I can't stoop like this too much longer."

"I don't plan on sleeping out here." I smiled. "Give me a few minutes."

"I thought tonight wasn't going to happen. Thanks for not hurting me like I hurt you."

"Do you love him?" I asked. I was looking straight ahead.

"No."

I turned to look at Trevor, looking through his eyes and into his soul.

I remained silent.

He stood, turned, and began walking towards the house. When he was several feet from the front door, his cell phone rang.

"This is Trevor," he answered quickly.

"I forgot to tell you I love you. Happy Valentine's Day!"

Trevor turned around and smiled. The phone was still pressed against his ear.

"I love you, too."

I hung up the phone and slowly sat back in the car.

About the Author

Kristofer Clarke is the author of Less Than Perfect Circumstance. He is an educator in the District of Columbia Metropolitan area. He holds a Bachelor of Arts degree from Middlebury College, and a Master of Education degree from Bowie State University. He is currently working on his next novel.

Visit Kristofer at www.kristoferclarke.webs.com

CPSIA information can be obtained at www.ICGtesting.com
Printed in the USA
BVOW010645240912

301136BV00001B/27/P